THE REALMGATE WARS

CALL OF ARCHAON

THE REALMGATE WARS

CALL OF ARCHAON

DAVID ANNANDALE

DAVID GUYMER

GUY HALEY

ROB SANDERS

BLACK LIBRARY

A BLACK LIBRARY PUBLICATION

Call of Archaon first published in 2015.
This edition published in Great Britain in 2016 by
Black Library,
Games Workshop Ltd.,
Willow Road,
Nottingham,
NG7 2WS, UK.

10 9 8 7 6 5 4 3 2 1

Produced by Games Workshop in Nottingham.
Cover illustrations by Paul Dainton and Antonio Luis.

A CIP record for this book is available from the British Library.

ISBN 13: 978 1 78496 294 4

See Black Library on the internet at

blacklibrary.com

Find out more about Games Workshop
and the world of Warhammer 40,000 at

games-workshop.com

Printed and bound by CPI Group (UK) Ltd, Croydon, CR0 4YY

From the maelstrom of a sundered world, the
Eight Realms were born. The formless and the divine
exploded into life.

Strange, new worlds appeared in the firmament, each one
gilded with spirits, gods and men. Noblest of the gods was
Sigmar. For years beyond reckoning he illuminated the realms,
wreathed in light and majesty as he carved out his reign. His
strength was the power of thunder. His wisdom was infinite.
Mortal and immortal alike kneeled before his lofty throne.
Great empires rose and, for a while, treachery was banished.
Sigmar claimed the land and sky as his own and ruled over a
glorious age of myth.

But cruelty is tenacious. As had been foreseen, the great
alliance of gods and men tore itself apart. Myth and legend
crumbled into Chaos. Darkness flooded the realms. Torture,
slavery and fear replaced the glory that came before. Sigmar
turned his back on the mortal kingdoms, disgusted by their
fate. He fixed his gaze instead on the remains of the world he
had lost long ago, brooding over its charred core, searching
endlessly for a sign of hope. And then, in the dark heat of
his rage, he caught a glimpse of something magnificent. He
pictured a weapon born of the heavens. A beacon powerful
enough to pierce the endless night. An army hewn from
everything he had lost.

Sigmar set his artisans to work and for long ages they toiled,
striving to harness the power of the stars. As Sigmar's great
work neared completion, he turned back to the realms and saw
that the dominion of Chaos was almost complete. The hour
for vengeance had come. Finally, with lightning blazing across
his brow, he stepped forth to unleash his creations.

The Age of Sigmar had begun.

TABLE OF CONTENTS

BENEATH THE BLACK THUMB

David Guymer

I

'You come to me offering death,' said Copsys Bule, stabbing his long-handled trident into the soft red soil. Blood or something distantly akin to it oozed lazily up around the sinking tines. 'A kingly gift, envoy, but death flourishes where I choose to sow it. I am a harvester of death.'

Kletch Scabclaw studied him with eyes that could have gleaned weakness from diamond. They were milk yellow, and glared over the mangy scrap of man-skin that he held pressed to his muzzle in the claws from which he had taken his name. The look on his furry, verminous face might have been one of disgust, though at what, or *who*, was something the plague priest kept for himself.

'A new age begins, they squeak-say.' Spreading his paws, the skaven irritably swatted aside a buzzing bloat fly. Through Bule's blurred vision it appeared to have three eyes, until the ratman snapped his claws and his vision once again became clear. 'War comes. Even to you.'

Bule snapped his head up.

The skaven immediately backed up a pace, hunched for fight or flight. Light on his foot-paws, he stood atop the rotten mush that went up to Bule's greaves. His right paw had gone for the weapon he concealed beneath his robes, and he hissed a warning through his scented rag.

Bule smiled, rotten flesh yielding to produce something too wide for a human mouth.

Slowly, Kletch held up his empty paws, then the gnawed-on nub of his tail. It switched over the ratman's head with irritation. 'I did not come-scurry all way from clan-burrow to fight-quarrel. The Black Thumb and Clan Rikkit were friend-allies in the Age of Chaos. Is written. Is remembered. Now we must-need fight tooth to claw again.'

Bule turned his back with a mild shake of the head. Withdrawing his bloodied trident, he stabbed three new aeration holes into the soil, the tines spearing an inch deep before hitting something unyielding. Baring the black stubs of his teeth he gave a grunt of pleasure, planted his foot to the back of the fork-head, and rocked back and forth on the handle.

Levering the trident against his bloated girth, he turned over the unyielding patch in a waft of decomposing flesh.

The human corpse tore off its blanket of topsoil and flopped over. A face that was grey-black and runny and lovely as a crop of sweet tubers fresh out of the ground stared up at the slow circling stars with the clarity of the dead. Disturbed maggots and worms squirmed under the starlight, as if divulging some great secret under torture. Bule watched them re-bury themselves, lulled by the drone of a billion bloat flies and the rank cackle of crows.

Wriggle. Wriggle.

'*Rotbringer*,' the skaven prompted him.

Bule pinched his eyes wetly, mind asquirm with worms and portent. The ratman continued.

'The lightning men hit clan-burrows in Cripple Fang, Untamed Lands and Putris Bog. Even clan-cousins from far Ghyran come-flee, tunnelling the realm-places to bring word of war.'

Shouldering his trident, Bule turned around suddenly enough to elicit a low squeal of alarm from the plague priest of Clan Rikkit. The ratman leapt to one side, reaching again for his concealed weapon, but Bule merely squelched through the spot he had been occupying as though he were a zombie suddenly impelled to be elsewhere.

'Bule. *Bule!*'

Copsys Bule ignored him, his armour emitting a mould-muffled *clank* with every step. Several of the spiked plates were split apart at the joins, but the damage to his armour had been inflicted not from without but from within. Corpse gasses distended his belly, opening up the plates from the inside like a fat grub eating its way out of an egg sac. Everywhere there remained living skin, swellings, boils and tumours caused further buckling, mottling the once-green metal to black.

Not since before the Age of Chaos had Bule known an equal, and his gardens brought weeping harvest to lands from the Bloodbloom Fields in the south to the Avalundic Ice Kingdoms in the north, from the peat bogs of Murgid Fein to the unconquerable Rabid Heights and their gargant kings.

His demesne was too vast for one name.

It encompassed the Pox Sands, the great Bloat Lake and the Plantation of Flies – fleshwork patches stitched with irrigation ditches that steamed with blight and hummed with spawning daemonflies. As far into the bubonic haze as the eye could see, scrofulous, once-human things tilled the soil with rakes and hoes, or waded into pools with long prods to turn the bloated corpses that floated in them, gestating towards ripeness. Hundreds expired in the time it took Bule to walk past them, and were dragged away to the nurseries to replenish the soil in their turn.

But it was the nature of lesser beings to attach small names to great things.

They called it the Corpse Marshes.

Seemingly at random, *feeling* where the dead desired his knife, he squatted down into the mire. A sigh of simple pleasure escaped him. The crucified remains of men, women and children staked the ground in serried rows for a stretch greater than a man could ride in a day. Here could be found the bodies of almost every race, including several that no longer existed anywhere but as they did here now. For reasons fathomable to few but Bule himself, he called it his Living Orchard. A foetid breeze moaned through the dead, making them hum and sway, like lush-leaved trees in bloom. Drawing a curved knife from his arming belt, he sawed away a hand that liquefaction was beginning to pull away from the wrist. It was human. A nectarine blackness trickled from the cut. He licked it from his hand, eyes closed in ecstasy.

There was no plan in his mind of how his garden should be, but he knew what needed to be done towards its completion. And it would be soon. Very soon.

The thought thrilled him even as the part of him that had cherished these labours was saddened by their imminent passing.

'There are a great many of your kind here,' Bule said, aware that the ratman had followed him and was now crouching on an old wall behind him. Keeping his distance. 'Your fur. Your guts. You teem with life like no other.' He cut away another sagging limb with a clinical slash. 'Nothing rots as quickly as a skaven rots. Nothing embraces Grandfather Nurgle so completely.'

'Is that what you want-wish me to take back to my masters?'

'Ask me again come the high moon.'

'Why-why? What changes then?'

Bule licked his knife with a wide smile. Birds cried in fevered tongues, a diseased animal sagacity that he might one day have the fortune to fathom but half of. 'You come on an auspicious night. For the first time in thousands of years the stars will align my realmgate with another.'

'And then?' Kletch hissed, suddenly wary.

'Ask me again come the high moon.'

II

Fistula, First Blightlord of the Black Thumb, delighter in sickness and death, opened the orruk from hip to hip with a sawing reverse of his blade. A surprised snort issued from the greenskin's tusked helmet, but the fighter remained upright, tough as necrotic flesh and just as dead to pain. Holding its squirming guts in a fist the size of a buckler, it swung its axe at the blightlord with a roar.

Hardwearing, vicious – orruks were infamous. But the fever spreading fire through its veins from the infected belly wound made it sluggish. Fistula sidestepped the clumsy slash with ease then broke its shin with a heel jab. It was sweating. Most men would never know that an orruk could suffer the way this one now did. But still it would not yield.

Fistula appreciated that.

Dashing aside its weakening backslash on the flat of his sword, he stepped in behind its flailing trunk of an arm, close enough to smell the daemon plaguelings rampaging through its veins, then plunged his parrying dagger through its throat.

The orruk's mammoth jaws snapped spasmodically as Fistula tore his dagger loose and kicked the brute away. Blood from the torn artery sprayed in a rising arc and painted the open face of Fistula's helm green. He gasped. Partly to drink the wetness from the air. Partly for the raw pleasure of doing so.

Fistula looked down on the beaten orruk. It was still snapping its jaws even as it drowned in its fluids and its eyes turned white. Fistula could have ended it quickly, should have, perhaps, but endemic as the orruks were in the shadow of the Rabid Heights there were never enough to last. He looked up.

The orruks were still fighting in scattered mobs spread out along the length of the narrow gulch into which the Black Thumb had pursued them, but they were broken. Not in the manner of a human or Rotbringer host. They did not run. Rather, they held on with the witless tenacity of sick beasts. Hardy as they were as a race, all bore the stigmata of infection: weeping sores and crusted cuts that would not heal. For every hundred that lay dead with an obvious wound, a hundred more twitched on the ground with blood foam in their mouths and flies on their rotting flesh.

Gors and bestigors plunged headlong into the fray, hacking and goring with frenzied abandon. Rotbringer knights on maggot-riddled steeds galloped up the steeply climbing wall of the gulch to strike at the orruk warleader. The huge beast was surrounded by his biggest and most brutal, but was already heavily beset by the Tzeentchian warhost driving in from the opposite side of the ravine.

The Changeling host was a cacophonous legion of colours and shapes. Gold glittered. Strange voices whispered. Flames of every cast, smell and texture danced along the crossbars of banner poles, and suits of almost-sentient armour whispered secrets to the deepest subconscious of all nearby with a mind to hear. Daemonflies buzzed over everything and everyone. Blight hounds ran along the flanks, pulling down the isolated and the maimed. Giant slugs burrowed up from under the hardpan to swallow Tzeentchian warriors whole while plague drones and sleek daemonic screamers swept at each other in pitched battle for the skies.

The orruks had become almost incidental.

Fistula read the kindred mood in his opposite number, the hunger, coming from somewhere out there in the gulch. They had both come to torment prey, but now, starved of a true challenge, they threw their warriors at the other with greater ferocity than they had ever before.

It was something that Copsys Bule had become too fat and old to realise. Even the most rapacious of plagues could be tamed, lingering only on the scraps left by those they had once devastated in their millions.

A stamp of hellsteel and an ebullient cry called Fistula back from the abstract of the battle. Through a congested melee of putrid blightkings and sickening orruk fighters half again their size, a Chaos warrior encased in full plate armour of azure and gold barged towards him. His helm was solid metal, with only the etching of half-lidded eyes through which some enchantment perhaps permitted him to see. From the sides, golden horns spiralled inwards towards infinity. The Tzeentchian knuckled aside an orruk and roared the final strides with his broadsword swept high overhead.

With a shout, Fistula pivoted on the spot and smacked his saw-toothed blade hard into the larger blade's descent. It was not a parry. He struck the Tzeentchian's broadsword as though meaning to do it harm. The impact arced up his arm. He felt it vibrate in his teeth. Reflex action shocked his fingers open and would have lost him his blade if not for the blood and pus that pooled endlessly into his grip from infected calluses and glued palm to hilt.

The Tzeentchian reeled as though it had been struck on the head by a blow that had left its helmet ringing. Its heavy sword trailed, elbows locked in spasm with the aftershock of keeping a hold of his blade.

Fistula struck off the warrior's head with a single blow to the neck and laughed.

He was the opposite of Copsys Bule in most ways. Where the Lord of Plagues had become a bloated wreck of a man, Fistula's body was wasted, the favour in which he was held written in lesions on pared bone and in the ropey musculature that seeped and seeped without end. He was a warrior. A fever raged in his mind that no level of war could ever purge and his armour, lighter by preference, was etched with tallies of the blights he had tasted and the civilizations he had brought low.

'Secure the dead,' bellowed a cadaverous, jaundiced blightking wearing a cruel harness of scythe-edged plates and hanging mail. He lay into the orruks with a pair of matching knives, bloodily proficient in his preferred mode of killing. Fistula was one of the few to know him as Vitane. To most, he was Leech. The blightking turned and waved a *come now* gesture. 'Bring up the wagons. If we are not back by high moon it will go poorly for you.'

Rattling in under a fug of disease came a dozen wagons. Each was drawn by a team of six wheezing horses, their loose wheels the size of a man, their high sides scratched with the knife marks of individual warriors and with a splintered parapet of aged wood. Leprous harvesters in hoods and swaddling leaned over the parapet with hooks to draw up the dead. The drovers called a halt. The horses snuffled in their traces, hacking, puking, biting at each other's flea-ravaged coats.

Fighting his way to Fistula's side, Vitane looked down on the orruk still dying at his lord's feet. The leathery tissue was continuing to shrivel away, the liquidised remainder sinking around the bones.

'He will be unhappy. This one is worthless.'

Fistula sneered. Vitane was old enough to have fought with Copsys Bule from the beginning, lacking enough in ambition or favour to prevent his star being eclipsed by the man he now followed into battle.

'I am not here to scavenge and I am not here for Bule,' Fistula said.

They could not all dine off glories past.

Fistula scanned the confusion for the Tzeentchian champion. Warriors of every stripe filled the gulch from wall to wall with a riot of colour and noise. Even the sky reflected the vivid clash, the bubonic haze that blanketed Bule's demesnes turned a sickly turquoise by the rolling cumulus of Tzeentchian fire that followed the war horde from the north. Twisted trees covered in naked sores and weeping black foliage clung to the ridgeline. They swayed under the opposing winds.

Fistula shivered though he could not say why. His eyes narrowed.

There was something there, hidden under the drooping canopy. Fistula glimpsed a figure, or the suggestion of one. More a feeling than something he could later describe and claim with certainty had been real. He perceived a sense of robes, of a gaunt, skeletal *height*, but his overriding impression was one of watchfulness, of many, many sets of eyes trained upon every aspect of this moment in time. In a blink of the mind it was gone. The inkling of its prior being was a subliminal glamour that nevertheless refused to fully fade, as though he had gazed overlong upon a daemon and imprinted its corona of power onto his mind.

He shook his head, and with the blessed release of a peeled scab pulled off his helmet and wiped the orruk's gore from his hairless scalp.

The sense of watchfulness remained on him, a nagging question at the back of his mind. He felt judgement, though for what, Fistula doubted he had the faculties to comprehend. Nor did he care. He bared his teeth in anticipation and raised his sword to signal the charge. His own glorification was all that mattered.

Let it watch. Let it judge.

III

Kletch Scabclaw spread his arms out to either side while a skaven-slave hung the heavy ambassadorial cloak of Clan Rikkit over his shoulders. It was a bit much for the cloying humidity of the Corpse Marshes, and itched in hard-to-reach places that no garment so august should. Its fleas had been passed from priest to priest for two hundred years, and were now the hardy descendents of those that had survived the clan's full arsenal of pesticidal sorcery.

His dresser ducked under his arm and shuffled around to the front.

The slave was naked but for its own scrappy fur and the brands of clan and owner, but Kletch was only partially reassured by that. To his mind there were any number of innovative places in which a determined assassin might secrete a weapon. His yellow eyes drilled into the side of the slave's head. The wretch bared its throat with a whimper, stabbing its thumb several times in its panic to fasten the cloak's rat bone collar. Kletch fidgeted as the slave fussed.

It was too hot. The garish green light of the warpstone bra-ziers around the low-roofed tent was too bright. The spiced scent they gave off to hold back the reek was too sickly sweet.

'How much-long to high moon?' he asked of the plague monk seated against the wall of the pavilion behind his back.

'Soon-soon.'

Scurf's piebald fur was pox-scarred, so denuded of hair from his own incessant scratching that he resembled a game bird that had been abandoned before it could be fully plucked. The crusted word-bringer set his claw quill onto the stack of man-skin parchment on which he had been cataloguing the many new diseases they had encountered since their arrival in the Corpse Marshes and shrugged. 'An hour, I think-guess.'

Kletch wriggled his shoulders in discomfort. 'Something is about to happen-come. I feel-feel in my claws.'

'I feel-smell also,' said Scurf, always eager to concur.

The slave scurried over to the brass-ribbed chest sitting open by the hide wall of the tent, and returned with Kletch's warpstone-tipped staff. Kletch snatched it off the slave with a snarled rebuke. Feeling a little better, he gave the air a fresh sniff, opening his mouth to taste. Between the reek of putre-faction and his own efforts to keep it at bay, there was little left to be smelled, but somehow he knew, *knew*, that there was more than just the three of them present in that tent.

'You want-wish to go home?' asked Scurf.

'No,' said Kletch, meaning yes. 'Clanlords will not reward us for returning with paws empty. The lightning men hit them much-hard in lots-many places. Clanlords grow desperate. They... make bad decisions when they are desperate.'

The slave scurried back bearing a bottle filled with a green-ish red liquor that it poured into a goblet. Steam hissed off the cup as the liquid hit the lacquer. The slave bobbed its head low and presented the potation. Kletch eyed the rodent severely. With a gulp, the slave brought the cup to its lips and took the daintiest sip.

Kletch took the goblet from his retching slave, stole his nerve, and then downed its contents. He grimaced, throat tightening, musk glands clenching, and stuck out his tongue. '*Blegh!*'

'Best-best potions taste worst,' said Scurf sagely.

Clan Rikkit had once been part of Pestilens, before a tunnel collapse in the ways between worlds had separated them from their brethren. They still retained many of the old immunities, but the cautious rat was the healthy rat.

'This all a waste of time anyway,' said Scurf, picking up his quill once more and dunking it in the shelled ink bug still twitching on his table. Scratching away at the parchment, he went on. 'He has many warriors, but this not the Copsys Bule used to frighten my litter when I was small-young.'

Kletch was unconvinced. Bule could afford to let the world pass him by for a millennium or two if he chose to do so, of that he was certain. And if Bule was any less than the tyrant of clan legend then Kletch was glad that he had not been the envoy sent to treat with *that* Lord of Plagues.

'One hour more we can wait. Let us see this over-done, but have all my warriors ready to go.'

'Yes-yes,' said Scurf, carefully folding his quill and packing it away.

Kletch twitched aside the tent flap and slipped out into the muggy night with wrinkled nose and downcast eyes. Two from the two-dozen plague monks quietly chittering their praises on the broken ground outside of the tent fell into step behind him.

A colossal fortress-temple had once stood here, built by a people who had worshipped the stars and raised towers of incredible scale that they might feel the distant objects of their faith more keenly. For all that their eyes had attended the heavens, they had clearly also been masters of stone. Many of the great structures still stood though they were ruinous now, verterbral columns of stone that had been yellowed by blight, weather and war. Copsys Bule called this place the Hanging Gardens, named so for the thousands upon thousands of dead and dying strung up from its moss-clad defensive walls. Those still alive writhed in fever so that the walls themselves appeared in motion. Their mouths moved but no evidence of their torment could be heard from them, not above the flies.

To count the flies was to court insanity. They were infinite, swarms within swarms, billowing over the corrupted fortress in such numbers that at times they were as the chitinous outer wings of a beetle closing over the world and shutting out the sky. At such times the drone was a gnawing on the boundary between earth and heavens, between real and unreal. At other times it was simply maddening. It set the teeth on edge.

The Clan Rikkit camp pavilion was set up on the rubble where the innermost gate had crumbled to create a rockery populated with razor weeds that were watered each day with the blood of year-dead men. It would foul a charge as surely as any gate ever would, assuming any enemy had the fortitude to survive as far as Bule's innermost defensive line.

From that vantage Kletch had an unimpeded and deeply unpleasant view.

The Corpse Marshes were monstrous. It reminded him only somewhat of the honeycombed pox caves of Murgid Fein, where diseases were bred, mutated and harvested from slaves of every race. But here the scale was far more epic. The very fabric of the world for as far as his dim eyes could show him felt rotten, *perished*. The reports of all of his senses scurried about his mind to decry its wrongness and even he, master of the industrialisation of degradation, felt sickened by it.

A geyser of corpse gas rippled upwards and outwards from a sinkhole further down near the gatehouse. Grime spattered back over the rotten gates and the band of warriors marching home over its splinters. A column of plague beasts and meat wagons followed them. Kletch recognised Fistula's pack: the most useful of Bule's warriors, but a drop in the septic ocean of his horde.

Leaning against his staff, he settled in to wait.

'Another day spent in genuflection to our lord's placidity, envoy?' said Fistula as he tramped up the slope, evidently bound for the same destination as Kletch. The champion was spattered with loose gore and beaming, contempt for all and sundry and for Kletch in particular vibrant in his bloodshot eyes.

The blightlord walked over, laden carts drawn by withered, pestilential beasts creaking on behind him. Kletch stiffened with immediate suspicion and sniffed at the flies buzzing lazily after the vehicles' cargo. The experiments of Clan Burrzik in breeding eavesdropping mosquitoes had faltered as a consequence of the clan's incompetence, but one never knew. One never knew.

'Maybe,' he said, then chirred something conciliatory and gestured with his tail to the top of the hill.

There, encircled by a ring of luminous white pillars that in their cleanliness exuded a sense of power and prominence, was a marble archway carved with astrological constellations and runic notations. It stood bare to the stars as if waiting only on their call, and even inert as it was, the sight of it sent a frisson of imagined dread running to the tip of his tail. He could understand why the ancients here had built such a monument to the heavens.

He licked his gums nervously. 'What does Bule want-think will happen tonight?'

'I can tell you what *I* think will happen.'

Kletch caught the blightlord's look and read the need there. Battle. Survival. Aims not identical to his, but with cunning words and enough will perhaps complementary ones. He glanced upwards again to mark the approach of high moon, his neck, accustomed to tunnels and caves, already sore from continually doing so. That was when he noticed what had been worrying at him since he left his tent.

The stars were moving.

IV

For a count of years numbering seven times seven times seven times seven, Copsys Bule had tended his garden. He did not know how many millions he had pulled out of the ground since that first day. Unlike some, he kept no lists, no ledgers, except that which existed in his mind. He knew only that his god saw it as good.

Turning his knife so that it was point down, he pushed the blade into the mushy chest of the body spread like soft grey cheese over dry bread across the trencher table in front of him. There was no resistance. It was like cutting into marrow jelly.

Flesh separated in a great swelling of maggots as Bule carved from collar to coccyx. A comingling of organs and body juices dribbled from the gash. The smell was pure ambrosia. His belly gurgled. Decay was a master gourmet. It loosened the fat, softened fibres and pulled meat from the bone. It brought out a depth and range of flavours that the impatient flesh-eaters of Khorne or the squeamish that burned their meat with fire could never experience.

He licked the juices from his knife blade, mouth distending to accommodate his entire fist. The panoply of tastes and odours gave him shivers and he closed his eyes.

The added spice of plague magic, the power of new life, tingled on the tip of his tongue and then diffused through him like a warmth. He withdrew his hand, sucked clean, and then hung the knife from one of the curing hooks that protruded from his armour.

'All. Ready,' snuffled Gurhg, the bray shaman thumping the ground with a skull-topped stave as he walked around the stirring realmgate. Standing behind the sagging trenchers in an octed around the realmgate, blightlords and champions watched solemnly. The shaman raised his bull snout and snorted, bone fetishes and feathers tinkling from blistered horns. He closed his eyes and emitted a low sigh that made the hanging flesh of his throat quiver. 'Feel. Him. Stirring.'

Bule spread his arms with a smile. Torchlight flickered from sconces set in the columns. Brass tocsins played by hooded slaves with wire brushes hummed a sonorous chorus.

'Feast, my children.'

To a great squishing of meat and crumbling of rot-softened bone, the gathered worthies of the Rotbringers tucked in with a hunger. Bule watched them all, hands across his swollen girth. There was Fistula, ever prideful, ambitious, filling his mouth with the same abandon as the others. Beside him the old bloat hound, Vitane, sucked jelly from his fingers and laughed at a joke. Their greatly honoured guest from Clan Rikkit was hunched behind a corner trencher, nibbling diplomatically at a bit of bone and throwing uneasy glances up at the sky. Copsys Bule basked in the paternal glow.

It was nearly time. The magic was rising, and Bule could feel the realmgate responding. For a moment he could *feel* the connections that ran through the Eightpoints to some other place, some other realm, where one far mightier than he tended a garden of his own. He looked up. The moon was approaching its zenith. The stars were in alignment, brighter and clearer than Bule had ever seen them before. One of them momentarily grew brighter.

Bule examined the moving constellation with wide open eyes. Yes. *Yes.*

The star grew brighter, brighter, shining out the others around it and projecting a beam of starlight directly onto the realmgate. Bule grunted at the sharp glare and shielded his eyes with his arm. As the light dissipated, he looked immediately back to the gate.

A slender-bodied lizard wielding what looked like a dart-pipe and a spear was now standing on the pedestal before the gate. It stood on its hind legs like a man, shorter even than Kletch Scabclaw and more wiry still. The black colouration of its scales mottled to white as Bule watched, matching itself almost seamlessly to the marble hues of the gate behind it. His eyes continuing to recover from the flash, Bule noticed a hundred or so more of the little creatures, spread out in the shadows around the gathered Rotbringers.

A strained silence fell over them all. Even Gurhg noticed and stopped chanting.

The lizard-man lowered its head, spines engorging to raise a vivid frill. It emitted a warbling chirrup then lifted its dart-pipe to its beak.

For one so vast, Bule could move like poison through a panicking man's veins when quickened to do so. That he had not been so roused in over a hundred years was nothing. He was Copsys Bule, the Black Thumb, and his knife was in his hand and wrist deep in the lizard's still-shattering ribcage before the creature had drawn its breath.

The lizard's nictitating eyelids fluttered in shock. Already its scaly skin was beginning to blister with the lesions of Nurgle's blessed rot, daemonflies pupating inside the wound in its chest, but to Bule's surprise what emerged from that wound was not blood but pure, cleansing starlight.

Scalded where it touched his arm, Bule tore his hand back, ripping a chunk of the lizard's chest out with it. It shuddered and fell, vanishing in a cascade of glimmering motes before it hit the ground.

Clenching and unclenching his fist around his knife handle, feeling the burned, *cleansed*, tissue pulling, Bule grunted at the barely comparable sensation of a metal-tipped blow dart puncturing his neck. He felt the venom enter his blood and would have laughed at its impish ineffectuality had he not been building towards such a fury.

This was his moment, his time. The signs had been guiding him for centuries towards this night.

With a snarl that came from deep in his monstrous belly, he turned and flung his knife. It spun end over end, so fast it appeared as a solid discus, and punched a chameleon lizard from its feet in an explosion of light and bone.

Blow darts and javelins droned around him like hornets, snuffing out the torches with the wind of their flight, and falling on the Rotbringers. They bristled from unfeeling flesh, rattled off heavy armour and even downed a handful of the mighty warriors before they had a chance to react. The beastman, Gurhg, dropped to his haunches and backed into a trencher table with his head down. He found Kletch already under it.

Air rippled inside the arch of the realmgate.

It was subtle but there, the power awakening in direct response to the plague magic that Bule had nurtured in his garden for two thousand four hundred and one years. That power was still rising. Nothing would stop it now.

Copsys Bule looked again at his hand, free of blight for the first time since he knew not when.

'Kill them all!' he shrieked. 'Let none of them touch my garden!'

V

Fistula was more disoriented than angry. He was drunk on meat and cankerberry wine, and on a power that he could not put name to but which filled him with a fever swirl of thoughts. The discordant moan of tocsins droned through his mind, though they were playing a cadence of battle now rather than of ceremony. The taste of meat was in his mouth, but it was fresh, torn not from the embrace of Copsys Bule's soil but from the struggling bodies of the living.

He spat out a mouthful of blistering starlight. Or tried to. His throat burned, however hard he wretched and gagged.

Goaded into lucidity on a knife-edge of pain he struck down a lizard-man that was hissing in cold-blooded consternation at the chunk bitten out of its wrist. It disappeared in a drizzle of glimmer dust. Two more took advantage of the light-shock to blindside him. They came with spears held short.

Fistula caught the haft of the first spear thrust, then with his sword hand punched it in half. The lizard stumbled. Turning his body across and through it, he pushed it on its way to the ground, spitting his sword out to arm's length to impale the second. Light exploded from its back around the tip of his sword. This time he was ready for the glare. Eyes already narrowed, he spun quickly away, stamping on the first lizard and grinding the light that bled from its fractured skull under his boot.

Something small and metallic spanked his pauldron guard. Darts tipped with starmetal zipped by. He saw a burly Rotbringer with a cloak of festering hide go down under a volley of them. Another took a freak hit, a dart straight down the ear, dropping the warrior like his weight in dead meat.

From somewhere, screaming. Melting flesh and starlight.

Every one of these warriors was a master of war, the mightiest of mortal champions uplifted to near daemonhood by the Lord of Decay. But they had forgotten what it felt like to be challenged. After millennia of pointless warfare they had forgotten what it truly was to fight.

Fistula clutched at his gut with his off-hand.

He felt ill, stricken, a great swelling pressing up from inside his chest. Pressure climbed up his throat, as though he were a snake trying to regurgitate a man that had been too large for him to swallow. A bilious taste flooded his mouth and, on unconscious reflex, he doubled over and vomited forth a torrent of foulness and corruption.

The lizard-men caught in the flow died instantly and in agony. The Rotbringers similarly touched were healed as if by the beaming intercession of Grandfather Nurgle himself. Maggots squirmed over open wounds. New and glorious infections puckered flesh that had been rankly cleansed by the lizards' light.

Swallowing several times to assure himself that he too was whole again, he looked about for more enemies. There were none. All around him were in advanced stages of rot or already returned to whatever heavenly body had spewed them forth.

He panted, heart racing. Was that all?

'Kill them all!' he heard Copsys Bule shout, a shrill note of fury screwing his voice tight. 'Let none of them touch my garden!'

Fistula shot around to look down the slope. His heart thumped hard for joy.

Light knifed frenziedly from the heavens. Flashes blossomed within the fug of flies, then glowed and spawned warriors. Many of them were bigger than the lizard-men he had just slaughtered. Some of them were a lot bigger. That first wave must have been some kind of advance party. Scouts. Assassins, perhaps. This was an army, coming down in conventional formations.

Accompanied by tocsins and bells and calls to glory, warriors of the Rotbringers mustered over the old corpse-hung curtain walls to oppose them. Bule commanded the souls of a hundred thousand, and although more than half were scattered wide over the Corpse Marshes and beyond, what remained was a mighty host indeed.

He bared sharpened teeth, a feral grin. Now for notice. Now for glory. This was going to be a fight.

'You want war?' Bule roared at the stars, and the very ground beneath seemed to tremble at his words.

Someone had passed the Lord of Plagues his helmet, and his voice boomed from inside the steel. In both hands he gripped the haft of the trident with which he tended his garden, veins standing out from bulging biceps as he continued to howl without words. God-gifted power oozed from him, turning the air around him syrupy brown. Sickly, cyclopean figures began to take shape there. They were horned, drenched in mucous and stooped over serrated swords that reeked of soul-rot. Nurgle's tallymen. Plaguebearers. From the strain in Bule's bearing it was though he passed them from his own body. In a sense he did.

Fistula howled, maddened by battle-lust and plague.

Bule crashed the brass ferrule of his trident into the ground and screamed.

'I will give you war!'

VI

Kletch Scabclaw ran in the middle of the Rotbringers' counter-attack, where he felt naturally safest, ducking, weaving, leaping between pockets of solid ground. Not that he felt all that safe. Beastmen thundered downhill like rabid animals while Chaos warriors, each with their own maddened cry on their black lips, battled each other to be the first to meet the enemy and in their blundering almost dragged Kletch under more than once. Of course, the plague monks of Clan Rikkit could be just as zealous in battle, but only with the inspiring words of their priest in their ears and the fumes of his blessed censer in their snouts. As well as being unruly, the horde was not as sufficiently numerous as he would have liked. That wasn't exactly helped by those who were continually peeling off to strike out at the lizard-man skirmishers firing down on them from their flanks.

The lizards scampered with near-impunity over walls and pox moats that, judging by the clear lack of defenders, the Rotbringers had considered impassable.

The Rotbringers had been fools.

Even by Kletch's own standards, the lizards were light on their feet. Their bones seemed to be hollow, and with little else to them but light they skipped across floating corpses as cleanly as if they were solid ground. Only the moats themselves gave them pause – fecund nurseries of disease that hummed with deadly daemonflies – but they served only to funnel the rabid Rotbringers through their own defensive works where they were easy pickings for the lizard's dartpipes.

Skinks.

Kletch shivered, some deep residual instinct to freeze and play dead almost killing him there amongst the running column of Chaos warriors, beastmen and mind-plagued fanatics.

He kept running, not watching, his pre-conscious replaying him impressions of jungles he had never seen, of stepped pyramids he had never visited, the terror of being prey in a land he had never called his. He had not seen or heard of these lizard-men, these seraphon, before now, but deep down he *knew* them, and it was a knowledge that a thousand generations of new lands and new enemies could not wipe from his racial memory.

He leapt from one patch of solid ground to another, then another, easily outpacing the beasts and once-men that ran around him. His heavy cloak slowed him only a little, flapping out as he made one long leap, landing on a leaning root of a column. Sinking around his staff onto all fours, he sniffed the air for the musk of his own.

Useless. The whole castle was thick with decay. With a snarl, he resorted to using his eyes.

Despite the lizards' – the *skinks'* – success in drawing the Rotbringers into more difficult terrain, the bulk of Bule's horde were still charging for the good ground where the main outer curtain walls converged on the gatehouse citadel. He could hear the drums and horns, the shouts and the roar of beasts. Skaven eyesight grew dim over any kind of distance and for that, today, he was grateful.

'Go around!' he squeaked, gesticulating furiously from his pedestal to the band of Rotbringers that were wading into a stinking brown pond to get at the brightly scaled skinks on the other side. 'Go get. Kill-kill. Go!'

To no surprise of his, the Rotbringer's champion plunged on into deeper water. The warrior was an idiot. He'd earned the dart in the throat that dropped him face down into the mire a moment later.

The skinks were making a mockery of the heavily armoured blightkings, making them look sluggish. The daemons were another matter.

Every sore on Kletch's body wept, every ache seizing and filling his wiry body with pain as ten of Nurgle's tallymen strode onto the pox moat, walking weightlessly upon the scum that floated on the surface and through the stinging daemonflies. The cold-blooded star-creatures barely reacted. Kletch watched as a skink shaman rustled his feathered cloak, flying over the plague-bearers' heads to land in a swirl of red and gold on a stump of wall behind them. There, he shook his staff, exhorting a hail of darts from his kin that fell amongst the closing daemons.

Kletch snickered. Everyone knew that daemons could not be killed that way. But the tallymen fell by the handful, if anything even more vulnerable to the seraphon's envenomed darts than the mortals they marched beside.

With a snarl, Kletch reached inside his cloak for his weapon, eyes locked on the shaman.

'See-smell how tough you are. Kletch not afraid of scrawny scaly-meat.'

The faintest trace of reptile musk warned him of the danger just before an ear-splitting shriek from above re-triggered every instinct he had to freeze, run, hide. *Terradon.* The giant reptile swooped overhead, banked gracefully under the effortless direction of its skink rider, then dropped a boulder from its hind-claws. It came down like a meteor. It *was* a meteor.

With a terrified squeal, Kletch leapt from his column, arms and legs churning as the spot he had been standing on was annihilated, the air at his back electrified by a starlight explosion. His tail peeled. His cloak caught fire. He landed in a roll, steaming from fur and clothes and from the accidental release of fear musk down his leg.

'Scratch and sniff,' he swore.

Patting himself down, he brushed a string of darts from the back of his cloak. He swallowed the bad taste in his mouth. Dropping to all fours to make himself less of a target to any skinks looking to pick off survivors, he scurried from the path, zig-zagged through a verge of bloodgrass that stuck up from a hummock of dead men and horses like pins, and then dived into a wild patch of bruise-coloured bushes that clung to a ledge growing out from the second curtain wall. A few tail-lengths in he poked his head up through the scratching branches.

Below, clanking streams of Chaos warriors fed into a blurrily defined blob of screams and steel, a blood-and-lizard stink spilling out over half a league of the Hanging Garden's heartlands. He didn't need the eyes of a surface-dweller to see the blocks of bulky lizard warriors – *saurus* – grinding in under their golden icons. He could see well enough the giant reptiles that towered over all with swaying howdahs on their backs, even if he couldn't quite count the horns on their bony head shields.

The seraphon were being held back for now. Nothing stood up to attrition like a warrior of Nurgle, and Copsys Bule commanded monsters of his own. Kletch sniffed the air and shivered at the sharp, unmistakeably vile scent.

The Lord of Plagues was down there. Good riddance.

'*Scabclaw-master!*'

Kletch hissed angrily to mask his surprise, but this time held onto his musk. Scurf was scurrying through the flesh-drinking grasses, surrounded by a clawpack of stormvermin mercenaries in muddy black plate mail and wielding vicious-looking halberds. Several hundred raggedy plague monks followed, individuals breaking every so often to sniff the air, lash their tails in fear, and then hurry on.

'Lightning men!' Scurf squealed.

The word-bringer was in the same stained linen cassock he'd been wearing an hour ago, but had, apparently in great haste, donned a mail coif and was clutching a cracked tome that he held onto like a shield. He waved a rusty scimitar at the stars. Flies eddied and swarmed, a billion billion, but the stars behind no longer moved. An unnaturally intense constellation in the shape of a squatting toad glared down with eyes tinged red.

'Fool-fool,' Kletch snapped. 'This is something other.'

'Something new?'

Kletch shook his muzzle. 'Something old.'

'The claw-packs are ready to leave-go,' added Scurf. He glanced down to the battle and gulped. 'Very-very much-ready.'

Kletch bared his teeth, yellow eyes shining. This might all just work out after all. If Copsys Bule was defeated, as looked likely, then the clanlords could hardly blame *him* for failing to secure an alliance that the Lord of Plagues had never appeared to want at all. And if the weakened Lord of Plagues somehow managed to secure a pyrrhic victory? Perhaps then the generous backing of Clan Rikkit would appeal to him more.

'This way,' Kletch hissed.

Darting back into the bloodgrass, he wove through it, driving purposefully away from the main seraphon assault. Corpses at varying stages of rankness wobbled underpaw, tipping, sinking, at times disintegrating before he was able to leap clear and plunging him into foetid water. He spluttered a wordless prayer to the Pestilent Horned Rat that the tonic he had drunk would continue to prove effective. Keeping his head down and his nose clear, he scurried on. He was moving inside the circle of the inner walls to the far side of the fortress-temple. From there, with luck, he would be able to clamber down and escape without great difficulty. He upped his pace, becoming a blur of fur and movement.

There was nothing in all the realms quicker than a skaven with a battle to escape, but Kletch was not yet so anxious to flee as to allow himself to pull ahead of his brother monks.

Not for the first time – and he fervently hoped not for the last – sound skaven thinking saved his hide.

Crashing through a canopy of hanging dead, a lumbering reptile as massive as a barded warhorse snapped the lead clan-rat up in its jaws, trampling three more before the saurus riding it could rein it back.

Its predatory head was huge and low-slung, supported by a monstrous neck and counter-weighted by a thick tail that tacked menacingly in advance of its movements as it turned. The skaven in its jaws was shrieking. A savage yank of neck and jaw and the beast bit the pitiful creature through, sending legs and torso flying over opposite shoulders. A rake of its vestigial forepaws claimed another.

Scurf issued a rallying squeal, backing into the stormvermin clawpack as the beast completed its turn and snorted in his nose. He whipped up his book of woes with a frightened squeak as the saurus' mace came down.

The book was mouldering parchment bound in cracked leather.

The mace was meteoric stone.

Hurriedly withdrawing from the smashed word-bringer, the stormvermin lowered their halberds, throwing up a wall of hooked blades between them and the beast. The reptile – *a cold one* – snapped contemptuously, taking off one of the blades and eating it.

The saurus hefted its bloodied mace and with cold calm scanned the skaven scattered across the grass before it. Every scale armouring its grossly powerful hide was chipped and scarred. Its eyes were old. Beautiful works of golden plate clad vulnerable spots such as its throat and wrists. It shone like the light at the end of all the skaven's tunnels.

Pumping its mace up into the air, it gave a roar that shook the air. With answering roars, a full cohort of glittering saurus warriors marched into the open.

Kletch squealed for order, for ranks, shoving his way to the back of them as he did so. These saurus were on foot, armed with spears and shields, but it scarcely mattered. Each one was twice the size of an armoured stormvermin and looked the match for any six.

With frenzied squeals, the plague monks charged. The saurus trampled them without appearing to notice and slammed into the line of stormvermin.

'Hold. Fight! *Kill-kill!*' shouted Kletch, growing ever shriller as the lizards' massive line troops ground their way through his.

A rustle from the tall weeds to the right made his heart sink. There were more.

Hacking wildly at the bodies that came at him on nooses from all sides, Blightlord Fistula ran through, savaging a saurus from behind before the cold-blooded brute had even realised he was there. Coming under a swarm of flies, his putrid blight-kings piled in behind him.

This was a more even fight. The blightkings were Bule's elite and, Kletch knew, Fistula's were the best. He was not at all surprised that the first blightlord had been amongst the reckless few to be dragged out into the swamp chasing skinks.

'In! In!' Kletch squeaked, urging his warriors on.

Scenting blood, the clawpacks and surviving plague monks pushed forward, wedging the saurus between two sets of enemies.

Observing the reverse in fortunes with an impersonal, calculating detachment, the saurus pointed its cold one towards Fistula and roared its challenge. The first blightlord ran at it with a yell, both weapons out at his side, armour dripping with bile.

The saurus struck first. The cadaver-thin blightlord parried the lizard's mace with a blow that would have broken both of their arms had either been a lesser being, then rolled out of the lunge of the cold one's jaws. His knife chewed down the side of the beast's neck and spat out scales. He dodged back, turning a crunching side kick from the old saurus on his vambrace, then charged back in.

The saurus was wheeling his furious mount when Fistula stepped onto a plague monk's mushed body and, using it a springboard, vaulted over the reach of the cold one's flailing *snap*. Sliding down the beast's spiny neck, he slammed bodily into the saurus and punched a knife towards its neck. It moved just fast enough to take it in the shoulder. If it felt either surprise or pain it didn't show it. A shattering head butt snapped back Fistula's head and sent him crashing over the cold one's flank and down to the sucking ground. The cold one stomped on his breastplate, pushing him deeper under.

Then Kletch withered away the saurus' head with a bolt of plague magic.

The cold one issued a defiant roar that shook the eardrums long after it vanished into the same cloud of light that reclaimed its master.

Shivering off the giddy tingle of the warpstone fumes from his pestilent censer, Kletch secreted the relic back into its pouch underneath his robes. He had taken the weapon from the clan vaults to deal with Copsys Bule, but it smelled like that was one precaution he didn't need anymore.

'He had me.' Fistula's laughter bubbled crazily, riding down from some wild adrenaline high.

'We should be going-gone. Before more like it come.'

'Going?' Fistula sat up straight, face flushed red and cut in half by a razored smile. 'I would fight more of your lightning men.'

'They are not lightning men,' Kletch snapped, suddenly lacking all patience for the stupidity of others. 'The lightning men are... are much worse.'

'Worse?'

'Come with me,' Kletch hissed, sidling closer, tail switching side to side. 'Bule is old. Leave him to rot in his garden. Come kill-slay with Clan Rikkit.'

Fistula looked to his warriors. Kletch bared his fangs in a grin. He wouldn't be returning to the clanlords with empty paws after all.

VII

Copsys Bule was untouchable.

Of the lizard-men that came close, only the very mightiest amongst them could make it within reach of his weapon before Nurgle's Rot left them crippled and blind. And yet on these star-lizards came, fearing neither death nor disease.

His trident struck like an adder, piercing the throat of a heavily scarred lizard and exploding through the back of its neck. With one huge scaly hand it grappled with the haft, swinging a glowing starmetal axe with the other. Bule yanked back on his trident, pulling the impaled scar-veteran into a forward stumble and sending its axe stroke flailing harmlessly past his shoulder. An open fist to the gut punched the scar-veteran off his weapon's tines, two feet through the air and onto its back. Bule closed the distance, trident spinning once, twice, overhead, and then smashing through the lizard-man's chest. With a heave, he drew the trident up, the weapon arcing back overhead to its full extension to polearm the spear warrior that had been charging his supposed blindside.

With the rest of his horde struggling to hold their line, Copsys Bule took another forward step.

A powerful lizard in golden armour blocked him. The blinding might of Azyr screamed between the joins of its scales, and the roar of its challenge was like that of a furnace. Saliva stellar white hissed from its jaws as it brought up a primitive-looking two-handed blade.

Bule turned the hacking stroke with a loop of his trident, then took the haft between both hands and drove the ferrule into the sun-lizard's groin. The warrior emitted a grunt and staggered back, unhurt, throwing a punch that caught the haft of Bule's weapon. The struck trident popped out of Bule's fingers and landed in the mud behind him. It was the deft, impish move of a master of unarmed combat.

With a celestial roar, the sun-lizard swept its weapon overhead.

Spinning and dropping, Bule planted his knee on the ferrule and slid his hand under the trident's haft. Halfway along, a flex of the fingers bounced it up, reversed against the slope of his shoulder, just as the sun-warrior charged in to deliver the deathblow.

There was a heavy crunch, a sigh, the burn of starlight raining across his back.

Bule turned as he rose, swinging his weapon out like a scythe, letting fly, and sending the dying sun-warrior cannoning into the head of the hulking lizard giant that had just strode into view. Both went down in a mighty crash. The sun-lizard vanished in a flash of sunbeams. The giant, merely unconscious, did not rise again.

'Is this it?' he cried, laying out a murderous sigil of overlapping figure-of-eights. 'Is this all that you have?' To kill again, and to kill swiftly, felt glorious. Colours were vivid, scents sharp, cries like bells. He was a man awakening from a coma and remembering that he was furious. 'Do you even realise whom you face?'

He shovelled down another lizard-warrior on the flat of his tines, then span, alerted by the prickling sense of something approaching from behind.

A robed figure stood there on the writhing carpet of sickening lizards. It regarded him through the haze of flies, neither noticeably human nor obviously reptilian. Daemonic perhaps, yet not. Its head was angled like a hoe with a row of eyes along its ridge. Some of them examined Bule archly, others with compassion, mirth, and contempt. In spite of himself, of what and where he was, Bule felt a chill.

Blind to their visitor, a cohort of warrior lizards charged through the hazing flies. They died one by one. The inhuman apparition did not react, but, despite having no obvious mouth, Bule had the impression that it smiled at him, as though he were a bloat hound that had earned a treat.

A tremendous death bellow drew his attention away.

There, the mighty plague maggoth that had been rolling over the lizards' advance with a wedge of Rotbringers in train collapsed in an avalanche of folds. A sunbeam split the monster from shoulder to navel and the armour-plated head of some apex reptile butted it aside. Fixed to the lizard creature's back was the silver and star-metal housing of some inscrutable god-engine, which clicked and reset amidst a glow of energies. The Rotbringers retreated, their forward push stymied. Bule was aware of the enemy pouring forward on all fronts now as his own defences began to crumble. With a snarl, he took his trident overhand like a javelin and made to challenge that armoured reptile's invulnerability.

'*He seeks a champion.*'

The apparition's robes whispered as it followed him. Its clothing was made not of hides or cloth but of eyes, and the susurrus it made was the sound of hundreds of blinking eyelids, rippling white, green, black, and every other colour that skin came. It moved without truly moving. It spoke without speaking.

'*Seek him, champion.*'

Turning, gesturing without anything so prosaic as a pointed finger, the figure directed Bule's gaze to the realmgate. The skin within it flexed. The stars above it wheeled. Even from afar Bule could see that the view within was no longer of the garden with which it had previously been twinned. Fury returned to him redoubled. *Disbelief.* It was not mere bad fortune that had brought the seraphon upon him with the aligning stars. They had come for his realmgate.

Somehow they had manipulated the Eightpoints to change its destination. How? The magic involved in enacting such a feat was godlike!

The apparition hissed in sudden distress. Its cloak shimmered with many colours, every eye tightening shut as though simultaneously blinded. And then in a searing moment of universal light, it was gone.

'Grandfather!' Bule cried, light like a fire in his eyes. 'Aid me!'

Shading his eyes with one heavy arm, he peered into the oncoming host.

Floating on a cushion of force above the golden spears of its warriors came the source of the light. It was as if a star had been called down from the heavens and condensed into a brittle caul of bone-brown wrappings and dry flesh. Its presence alone was massive. From its palanquin, the mummified creature regarded the battle with the distant disinclination of an inhuman god. Instinctively, Bule understood that here came a being that had known power long before some daemons had even come to be. He felt himself drawn spiritually towards it, the golden funerary mask that picked out its amphibian features in jewels swelling to fill his mind as the universe subtly reordered around it.

It made no word or gesture, but somewhere in the cosmos something gave.

The heavens opened.

Bule howled impotent fury as the stars glimmered and fell, plucked from the sky, and smashed into his horde.

The first meteorite hit at an angle, obliterating a dozen Chaos warriors utterly and blowing a crater hundreds of feet wide. Then came the rest. The ground shook under the fury. The sky turned white, light and sound reaching an intensity where they sublimated into one, a single shrieking colour in Bule's inner eye, and even the daemons burned in fire.

Bule struggled gasping onto hands and knees, tripping a warrior lizard running in behind him with a backward kick and riding it face-down into the filth until it stopped thrashing. He stood up, dazed senseless by thunder. Waves of power smashed out from the advancing palanquin. It was almost impossible to stand against it, but in a tremendous feat of will, he stood. He shook his head.

'Aid me!'

Nothing. Nothing but the awesome presence of this starmaster.

Moving with difficulty, he turned and staggered back the way he had come. Never in his life had Copsys Bule run away, but Grandfather Nurgle did not know defeat.

With every waning, he would wax again.

VIII

First Blightlord Fistula stepped out of the realmgate and onto another world.

The air was syrupy, hot, sweetened by the sweat of fat citrus-scented leaves and by the bell-shaped blue flowers that he and his warriors crushed underfoot. He looked around in amazement, turning ponderously. He felt... *weightier*, as if the sky itself pushed him down under its palm. And the sun – forgetting for the moment that it should be night – was over large and buttercup yellow. Winged creatures rustled through the leaves above. And from somewhere, screams.

He pulled off his helmet, wiped his running nose, and drew deep.

'New lands.'

Soon all that was green would be a verdant collage of yellows and browns and leaf-rust reds. It would be the cradle of a new land's blight, the metastasis from which a new canker would swell. And all of it was his.

'Over here,' growled Vitane, crunching through the under-growth in the vague direction of those screams.

Fistula acceded to the old blightking's instincts for pain and followed. After a few minutes of unexpectedly heavy going through the dense foliage of this foreign land, the warriors were, to a man, blowing hard, their armour hanging loose on straps. The screams got nearer. More abject. Chesting aside a branch, too weary to bother his arm with the task, Fistula pushed ahead into a sun-drenched clearing.

Varicoloured lichens and mushrooms covered the split bark of the fallen log that dominated the clearing. The cries were coming from the other side of the log.

Shading his eyes from the visceral brightness of the sun, Fistula saw the bray shaman, Gurhg, who was easy enough to pick out with his totemic staff and cloak woven with bones, even within a knot of his followers. There were perhaps two-dozen, stomping about and smashing horns – re-establishing domi-nance hierarchies and staking claim to new territories. Gurhg stood hunched and swaying in the middle of it, nodding his goat head approvingly as six men and a woman bound to a line of hastily woven racks screamed. The wails of the seventh man were of a different order. A beastman with the face of a horse and a line of horrendously infected iron piercings through its top lip diligently flensed the human with a blunt knife.

Fistula smiled. There were people here. Good. It had been too long.

'Blightlord.' Arms spread, snout turned to bare the throat in that odd gesture of his, Kletch Scabclaw padded towards him through the forest. The skaven envoy fussed at the clasp of his cloak, but despite his obvious discomfort he did not seem inclined to take it off. At the treeline, he bobbed low and with-drew with a hiss, averting his eyes from the sun.

'Where are your warriors?' asked Fistula.

'In woods. Less brave rats than I must cower where sky is less bright-strong.'

'Good.'

Fistula looked across the clearing at the brawling beastmen, and the blightkings now spreading out through the lichens to crash down and rest. It was not much, but it would be a start, and more would flock to him soon enough.

'I will have them seek-burrow for the way home at once,' said Kletch, stamping his foot-paw anxiously.

'Good...'

Fistula put his hands on his hips and turned his face full on to the sun. It was his. It was all his.

Something heavy and wet tramped up through the woods behind him. The wheezing breath on the back of his neck was thick with the stench of stagnant meat.

'I began my quest with less. I can begin again.'

Fistula spun around.

Bule.

'I see now,' said Copsys Bule, unhelmed, smiling blackly. 'I see what I have been missing.'

'This is mine,' Fistula snarled, baring his blades. Some withered instinct for self-preservation kept him from using them, some dim recognition that the gods too had their favourites. He backed into the clearing. Bule moved towards him, Fistula continuing to retreat until the fallen tree prevented him from going any further. He dropped into a fighting crouch. 'I will not let you turn my conquest into another garden. You have forgotten how to do anything else!'

The Lord of Plagues spread his arms in forgiveness as he passed from the tree line and into the sunlight. His eyes squeezed shut against the sudden glare, but still Fistula did not think to attack. Mosses mottled and died where Bule trod. Insects dropped dead out of the air as he breathed it. Throughout the clearing beastmen, skaven and blightkings alike stopped what they were doing and abased themselves.

He came within sword's reach, knife's reach, arm's reach. Fistula lowered his weapons. He felt lethargic. His skin was hot.

Dropping to one knee in front of him, Copsys Bule leaned in and embraced him.

Fistula made an attempt at fighting it, but he felt so weak. His breath drained up and down like fluid. He shivered with chills even as fever sweat poured down his skin. Jerking in his determination to fight, he struggled as the Lord of Plagues cradled him, lowering him to the ground. Fistula tried to stare hatred at him, but failed even in that. Delirium fogged his eyes and opened his mind to wisdom's flood.

Sorcerers robed with eyes. An army of champions. Chaos united. A three-eyed king. Round and around.

'I'll. Fight you. Forever,' he swore.

'Grandfather Nurgle does not want us to submit,' Bule smiled. 'He wishes us to rage.'

The last thing Fistula saw before Nurgle's Rot fully entered his mind was Bule turning towards Kletch Scabclaw, arms open in blessing and friendship.

IX

Copsys Bule broke up the earth with his trident. A tangle of roots knotted up the soil, making it tough, and before long he was breathing hard, a burn spreading through his shoulders. It felt good. The simple labour eased his mind and his muscles. The repetitive activity gave him the chance to think, and to order his thoughts.

He had much to think upon.

'There,' he said, giving the ground a vigorous final crumbing, then stabbing his trident to one side. He ran his arm across his lank-haired brow, then turned and nodded.

Vitane slid his toe under Kletch Scabclaw's body and rolled the corpse into the rill that Bule had prepared for him. Flies crawled over the ratman's lips. His eyes were the black of rot-pickled eggs and the smell had that same astringent piquancy.

'So much life.' However many skaven he buried, the truth of that still filled him with wonder. 'My garden will thrive here.

It is as I said to you, envoy, no other race gives so thoroughly of themselves to Grandfather Nurgle.'

The skaven did not answer and nor did Bule expect him to. He would live again, of course. That was Nurgle's promise to all. The ratman's flesh would nurture many millions of short and wondrous lives, his decomposition would bring bounty to the ground in which he lay, but never again would he talk, think, or interfere in the ambitions of a Lord of Plagues.

Pulling up his trident, Bule proceeded to bed the skaven in.

The humans would go here, and here, either side, where their decay would be accelerated by the skaven's proximity. One of the other rat-men he'd dig a plot for over by the south-facing tree line where its remains could feed the poplars there. They were fast growers, and the rot would spread quickly. Already their leaves were beginning to wilt and brown at the edges. Birds hawked up a thin and sickly chorus of phlegm on the bowers.

He could see it now. He did not know how this was to end, he never had, but he knew how to begin.

'*Archaon.*'

Fistula was fetched up against the log, shivering like a man just fished in full armour from an ice pail. He muttered non-sequiturs under his breath, tired, for the moment at least, of raging them at the forest. His eyes rolled, like bones cast by a feverish shaman, and his brush with Nurgle's Rot had bequeathed him a circlet of rugose blisters that rimmed his bald head like a crown. Bule examined the stigmata. There was a sign there, he knew it, but of what?

'He grows more lucid,' observed Vitane.

'Nurgle favours him greatly.'

'A lord of flies,' Fistula murmured, shaking. 'A king with three eyes.'

A sign. Definitely.

Taking up his trident, Copsys Bule pushed it into the ground and began again.

He had much to think upon.

EYE OF THE STORM

STORM

Rob Sanders

The sorcerer opened his eyes. All of them.

The Many-Eyed Servant. Disciple of Tzeentch and subject of Archaon, who was the Everchosen of Chaos and the Ender of Worlds. Envisioner of sights unseen.

The Many-Eyed's gaze reached far, for he saw as gods do. He was Archaon's eyes. His gaze reached across the Mortal Realms. Searching. Searching for those who would become giants among men, warriors already pledged to ruin, who themselves searched for greater meaning and dark service. And there was no warlord of Chaos darker and greater than the Everchosen, for Archaon was Exalted Grand Marshal of the Apocalypse.

The Many-Eyed missed nothing. He saw through the living and dead, the inhuman and inanimate, and through the eyes of daemons, glinting in shadow. Coins fell from the lids of corpses, laid out on funeral pyres. Statues blinked the dust from their stony orbs. The eyes of cutthroats, kings and all wretched existence in between were spyglasses of the soul, through which the great sorcerer observed. Even the mind's eye was the sorcerer's to see. The play of pictures in the blackness behind the face. Memories churned up from the past. Secrets kept and fantasies imagined.

The daemon sorcerer looked for warriors worthy of his master's blade and plate, seeking out the darkest potential amongst a sea of butchers, corrupters, deviants and witchbreeds. True paragons of Chaos, like Archaon himself. Knights of Ruin, ready for the Everchosen's invitation in symbol, sign or vision, so that they might pass his test and join his baleful ranks – the living, armoured embodiment of Archaon's wrath, visited upon the Mortal Realms.

The Many-Eyed blinked his way across the worlds of men. He saw as the beasts did, and as the denizens who would act like beasts. In the forgotten reaches of the realm of Ghur, on a storm-lashed wasteland that savage nomads and wind-worshippers knew only as the Blasted Plain, the sorcerer found who he was looking for.

Orphaeo Zuvius. Blessed of the Great Changer. The one they call the Prince of Embers.

The Many-Eyed looked on Orphaeo through the eyes of the Tzeentchians that he led, the twisted wretches of his warband. In the cerulean plate and skirts of his half-robe, Orphaeo Zuvius pressed his slender body against the storm. The skies were bleeding and the winds streamed with blood, while grit plucked at his unholy vestments.

Zuvius steadied himself with the length of a wicked glaive. He walked with the polearm like a sorcerer's staff. It was a daemon-forged weapon, a shaft of sculpted metal crowned by a blade fashioned in the shape of Tzeentch's willowy symbol. It was called *A'cuitas,* and it was a gift from Zuvius' patron.

The Many-Eyed came to know this as he opened the ensor-celled weapon's eyes – for it had three, like his master, the Three-Eyed King – one that opened in the fat counterweight of the glaive's pommel and two set in either surface of the blade. The Many-Eyed took this as a good omen. From A'cuitas, the sorcerer commanded a better look of the champion's grue-some features.

Helmless, his face was a web of melted skin stretched across scorched flesh. The skin strands squirmed continuously across scalded features that might once have been handsome – fea-tures now contorted with self-satisfied determination and dark humour. Threadbare tresses of blue hair streamed from his head. Zuvius licked his smeared lips with a silver tongue: another of the Great Changer's gifts.

The glaive's blade blinked in the bloodstreaming storm. Now the sorcerer saw through the eyes of the Prince of Embers himself. Zuvius looked up at Mallofax, who sat atop the perch created by the blade's billhook. The creature was a familiar – a reptilian bird of cerulean plumage. The damned thing spoke to Zuvius in an ear-bleeding squawk that only the champion seemed to understand. The Prince of Embers nodded and looked back at his warband, trailing through the maelstrom of blood and wind-borne grit.

Trudging across the Blasted Plain in his wake were Sir Abriel and the remains of the king's household guard. Formerly charged with the protection of the royal family – for the Prince of Embers was royal indeed – the knights were now shadows of their former selves. Gone was the lustre of their plate and the mirror-finish of their weaponry. The Great Changer had twisted them as he had done the prince. They were but slaves to darkness, gangling horrors. The knights' besmirched plate had fused to their bodies and stretched with their unnatural step and reach. Covered in the glowing sigils of ruinous sorcery, they were now the Hexenguard of Orphaeo Zuvius.

Behind the knights, in their shredded cloaks, were the Unseeing – the Tzeentchian sorcerers who completed Zuvius' warband. Blind wretches, the Great Changer had taken their sight and cursed them with terrible, warped visions of the world about them. Striking out with their powers, the Unseeing turned their enemies into the frightful realisation of their horrific imaginings. With crooked hands on shoulders, the Unseeing formed a line of the blind following the blind – and all following the crunch of their master's footsteps.

Zuvius closed his eyes against the bloodstorm. Behind them and in the blackness of his lids, the Many-Eyed found light and the roar of flame. The prince's past was never far from his thoughts – an appalling vision of death and destruction that formed a dark stillness within the madman. It was the eye of a storm, a vision from an age long ago, before Zuvius and his warband were the twisted things they had become. A memory that would not be forgotten, floating to the surface of Zuvius' mind to sicken and be enjoyed.

Night. The walled city of Stormhaven, ablaze. The tower tops writhed in unnatural blue flame. The people screamed for their lives and then their deaths. The king was dead. Long live the king! The household guard stumbled from the north gate, the only one that was open. The others had been locked shut from the outside. People died like animals behind them, barging and clawing – swallowed by the blue flame. Sir Abriel and his men hacked and coughed, the power of change already finding its way inside them.

With them was Orphaeo – youngest son of the king and the only surviving member of House Zuvius. Surviving – but only just. He too had received the touch of change. Licked by the furious flames, Orphaeo was horribly burned. His face. His head. His hands. He did not cry out in pain. He was calm. The red raw muscles of his face remained uncontorted. He gave the order. Sir Abriel and his soot-smeared knights could not believe what they were hearing.

'Seal the gate,' the prince told them, stumbling away from Stormhaven's mighty walls. There was disbelief, disagreement, dissention even. But Orphaeo Zuvius was now the king and his will was absolute. Burying their doubts, the knights sealed the towering north gate, trapping the screaming innocents inside. They hoped that their liege had a good reason for acting so.

He did.

Ascending the nearby foothills, Zuvius turned to watch his city burn. A city loyal to the God-King, whose walls had stood against storm and ruinous savagery for generations. The prince felt the heat of the fire on his blistering face. He fancied this to be the satisfaction of the Great Changer, bathing him in the warmth of approval. It was a feeling that his face would not allow him to forget.

Mallofax circled the roaring, spitting firestorm of the burning city, the sapphire flames reaching for the heavens. He swooped in to land on Zuvius' shoulder. Abriel hated the prince's pet but the dread spectacle of Stormhaven ablaze meant that he barely noticed the scaly, feathered thing. If he had known that it had been Mallofax that was responsible for Stormhaven's fall, he would have cut the bird out of the air with a swing of his longsword. For it was Mallofax, flying over the walls and arriving one day on the prince's balcony, that had spoken of such horror to Orphaeo Zuvius, that had taught the prince the secrets of sorcery, the arts of manipulation and the power of change. That, as Tzeentch's emissary, had empowered Zuvius to turn brother *against brother, son against father and the people against their king, all culminating in riot and treachery, atrocity and flame.*

Sir Abriel and the household guard gathered about their young king. He was not their king, however. He was no one's king. He was forever the Prince of Embers – heir to the glowing ashes of a razed kingdom.

Zuvius watched the palace towers fall. He watched his own topple, falling like a mighty felled tree through the flames. Its tower top smashed into the city walls before the prince, knocking brick and stone from the defences. Zuvius stood transfixed. The bright blue fires within the city lit up a symbol rent into the wall.

'What is that?' the Prince of Embers demanded. Mallofax twitched his head and turned a glassy eye towards the damaged wall. The bird squawked. Through the soul-curdling sounds Zuvius heard the familiar's dark words.

''Tis the mark of the Everchosen,' Mallofax told him. 'An invitation.'

'To what?'

'The Exalted Grand Marshal calls,' the bird squawked. 'The Architect made you but Archaon will break you. You are to be forged anew, Zuvius, like I taught you. Listen to the screams. Look into the fire. Tell me what you see.'

Zuvius watched as the blue inferno flared up through the damaged wall, reaching for the battlements. In the lick and flicker of azure brilliance, the Prince of Embers saw a far off place take form.

'I see a storm within a storm,' he said to Mallofax. He squinted at the blaze.

'And?'

'Rising from it is a landform, sculpted by the storm,' Zuvius said. 'A mesa, shaped like a great anvil, with a path leading up to it.'

'The Beaten Path,' Mallofax told him. 'Your mettle is to be tested there, for the Everchosen selects only the best warriors of Chaos for his inner circle of death and dread.'

Zuvius nodded to himself. 'You know this place?'

'Of course,' the bird said. 'The storms you speak of rage across a distant wilderness called the Blasted Plain.'

The Prince of Embers jerked his shoulder, prompting the familiar to once again take flight.

'Then lead on,' Zuvius said. 'It would not be wise to keep the Everchosen of Chaos waiting.'

The Blasted Plain was living up to its name. Orphaeo Zuvius put one foot in front of another, forcing his way on through the streaming haze of crimson. There was nothing there but a maelstrom of everlasting gales and the blood of those claimed by the storm. The prince's hair and robe skirts twisted and tangled in the wind, while Mallofax's plumage was a constant ruffle. More miserable still was the twisted thing that had been Sir Abriel, and what remained of the Hexenguard and the sorcerers of the Unseeing who followed.

They had reason to feel misery. They had been wandering through the bloodstorm for weeks. Their cloaks and robes were in tatters and their plate scratched and dented. With only the beady eye of the bird Mallofax to guide them and the nods of his beak to indicate their heading, Zuvius and his warband moved from squall to squall. The storms that tormented the Blasted Plain were filled with whirls and eddies. In places, the Tzeentchians were drenched in fat droplets of gore that rained down from a crimson sky, while in others the gales and tempests turned the blood to a diluted smear. Exposure was not the only danger in the perpetual storm. Whirlwinds snatched up shrieking sorcerers of the Unseeing, lifting them into oblivion, while on the rocky expanse, sudden gusts lifted grit and pebble from the ground, blasting them through the Hexenguard like grapeshot from a cannon.

The Prince of Embers left a trail of corpses in his wake. What had been an army of Chaos knights and witchbreeds was now a warband numbering fewer than forty dark souls – still a potent force, but the trials of time, the perversities of the weather and enemy encounters had taken their toll.

He did not regret his decision to brave the Blasted Plain in search of the Beaten Path. He had been chosen. Those knights and sorcerers who had fallen had been unworthy of the Everchosen, and unworthy of him. Zuvius was to be tested. What kind of prospect would he be if he couldn't even reach the site that had been chosen for his trial? Zuvius pushed on through the bloodstorm. He could not allow it to defeat him.

Still, the depleted ranks of Zuvius' grand warband did not bode well for the challenges he knew to be ahead. He would have to supplement his numbers with lost wretches looking for direction and dark purpose. Fools were never in shortage. The Prince of Embers would give them purpose and they would give their lives in service of his destiny.

The Chaos champion heard Sir Abriel call something unintelligible through the storm. It was all the twisted knight was capable of now, beyond the devastating reach of his bladework. Peering at him through the bloody curtain of rain, Zuvius saw that Sir Abriel was pointing off to their right with the freakishly long fingers of his warped gauntlet. Following the direction the finger indicated, Zuvius squinted at the outline of tents in the distance – some kind of encampment in the wilderness.

'Food. Water. Shelter?' Zuvius said, shaking Mallofax on the glaive.

'Death?' the bird returned. Zuvius looked around. After

weeks out on the Blasted Plain he honestly thought his war-band wouldn't care.

'We're more than a match for a few nomads,' the Prince of Embers hissed, almost insulted at the insinuation of their vulnerability. Recent encounters and the toll of the storm had depleted his numbers but the Hexenguard and the Unseeing were more than capable of bringing horror and death to a tribe of wind-worshipping savages. Zuvius lurched through the storm in the direction of the camp.

'Onwards,' he called. With warped appreciation, the knights and sorcerers of the warband followed their master.

Zuvius pulled back the thick flaps of stitched flesh. Inside, the huge tent was a structure of giant bones. It was like stepping inside a giant ribcage. Torches flickered smokily. Zuvius immediately got the impression of many bodies – no doubt the tribesmen and savages he had been warned about. As Mallofax had predicted, the place stank of old blood and death.

The Prince of Embers stepped forward with confidence, allowing the Hexenguard and his sorcerers in. Regardless of the horrors they could inflict, the Unseeing did not make for an intimidating sight. The twisted knights, however, in their ghastly plate and glowing sigils, would be more than enough to startle the tribesmen. Then they would come to know that warriors of the Ruinous Powers were among them and that the sight of these doom-laden forms would be their last.

As Zuvius blinked blood from his eyes and adjusted to the gloom, he came to realise that he was not standing among scrawny nomads. Instead of wind-worshippers, the tent was filled wall to wall with muscle. Red flesh and scar-markings confirmed Zuvius' fears. They were not the first warband to take shelter in the tribesmen's tents. Barbaric servants of the

Blood God had beaten them to it. Looking down, the Prince of Embers saw that he was standing in the splattered remains of its previous occupants.

Casting a gaze across the tent, Zuvius made a quiet estimate of his rivals' strength. It was a veritable warband, all armed to the teeth, with perhaps more in the other tents. Zuvius had nothing approaching their number. A ripple of brute surprise passed through the barbarians, followed instantly by snarls and the wrinkle of lips. Muscles twitched to tautness and weapons scraped as they were snatched from the tent floor. Zuvius saw bloodreavers of the Goresworn, obvious from their decorative scarring. Other savages he recognised from their brazen cuisses and greaves, rattling beneath the broad red musculature of their chests. They were the wrathmongers of Khorne, blessed with the unyielding fury of their Ruinous god.

A stitch-faced chieftain and a wrathmonger closed on the Tzeentchians. The chieftain drew wicked blades from a selection of leather sheathes, holding them like talons in his gore-stained hands. The master of the wrathmongers, wearing the fanged skull of some daemon creature as a helmet, dragged the blood-rusted chain of a flail behind him, ready to yank it forward and hurl the hammer head attached to the length.

'Fight or flee?' Mallofax shrieked, flapping his wings and hovering above Zuvius and his warband. When the champion of Tzeentch didn't answer, the familiar repeated, 'Fight or flee?'

'Neither,' the Prince of Embers said. The Tzeentchian didn't move. He made the effort not to straighten and his glaive remained upright in his hand like a walking staff. He didn't want to provoke the savage disciples of Khorne any more than he already had by simply being there. At the same time, he wanted to present the calm front of a champion too powerful to be threatened by warriors of the Blood God, even in such number.

'Mine,' the chieftain hissed.

'The scraps, perhaps,' the wrathmonger rumbled.

Sorcerous sigils burned bright on the plate of the Hexenguard as the ghastly knights formed up in front of their prince with their notched longswords and battered shields.

'Stand down,' Zuvius said, his tone perverse and playful. Sir Abriel was unsure. He issued some kind of question from the hole in his face that he used as a mouth. The chieftain and the wrathmonger advanced, their men drawn up behind them.

Zuvius' eyes moved beyond the furious warband. Rising from a throne of stained skulls – the nomads', the prince presumed – was a champion larger still. A deathbringer, an exalted champion of the Blood God. Though he had been a man once, Khorne had blessed his chosen with hulking brawn. The warband leader was a veritable wall of muscle. The teeth of great beasts jangled on sinew necklaces while a pair of bull's horns erupted from his malformed skull. His hands were encased in bone weapons – pronged gougers that extended like a pair of claws. On his back, he carried a battle-axe, the blade of which was as broad as the champion himself.

'Hold,' the monstrous champion said. His voice was deep, like some bottomless trench reaching down into the bowels of the realm. His dogs of war stopped in their tracks, as if they had been yanked back on a running chain. The Goresworn came to a halt at the champion's command. They parted to let the deathbringer through.

Zuvius could see the champion's mind at work – which was something to be said of such savages. A hardening of the eyes. A tautness in the lips. Zuvius reasoned that the deathbringer had probably fought just about everything that lived and breathed on these plains. He had faced the sorcerous servants of the Great Changer before. Unlike his lieutenants, he was cautious. Wisely so, Zuvius agreed.

'What are you doing here on the Blasted Plain?' the warrior called across the tent. 'Speak fast and true or the bloodreavers here will smash your bones for the marrow inside. The wrathmongers will simply kill you out of spite. At my order, your blood will join that of the storm, in honour of mighty Khorne.'

Zuvius felt the eyes of all on him. The barbarians were aching for the violence to come.

'That would be ill advised,' the prince told him, playing for time. Zuvius' mind whirled. The Khornate savages within the tent would swamp them. Others, responding instinctively to the sounds of battle, would come up behind the Tzeentchian warband. It would be a slaughter, standing on the blood and bones of a previous one. Zuvius tasted the air with his silver tongue. Swords and sorcery couldn't take him where he needed to go. He would have to rely on one of his other god-given talents. 'For then you would not hear what I have to say.'

'And why would the great Skargan Fell-of-Heart need to hear the lies of filth witchbreed like you?' the Goresworn chieftain hissed, looking back at his master.

'Because even if only half of what I tell him comes to pass,' Zuvius said, 'then his ascension will be assured.'

'What ascension?' Skargan rumbled.

'The Everchosen calls for you, mighty one,' the Prince of Embers lied.

'Almighty Archaon?'

'Aye, my lord,' Zuvius said. 'The Exalted Grand Marshal of the Apocalypse asks only for the greatest warriors of the age, and he has called for you.'

'I'll cut that lying tongue out of your mouth, Tzeentchian,' the chieftain promised.

'Kraal, son of Zhufgor, let the sorcerer speak,' Skargan Fell-of-Heart said. The bloodreavers seethed about their chieftain while the wrathmongers foamed at their snaggle-toothed mouths. 'How came you by this knowledge?'

'A vision, my lord,' Zuvius said.

'Visions and enchantments,' Kraal, son of Zhufgor, spat in disgust.

The deathbringer's mouth curled into a snarl. He nodded his great horned head. A member of the Goresworn stepped up behind his chieftain, slipping his reaver blade beneath Kraal's chin. In a moment it was over. Zuvius felt the speckle of warm blood across the sensitive flesh of his face. The chieftain dropped and his killer stepped forward.

'Voark, son of Kraal,' the deathbringer said, 'the Goresworn is yours.'

Voark nodded his murderous appreciation.

'Sorcerer: speak.'

'I saw a vision in the flames of a burning city, exalted one,' Zuvius said. 'Skargan Fell-of-Heart, wearing the sigil of the Everchosen. The Exalted Grand Marshal of the Apocalypse is gathering his troops, deathbringer. Khorne knows you belong among them.'

Skargan narrowed the bloody orbs of his eyes at Zuvius.

'Your sorceries will not work on me,' he told the prince, tapping the talon-tip of a gouger against his bronze collar. 'The Blood God will not allow it.'

Zuvius nodded. He had seen such artefacts on Khornate champions before – the Blood God was eager to protect his butchers from the manipulations of magic. But the Tzeentchian did not need such powers.

'Come between the Ender of Worlds and his chosen?' Zuvius said. 'Not me, deathbringer. Not for all the dark glory in the realms. I know my place – in this, as in all things. I am merely the messenger.'

Skargan Fell-of-Heart looked to Voark, son of Kraal.

'Tell me more of your vision, sorcerer,' the deathbringer commanded.

'You must walk the Beaten Path, exalted one,' Zuvius said, 'to a place of testing – so that the Everchosen may judge if he chose wisely.'

'A battle?' Skargan said with a gory glint in his eye.

'I suspect, my lord.'

'You know this path?'

'I do,' the Prince of Embers said. 'And I have seen you walk it to glory.'

'What do you get out of this, sorcerous mongrel?' the death-bringer spat. Zuvius thought on the question.

'Nothing, mighty champion,' the prince told him. 'But I cannot deny destiny or the will of the Everchosen.'

Skargan scowled. Zuvius could see that the monstrous warrior didn't believe him. The prince watched as a flicker of doubt crossed the warlord's features. To disbelieve a servant of Tzeentch was one thing – common sense even – but to defy the will of the Everchosen of Chaos was something else entirely.

'Then you shall guide me along this path,' Skargan said. He turned to address the warriors in the tent. 'And if I seem displeased with this sorcerer and his wretches or you see them doing something that you know would displease me, then in Khorne's name – kill them.'

'As fair as you are wise, my lord,' Zuvius told Skargan Fell-of-Heart.

* * *

Orphaeo Zuvius forged on through the storm of blood. His warband trudged laboriously through a mire of rising gore, while Mallofax flapped his wings and shivered his feathers, shaking crimson droplets from his plumage. The Prince of Embers was now surrounded by Khornate killers intent on his blood. Looking back along the ranks of the Hexenguard and the sorcerers of the Unseeing, Zuvius could see the horde of Skargan Fell-of-Heart following them through the maelstrom. Two wrathmongers strode either side of him like a brute escort and Voark, son of Kraal, walked at the head of the bloodreavers, who swarmed about their beloved deathbringer, shielding Skargan as best they could from the storm with their number.

When Zuvius had seen the true size of the deathbringer's horde he knew that he had made the right decision in not attacking the Fell-of-Heart and his butchers. Skargan's warband numbered hundreds of battle-hardened warriors. To destroy them would have cost the prince dearly, perhaps even his life. Skargan and his horde had come to the Blasted Plain to honour their god, baptised in a bloodstorm they thought to be a manifestation of Khorne. They did not know that the storm existed only to scour the plain and claim the unwary. Mallofax had told his prince that the Blasted Plain was a cursed place. Nomads, wind-worshippers and travellers found eventual death in the perpetual tempest, their blood becoming one with the rains.

And the rain came down harder than ever, strumming fat droplets against Zuvius' plate. As they moved across the Blasted Plain, the Chaos champions left corpses in their wake. Moving from maelstrom to maelstrom and subject to the perversities of the storm, both Skargan and his sorcerer guide had lost members of their warbands. Twisters suddenly made landfall, stirring up the shallows and snatching bloodreavers up into the sky. One of the hulking wrathmongers was claimed by a sinkhole in the flooding mire. The temperature would change rapidly: in one moment red icicles hung from the plate of the Hexenguard, then an hour later Zuvius would lose a sorcerer to a balmy haze of swirling red steam.

'What is it?' Zuvius asked as Mallofax began to squawk and flap his wings furiously.

'This storm has teeth,' the bird said cryptically. Zuvius gave the familiar a quizzical look before the patter of bone against his plate told him all he needed to know. As the rising gale whistled through his skirts and the ragged ribbons of the Hexenguard's cloaks, it carried with it teeth, fangs and splinters of bone. Zuvius felt a shard cut across his cheek. Another tore through his skirts and plucked at the flesh of his leg. As the tempest intensified about them, so did the hail. It shredded through one of the wrathmongers and turned a bloodreaver into a bloody smear.

'The hollow!' Skargan Fell-of-Heart bawled through the storm. The horde had just passed a flooded hollow and the deathbringer directed his savages down into it.

'Do we follow them?' Mallofax squawked.

Zuvius looked about as the Hexenguard closed in with their shields, giving their sorcerous lord shelter. It was their best chance to escape Skargan's warriors. Conversely, the storm might still eat them alive and the Khornate warband was not without its uses.

'Do we have a choice?' Zuvius said, marching towards the hollow, teeth and bone rattling against the metal of the knights' shields.

Slipping and sliding down into shallows, Zuvius looked up at the wind streaming blood and bone above. The hollow offered shelter but was flooded with a crimson murk that sloshed around their boots. Zuvius wondered how long the squall of razored teeth and bone shards would last.

'How much further?' Skargan demanded, pulling fangs from his red flesh. Zuvius didn't know.

'Not far,' the prince said.

'What does that even mean?' Voark, son of Kraal spat. He could not hold back his ire. Looking around for his own son, Skraal, the bloodreaver continued, content that there was not a blade heading for his back. 'This sorcerer-filth is trying to get us killed out here. Leading us from trap to trap.' One of the wrathmongers grunted agreement from nearby. Zuvius realised that he had to stop this before Voark ignited the Blood God's hatred of sorcerers in Skargan and his horde.

'Apologies, exalted one,' Zuvius said. The deathbringer's monstrous features creased with disgust. He despised any man who would beg for his life rather than fight for it. Voark allowed cruel glee to creep across his lips.

'I can hold my tongue no longer,' Zuvius spoke quickly. 'My vision revealed knowledge that I was too fearful to grant you.'

'What knowledge?' the Fell-of-Heart snapped. He eyes narrowed in fury. 'You would deny me all that you know?'

'Having met your chieftains, I could not believe it,' Zuvius said. 'No champion commands warriors as fervent and loyal.'

'Believe what?' the deathbringer fumed.

'That the bloodreavers and the wrathmongers would betray one another,' the prince told him, with as much grave sincerity as the Tzeentchian could muster through his sly lips. 'And through each other – you.'

Skargan looked incredulously at Zuvius, at the wrathmongers and at Voark, as if he did not know which of them to kill first. Voark made the decision for him.

'Turncoat wretch! I knew you were planning something,'

he shrieked, drawing his reaver blade and pointing it at the nearest wrathmonger. At Voark's accusation, the bloodreavers started to advance, only to be caught in the terrible arc of the wrathmonger's hammer-flail. Splatting through bloodreavers, the warrior roared in confusion, heaving his devastating weapons about him on their wrist-clasped chains. Others erupted around him, cutting down swathes of warriors with ugly swings of their flails. Agile bloodreavers leapt and ducked out of the weapons' devastating paths, those too slow becoming a splatter of flesh chunks and detached limbs. Running back at the crimson hulks, the bloodreavers swarmed the wrathmongers, climbing up onto their backs and globed shoulders, knifing and stabbing with their short, cruel blades.

For a brief time there was mayhem. Wrathmongers stamped fountains of crimson rainwater about them as they charged throngs of rabid bloodreavers. The warriors danced out of their path and slashed at them with their razor-sharp blades. Skargan Fell-of-Heart cut through the havoc. Grabbing his colossal battle-axe from his back, the deathbringer strode through the shallows and into the murderous clash. Smashing one of the wrathmongers down with the flat of the monstrous blade, Skargan shattered his skull helm and knocked him unconscious.

Turning savagely, he stamped out with his boot, landing a kick on the chest of Voark, son of Kraal. The warrior flew through the air with a crunch before splashing into the shallows.

'This is good?' Mallofax squawked from Zuvius' glaive.

'I'm not sure,' the Prince of Embers said. The ruthless violence and bloodshed about him was distracting. Being butchered by Skargan's savages was not part of Zuvius' plan, but having them butcher each other was not desirable either. He had acted to distract them from killing him, but he needed to harness their strength for the trials ahead. He had a feeling that he could not achieve his fell goals without their strength. Standing in the flooded hollow, Zuvius' sorcerous instincts twitched.

'Wait a minute,' he told the feathered familiar.

Zuvius saw a cloud forming through the bloody shallows of the hollow. The waters began to thicken to a muddy paste about the boots of the Chaos warriors, slurping and bubbling. Arms of pink brawn and sinew broke the surface of the unnatural mire, clutching with daemonic claws.

Zuvius watched as infernal horrors spawned from the water about them – a plague of Tzeentchian monstrosities drawn to the deliciousness of treachery and dissention in the ranks of the horde.

The hollow filled with the roars and screams of the Blood God's servants. Grabbed about the boots and ankles by the frightful appendages, they were dragged down into the sludge. Jaws formed in the fleshy surface of the shallows, brimming with row after row of jagged fangs, and Goresworn killers were swallowed whole. A wrathmonger had his leg chewed off, sending him into a sludge-punching fury, but his fist became entangled in the sinewy stickiness of daemon flesh.

Faced with a common enemy, the butchers forgot their former enmity and visited their rage upon the spawning pool in which they stood. Zuvius smiled to himself. The Great Changer, in all his perversity, had sent a blessing. The Khornate horde was once more unified in the face of a common enemy. They had swiftly forgotten their desire to end the prince. The daemon attack, meanwhile, was thinning out the dissenting forces. The appearance of the horrors not only gave Zuvius a chance to fight at the Khornate savages' side, but it would make them easier to manipulate than ever.

The sludge seemed like a single monster but from it individual creatures of nightmare rose, stretching themselves free. Wrath-mongers splattered the daemons within the monstrous arcs of their hammer-flails, while the bloodreavers struck grasping limbs from the creatures with their blades only to find two more erupt from gushing, pink stumps in their place.

The horrors seemed never-ending, scrambling free of their spawning pool like a plague of jubilant insanity. Their grotesque bodies were all fang-filled maw and beady eyes that frantically set upon new victims to maul. Clawed, muscular legs helped them to bound and latch onto Skargan's berserkers, while an eruption of supernaturally strong arms tore armour, limbs, helms and heads from the warrior-victims.

'This cannot be,' Mallofax shrieked above the carnage. 'These are the lesser playthings of our master.'

'The daemon horrors of Tzeentch,' Orphaeo Zuvius said, spinning the shaft of his glaive about him in willowy gauntlets. The prince's warband were not immune to the creatures' attentions. Infernal monstrosities dragged members of the Hexenguard down into the fleshy embrace of the pool to crack their plate in writhing knots of daemonic muscle.

The sorcerers of the Unseeing, meanwhile, clutched to one another in their blindness. Judiciously deployed, they were among the most powerful wretches at the prince's disposal. Their sorcerous powers could transform even the most deadly opponents into statuesque spawn of ruptured flesh and twisted bone, visiting the form of their dread visions upon the enemies about them. Against these formless monstrosities, their powers were all but useless. The daemonic horrors already took the form of the sorcerers' nightmarish imaginings.

'The Great Changer must be displeased,' Mallofax flapped. 'The Exalted Grand Marshal's invitation has angered him.'

'No,' Zuvius said, gritting his perfect teeth as he lopped off the clawed fingers of a reaching daemon with a graceful swing of A'cuitas. 'It is an honour. The joint damnation of this hollow strengthens our association with the Blood God's barbarians. Battle is like ale shared across a table to these brutes.'

As a member of the Hexenguard was pulled apart by two multi-limbed horrors, Sir Abriel splashed up through the slime to smash aside another monstrosity with his shield. Holding his glaive by the base of the shaft, Zuvius wheeled around, allowing the heavy blade of the weapon to lop limbs from the attacking creatures.

'Why do the Great Changer's daemons try to destroy us, then?' the bird squawked, unconvinced.

Zuvius turned A'cuitas around in his gauntlets, aiming the pommel of the glaive at the horrors emerging from the pool.

'For perversity's sake,' the prince said, with a grin of insanity. 'Why else?'

His daemon-forged weapon's searing blue eye opened. Lightning cracked from the glaive, causing the air to burn and the heart to jump. As the jagged bolt struck the nearest daemon, the thing seemed to rupture, exploding in a shower of pink slop. Aiming the sorcerous weapon across a line of advancing creatures, Zuvius had the lightning jump from monster to monster, turning one after another into flinch-inducing splatters of flesh.

Stomping through the curtain of gore, Skargan Fell-of-Heart was a destructive machine. His great axe was everywhere, chopping daemons asunder, lopping off limbs and cleaving the gibbering creatures in half. The clawing, strangling, savaging things climbed across his muscular frame only to be gouged free by the bone blades the deathbringer wore on each meaty fist. Flinging them off and down at the floor, Skargan sent them shrieking back to the fleshpool before stamping down on them with his boots.

'You!' the deathbringer roared at Zuvius. 'This is your doing.'

The Prince of Embers was tiring of the belligerent champion and his savage lieutenants. Thrusting A'cuitas forward, Zuvius impaled a creature before tearing the weapon back and turning it around in his hands. Blasting lightning into the stricken daemon, Zuvius coated Skargan with filth.

'Does this look like my doing?' the prince shot back, before passing the glaive behind his back and thrusting it to the side. The Tzeentchian horror coming at him opened its gaping mouth and attempted to swallow the weapon. The glaive blade was momentarily lost in the darkness before bursting forth out of the daemon's back. Zuvius turned to the approaching champion of Khorne. 'Does this look like my god favouring me?'

Skargan Fell-of-Heart considered the prince's words, with all of the calm thought of which he was capable. Furious at his brute conclusion, the deathbringer carved out a circle of destruction about him. Chopping. Hacking. Obliterating. His battle-axe dribbled ichor. The colour in the hollow was changing, however. The pink that had clouded the shallows and solidified to a spawning fleshpool was now dashed with azure. Every time a pink horror was mulched into formlessness, blue claws would prize the ruined daemonflesh apart. As the dying monstrosity rippled and quivered, a blue horror would climb out of its corpse, followed by another. Apart from its colour, each was identical in form to the foul being from which it proceeded.

Zuvius pursed his smeared lips. He was once more caught between the fury of the deathbringer and perverse circumstance. Looking up, he saw that the wind had dropped. The storm of fang and tooth was passing. The fat droplets of the bloodstorm still hammered down about them, however.

'It is an affliction of the land, exalted one,' Zuvius said. 'A hellish hole through which daemons bleed into the world. A flesh without end, my lord, living, dying and dividing. We must withdraw.'

'Never!' Skargan roared, tearing his gouging talons through a creature before batting three blue clawing beasts away with the flat of his axe blade.

'Get the sorcerers,' Zuvius commanded, sending Mallofax off in the direction of the Unseeing. The Prince of Embers would not die in some squalid hollow with a mindless berserker. As the sound of the bird's squawking led the blind wretches back up out of the hollow, Zuvius pointed a finger at Sir Abriel and the slope behind. Batting mad creatures aside with their knightly shields and cutting down horrors with their notched longswords, the Hexenguard covered their master's retreat.

Stepping back up the incline and towards the howl of the bloodstorm, Zuvius crackled lightning down on the creatures rushing Skargan. Dripping with pink and blue daemonblood that sizzled with sorcerous energy, and with monsters exploding about him, the deathbringer had a moment to take stock. His warband was dying, overrun by the daemon plague, despite the bloodreavers' savagery and the devastation of the wrath-mongers. A single decision separated Skargan Fell-of-Heart from annihilation.

Zuvius watched as the deathbringer exercised judgement beyond his powers. Skargan believed that the Everchosen of Chaos had demanded his dark service. Zuvius had put that belief in the champion's mind. Pushing several wrathmongers back up the slope and snatching Voark, son of Krall, from a small massacre of bloodreavers, Skargan bellowed his order across the hollow.

'There is no glory to be had here,' Khorne's champion roared, pointing his battle-axe back up at the storm. 'Onwards! To the glory of the Blood God and the Exalted Marshal!'

With Skargan's command cutting through the red haze of berserker rage, the horde began its staggered withdrawal from the hollow. Stumbling up the incline and away from the Tzeentchian swarm, the host re-entered the bloodstorm.

They were drowning. Drowning in blood.

The heavens broiled with fury and a crimson rain hammered down, flooding not just the hollows, cuttings and craters of the Blasted Plain but the storm-wracked wilderness itself. Zuvius and his Tzeentchian knights waded through the wounded waters. The Unseeing half-stumbled, half-swam. Mallofax flew, the bird buffeted this way and that in the gales that swept across the rising waters of the shallow sea.

Following the Prince of Embers through the deluge were the warband of Skargan Fell-of-Heart. Wading in disbelief through the waters, the Khornate warriors had never quite got over their rout at the hollow. Their champion's order to retreat from a fight and the soul-crushing demands of their trek through the storm and flood seemed to be breaking them. The cursed land and the daemons that haunted it notwithstanding, Zuvius had manipulated them with his lies. He had convinced Skargan to take this road to self-destruction and he was not finished with the deathbringer yet.

'Mallofax?' Zuvius called up through the storm. In the past hour, the prince had felt the blood slopping and splashing lower and lower against his plate. 'Are the waters receding?'

'We are on the Beaten Path,' the bird shrieked, swooping down onto the blade of A'cuitas. 'Look!'

Zuvius peered through the blood-streaming sky. A dark silhouette was rising above them, a feature so large and tall that even the unnatural storm's best efforts could not hide it. Zuvius recognised the mesa from his fiery vision, eroded by the erratic elements into the rocky shape of a colossal anvil.

Zuvius nodded absently at the bird. They were climbing, ascending the path that would take them up to the strange land. This path would test him, even more than it had already. Like a piece of bronze, Zuvius would be remoulded. The bronze had no comprehension of the blade it could become and the power over life and death it would wield. The Everchosen had selected his raw materials in Zuvius. The Tzeentchian hoped to now be hammered to hold an edge, to become a weapon worthy of Archaon's choosing. It was on the Beaten Path and the mesa that he would be tested and reforged. Zuvius pledged in the dark recesses of his heart to become that which would please the Everchosen of Chaos: a vision of death and destruction to earn the demigod's gaze.

'Deathbringer,' Zuvius called, prompting Skargan Fell-of-Heart to push roughly past several of his horde and slosh onwards through the shallows. 'The place I saw in my vision,' the Tzeentchian told him honestly, pointing to the silhouette of the anvil-shaped land formation. 'There challenges will be issued and destinies realised.'

The champion of Khorne didn't seem to hear Zuvius. Instead he barked a barely intelligible order to his warband, urging them on through the strength-sapping flood.

'Out of my way, sorcerer,' Skargan said, striding through blood and pushing past Zuvius, 'for gods help any wretch that stands in it.'

Standing aside, Zuvius issued an order to Sir Abriel and the Hexenguard, bringing them to a halt. The stumbling progress of the Unseeing was also checked by squawks from a hovering Mallofax. Zuvius let the spent savages of the Goresworn through, the wrathmongers stomping miserably up the Beaten Path after their master.

Several hours were spent ascending the weathered mesa. The

storm still raged about them, with dark droplets hammering into the rocky surface of the colossal formation.

Skargan stomped off across the mesa with his warband following in a loose, exhausted formation.

'I am here!' he roared, announcing his arrival with bombast only the blessed of Khorne could manage. 'Here to be judged. Judged worthy of your favour.'

The deathbringer's words were lost to the storm. The skies howled above but no answer came. The champion's face creased with anger. His horde gathered about him in expectation, driving the Fell-of-Heart's frustration further. They had travelled so far and given so much. He would not be humiliated in front of them. He would slaughter them all to a man before suffering doubt to cross their faces.

'Test me, Lord Archaon!' Skargan roared. 'End me if you can, Ender of Worlds.'

The blasphemy passed unheeded. Blood rained down. Skargan lowered his battle-axe.

'The Blood God's chosen is displeased,' Mallofax squawked. As Zuvius watched rage take the Fell-of-Heart, he knew what was coming.

'Ready yourselves,' Zuvius warned his Hexenguard and sorcerers.

'The sorcerer betrays the Exalted of Khorne,' Voark hissed through the ranks of the Goresworn. 'He lies for his amusement and that of his twisted god.'

Two of the wrathmongers flanked their furious master. Skargan himself steamed, his burning hatred for Zuvius and his sorcerous kind turning the droplets of bloody drizzle on his red skin to a searing haze.

'Unworthy...' the Deathbringer roared.

Sir Abriel's sword cleared its scabbard with a whoosh,

followed by the blades of the rest of the Hexenguard. The Unseeing began to moan. Blind though they were, they had some inkling of the butchery to come. They would recraft the enemies of their prince, sculpting, breaking and contorting his foes to uselessness and agonising death.

As Orphaeo Zuvius went to answer the champion of Khorne, it suddenly stopped raining. It had rained forever on the Blasted Plain – yet here on the Beaten Path and the rocky mesa, blood suddenly ceased to fall. The storm died and the clouds that boiled above them began to clear. Such was the unexpected change in the weather that Zuvius, Skargan and their followers forgot one another and looked up into the sky.

'What is happening?' the Fell-of-Heart asked.

'This is vision become reality,' Zuvius told him. 'We are about to be judged. Now we shall see who is truly unworthy.'

After the storm, distant thunder. The darkness was bleached clean by a blinding light. A swirling vortex of lightning streams fell from the sky and hammered into the mesa between the death-bringer's warband and Zuvius' Tzeentchians. The rock cracked with the force, sending spidery fractures through the surface of the landform. Everyone stumbled back, shielding their eyes.

Zuvius forced himself to look, despite the eye-scalding brightness of the intervention. The air burned. Snapping arcs reached out from where the lightning had earthed. The spreading storm created shapes from the crackle and static of bifurcating bolts, almost as though the power seethed across the surface of invisible figures that were already there. The crackle grew to a blinding intensity until finally, in a crescendo of light, heat and sound, armoured figures were suddenly among the Chaos warriors, having burned into reality.

'Stormcast Eternals,' Mallofax squawked in alarm. 'The God-King's vengeance made metal and flesh.'

Zuvius turned A'cuitas about in his gauntlets, causing Mallofax to take flight. The interlopers were no champions of Chaos, sent by the Exalted Grand Marshal of the Apocalypse to test them. These were not the legendary warriors of Archaon's inner circles, taken from the very ranks the Prince of Embers wished to join. These were warriors crafted beyond the Mortal Realms – the Stormcast Eternals of the God-King. Zuvius had never seen such champions of light. They had been a fantasy, a myth, a rumour – but now they were a searing reality. As they stood before him, it seemed impossible that they were anything else.

Clad in celestial silver plate, the Stormcasts were armoured perfection. Their helmets were moulded and close-fitting, presenting a cold mask of terrible impassivity framed in the spiked halo of their calling. Zuvius could almost hear the laughter of the Dark Gods. Tzeentch, revelling in his perversity. In Lord Archaon's trial, the Great Changer had presented Zuvius with both opportunity and certain death. The Everchosen had led him to his doom, into a trap with a sworn enemy.

A warrior – especially a sorcerous one – had to rely on more than a sword and the muscles used to swing it. Zuvius hadn't known what he would face at the end of the Beaten Path. He had tricked Skargan Fell-of-Heart into standing between him and whatever it might be. Perhaps the deathbringer might end them all and catch Archaon's eye after all. The Prince of Embers had to take that risk. Sigmar's living weapons, heralded by the thunder and riding the storm, had given him no choice.

'Exalted one,' Zuvius called over the crackle of lightning. Skargan looked through the lightstorm at the Tzeentchian. 'It's time. As I promised you: an enemy worthy of your blade. Here, on the great anvil of the world, Archaon means to craft a warrior worthy of his banner. In the fire of battle, you will be forged anew. I have seen it, Skargan. Here, in the eye of the storm, I have seen it.'

The Blood God's champion levelled his axe at the column of lightning that spawned the champions from its blinding brilliance.

'Only the faithful,' one of the Stormcast Eternals called, his words burning on the air with dread purity.

'Bring me heads,' Skargan Fell-of-Heart growled to his savages.

The first of the celestial warriors marched forward, undaunted. Skargan and his Khorne-worshipping savages were the kind of mindless barbarians that brought death and destruction to the realms. Zuvius felt a perverse glee in the clash of such warriors.

Advancing with bows of gleaming metal that crackled with a spiritual energy, the Stormcasts drew back arrows almost as long as a man was tall. As they held them there, the metal missiles glowed as though heated by some internal source of energy. With the arrows shafts of crackling brilliance, the Stormcasts let their missiles loose. As they left the bow, the arrows turned into bolts of lightning that shot forth in a streaming barrage too fast for the eye to follow. The loosed lightning blasted straight through members of the Goresworn, turning the impact sites on their chests into a molten vortex of flesh and bone before blazing on through a second and third victim.

The wrathmongers battered aside Voark's bloodreavers, swinging their hammer-flails about their hulking bodies. Zuvius saw the flails smash into the metal arrows with a resounding clang, but fail to turn the missiles aside. A celestial warrior came forth with an even larger bow clutched in his silver gauntlets, aiming it up at the crystal clear sky. Raising it to the heavens, he blasted a lightning storm up at the stars that then fell towards one of the wheeling wrathmongers. The barbarian had incredible reflexes for a warrior of his size and somehow dodged the descending blast of energy. Erupting into a maelstrom of furious arcs upon impact, the snaps and cracks of energy seized upon another wrathmonger and several nearby bloodreavers like a tentacled beast. At first stricken by the power coursing through their bones, the warriors began to smoulder and blacken, burning from the inside out. Crashing to their knees as the lightning storm died away, the charred remains hit the stone floor and shattered in a cloud of ash and soot.

Zuvius heard the clatter of shields as Sir Abriel and his monstrous Hexenguard formed up before their prince. The Stormcast Eternals would not be deterred, however. Stomping forward in their immaculate plate, they aimed the lightning of their bows straight at the ruinous knights. As all became blazing white before them and the metal crackled and snapped, the Hexenguard instinctively lowered their shields. Running forward, the knights set upon the warriors of Sigmar, smashing at burnished plate with their notched blades. Pushing back Sir Abriel with a stamp of his silver boot, a Stormcast stove in the ghoulish helm of another knight with the reinforced nock of his bow. Loading it once more, the warrior turned to blast a stream of lightning straight into a charging wrathmonger's head. The decapitated barbarian stumbled on several steps more before thudding to the ground.

The Prince of Embers could stand by no longer. It was in the nature of a Tzeentchian to manipulate, lie and allow others to assume the burden of circumstance in their stead. In presenting his sworn enemies, the Everchosen had assigned him a trial that could destroy them all. The Stormcasts were not some monstrous aberration of Chaos, a horde without number or champion blessed by the ruinous pantheon. They were an implacable foe for whom the destruction of all that Zuvius craved was absolute. The prince knew that he would have to throw everything he had at them.

Helping Sir Abriel back up to his feet, Zuvius felt his gauntlet creak about the A'cuitus. Dark desire drove him into a run and he hurled the glaive at the nearest Stormcast. A'cuitas closed its eyes as the blade of the daemon-forged weapon cleaved through the warrior's breastplate. The glaive sat there, embedded between the sculpted pectorals of the plate as something horrible happened within. With a blast of spiritual energy that knocked Zuvius back, the eye slits of the Stormcast's mask lit up. Something proud and lost died within the suit of armour. Like a bolt of lightning launching up from the realm and into the sky, all that the Stormcast warrior was disappeared in the momentary afterglow of the blinding arc of raw energy.

The death seemed to feed the rage of Skargan's warband, with the wrathmongers indulging their berserker fury and the bloodreavers throwing themselves at the advancing wall of celestial plate. Taking dark inspiration from Zuvius' kill, the slayers doubled their efforts, taking the fight to the Stormcasts that marched forth from the storm.

Wrathmongers swung their great hammer-flails about their mountainous frames, smashing Stormcast helms aside with one impact before taking them clean off with a second. Voark and his warriors swarmed Sigmar's Stormcasts, jumping, clutching and climbing – prizing apart plate from sculpted plate with the tips of their reaver blades. As another champion of Sigmar died nearby, skewered on the tapering blades of several Hexenguard, Zuvius ordered his warriors back. He looked up at the blood-swirling sky. He hoped that the Everchosen was watching, that the prince's sorceries, manipulations and slaughter had pleased monstrous Archaon.

'Form up,' the Prince of Embers called from behind the wall of warped shields. Lightning bolts crashed into the metal as the Stormcast Eternals unleashed the power of their bows at the knights. Sir Abriel and his gangling warriors staggered back. As Sigmar's celestial heroes pressed their advantage, the Prince of Embers willed them on. His knights had taken the fight to the mighty Stormcasts but it was now time to visit upon the God-King's warriors the true power at his disposal.

'Now!' he called. The Hexenguard parted their shields and pulled to one side, allowing the Unseeing through. The sorcerers thrust their gnarled, outstretched hands forward and the symbols tattooed into the flesh of their palms burned with dark enchantment.

Zuvius hadn't thought it possible for beings such as the Stormcasts to scream. The mesa was suddenly afflicted with horror as flesh, metal and bone contorted and changed shape. One moment the Stormcasts were sacred knights of purity and doom, the next they were horrific statues of twisted plate and ruptured innards. Blood pooled about the stillness of their forms as they suffered their final agonising moments frozen in place – warped representations of the sorcerers' nightmarish imagination.

As a bolt blasted over Zuvius' shoulder, Mallofax beat his wings for the sky, the bird shrieking and leaving behind a cascade of blue feathers. Stalking confidently forward, the Prince of Embers snatched A'cuitas from where it had fallen on the floor after striking a Stormcast down. He moved through the fray like a madman, untouched. The cold determination of Sigmar's holy warriors was nothing to him. The blood fever of Khorne's barbarians was nothing to him. The dark sorcery of the Unseeing and the swing of swords clasped in the Hexenguard's stretching limbs were nothing to him.

He spun his glaive about him elegantly, passing it about his wrist and across his back. With vicious turns of the shaft, Zuvius brought the blade down through the enemy, slashing ragged paths through celestial plate and flesh. Pillars of spiritual energy vaulted back to the sky at each merciless death like comets unleashed. The Prince of Embers sent the Stormcasts blazing back to their god, the Tzeentchian's devastating downcuts and heart-stabbing thrusts a whirlwind of death.

The Hexenguard moved up behind their prince in a wedge of dark plate and blade, forcing their ghoulish way through Sigmar's disciplined ranks. The Unseeing followed in a huddle, moaning and thrusting out their palms in sorcerous fear, turning armoured attackers to warped visions of plate and bone.

Zuvius was a force of serene destruction. He reached out with the length of his glaive to stab and stove in the masks of Stormcast helms. He swung the shaft of the daemon-forged weapon about him, smashing through the metal of bows and cutting gashes in the breastplates of advancing enemy warriors. He carved a path through the Stormcasts. Reckless insanity lifted his spirit as he ended those of pure heart about him.

He knew he had done well in the eyes of Tzeentch and the Everchosen of Chaos. A true warrior of Chaos served the Dark Gods not only to the best of his ability but through the abilities of the best. Skargan Fell-of-Heart and his host were battle-hardened slayers whose talents were best put to work in the service of a greater darkness than Khorne's simple bloodlust. Zuvius had put them exactly where he needed them to be, turning their strength againstthe warriors of the wretched God-King. Here, on a mesa crafted to celebrate Zuvius' victory, the Stormcasts and the mindless savages of the Blood God wasted their lives on one another.

Stormcasts marched out from the column of lightning with their glaives thrust out before them. The shimmering weapons were like sword blades mounted on shafts and the armoured warriors used them to cut bloodreavers in half. Slicing down through the savages of the Goresworn from the jaw to the hip, they marched on through the fallen flesh, coming together to skewer individual wrathmongers on their blades.

Zuvius felt the death about him as Voark, son of Kraal, was bludgeoned into the rocky surface of the mesa by a Stormcast with a glorious mace. He was avenged almost immediately by one of the wrathmongers who brought around the hammer head of his chain-flail in a brutal arc. It struck the warrior, smashing through the plate on his back and turning him into a shower of mangled plate, gore and blinding light.

The mesa was brightest about Skargan. As brilliant as the continuous column-stream of lightning was in bringing forth the God-King's warriors, the maelstrom of blazing death about the Fell-of-Heart was brighter still. Skargan was unstoppable, killing Stormcast after Stormcast for his god and the Everchosen. While his warband died about him – the Goresworn's savagery was no match for the Stormcasts' implacable, armoured advance, and the wrathmongers went to their deaths with reckless abandon – Skargan was a rock upon which the Stormcasts smashed themselves in the storm. He was death. He was fury. He was the exalted avatar of Khorne.

As the Prince of Embers approached, leading his warriors and killing with judicious flair, he saw Skargan gouge skulls out of masked helms with his bone claws, impale Stormcasts on his monstrous horns and smash bows from the cowardly grip of Stormcast Judicators. He broke armoured warriors in two with savage kicks and wheeled about him with his axe, the weapon taller than the deathbringer himself. He chopped through plate, he cleaved limbs from torsos and he felled mighty warriors of the God-King's holy storm. He tore heads and helms from bodies with his bare hands and rammed the shaft of the battle-axe back through throats and chests.

There was no stopping him. With the bodies of his warband about him, Skargan roared his challenge to a cloaked lord in immaculate celestial armour. Flanked by two of his brothers, the lord leading the host closed in, wielding a great halberd in one gauntlet and a warding lantern in the other. Zuvius could feel the soul-scarring magical energy coming off the lantern and flinched as it was unleashed. Skargan Fell-of-Heart cared nothing for its terrible light. His red flesh cooked on the bone at its proximity.

He killed the celestial leader's guardians, his axe screeching through their armour before sending their soulfire raging for the heavens. The lord came at the deathbringer with all the righteous fortitude of Sigmar himself. He smashed the warding lantern back and forth across Skargan's horned skull, battering and momentarily blinding the Chaos brute. For a moment, Skargan was caught off guard and stumbled. Wielding the length of the halberd in one gauntlet, the lord chopped at Skargan with elegant sweeps of the axe blade and thrust with the bladed spike that crowned the weapon. He smashed the bone claws of the gouger Skargan held up to defend himself and ripped through the smoking flesh of the Chaos champion's forearm. The lord landed a kick on the deathbringer's muscular chest with an armoured boot before cutting one of the monstrous horns from the warrior's head.

For a moment, Zuvius thought that he might have to face the mighty Stormcast lord himself. As the champion swung around the warding lantern for another disorientating blow, Skargan raised his axe with both hands. Instead of batting the magical weapon aside, the deathbringer's wrath-fuelled swing smashed the lantern into a blinding nova of magical energy. Surprised by his weapon's destruction, the lord staggered back. Skargan bellowed as the fierce flash of the lantern's destruction bathed his Khorne-pledged flesh in the God-King's scalding brilliance. He would not be stopped, however. Blindly back-swinging with his axe, he cut the halberd in two. Aiming with a slayer's instinct alone, Skargan brought his axe down and cut straight through the lord.

Plate, flesh and bone sheared away in two halves as the axe blade sparked. Zuvius watched the blinding essence of the warrior rocket into the sky. As it did, the column of lightning burning into the rock of the mesa crackled and spat to nothingness, leaving behind only heat and an afterglow.

'Hold,' Zuvius commanded. Sir Abriel and the remaining Hexenguard locked shields and waited, while those sorcerous wretches of the Unseeing who had not been skewered or blasted by the Stormcast Eternals grasped blindly for one another. They were not the only ones to have lost their sight.

The deathbringer was a mess, but an impressive mess. His red flesh was burnt and raw, smouldering about him. The bulging muscles of his arms, chest and back hung like ribbons where the God-King's warriors had sliced and stabbed, exposing rib and bone. One of his great horns was but a smashed stump while the champion's eyes were misty with the scorching brilliance of the warding lantern. It was obvious from the clumsiness of his movements that he was blind but he still clutched his battle-axe to him with the murderous talent of ten sighted warriors.

Mallofax flapped down to land on Zuvius' shoulder. The

sound seemed to spook the deathbringer, who looked about and then up into the sky, expecting the judgement and reward of Archaon, Everchosen of Chaos.

'Filth sorcerer,' Skargan growled. 'Is that you?'

The Prince of Embers turned A'cuitas about in his gauntlets, aiming the pommel of the daemon-forged weapon at the deathbringer. The eye opened in the metal.

'Aye,' Zuvius said. 'It is me. I have bad tidings for you, exalted one. You have been judged unworthy.'

Skargan's ugly features screwed up in fury. He peered blindly up into the blood storm.

'By who?' he roared, challenging the gods. 'By Khorne? By the Everchosen?'

'By me,' Zuvius told him. As the lightning leapt from his glaive and struck the deathbringer in the chest, Skargan Fell-of-Heart exploded. In an air-cracking blast of blood and flesh-scraps, the Blood God's champion turned into a crimson mist, thick and bitter. Zuvius cocked his head towards Mallofax.

'I sent him back to his dark god,' the prince said, a crooked smile on his lips. 'It's what he would have wanted.'

Orphaeo Zuvius didn't have to wait long for his judgement and reward. He had been reforged to the Everchosen's liking, and the bodies about him erupted in blue flashes. The unnatural lightning reached up into the sky with a whoosh and surrounded him. It sizzled in the blood rain, the licks and flames encircling the Prince of Embers and forming shimmering shapes.

'What do you see?' Mallofax asked of the prince. Peering hard into the heat and light of the furious vision, Zuvius looked about. In the surrounding energy, he could make out the outline of a great fortress.

'Jagged spires,' he said, 'towers and keeps, reaching up into horror-choked skies. Walls – spiked, colossal and thick. A fortress of ruin so large that it spans the Mortal Realms.'

'You see the Varanspire,' Mallofax told him, 'the fortress of the Everchosen. Your invitation is extended, my lord. You are worthy and he calls you to his service.'

The raging wall of flame that encircled them suddenly died. Everything became ominously still. The skies cleared to reveal a darkness beyond. Then came the flapping of wings. While Mallofax hopped between the prince's shoulder and A'cuitas, a flock of carrion birds descended from the darkness to feast on the flesh of the fallen.

'And where do we find this Varanspire?' Zuvius asked.

'It sits in the Realm of Chaos,' Mallofax said, 'linked to the Eightpoints, a nexus of gateways connecting the Mortal Realms.'

'A place of unrivalled destruction and death,' Zuvius said.

'Yes, my prince.'

Zuvius licked his mangled lips. He stabbed at the rock, tapping the pommel of his glaive on the surface of the mesa. The carrion birds took to the air in a swirling flock, startled by the impact. Mallofax flapped his wings also but retained his purchase.

'Invitation accepted,' Orphaeo Zuvius said. The knight that had been Sir Abriel followed with the Hexenguard and the sorcerers of the Unseeing.

'What now, my lord?' Mallofax asked.

'We follow the crows,' the Prince of Embers said, 'and trust in their appetite for death.'

THE SOLACE
OF RAGE

Guy Haley

In a castle fashioned from crystal, a weaver of destiny worked.

He, she, it – who could tell? None knew if the sorcerers had once been mortal or were daemon made. There were nine, or there were one, or there were both one and nine. In all things, including their number, they were mysterious. Or so they had meant to be.

The Many-Eyed Servant was one of the names of the nine, and it applied in this instance to a tall, skeletal figure, impossibly thin, with limbs like reed stalks and a body to match. Atop a strand of a neck balanced a broad head, disturbingly smooth and featureless save for a line of eyes along its ridge. A body of this sort was nought but a garment, and not the most important that it had occasion to wear. In this form, the Many-Eyed Servant's cloak defined it, name and nature – a long covering made of eyelids that fluttered and blinked, from behind which moist eyeballs of every hue peered out curiously.

The Many-Eyed Servant dabbled long fingers in a pool of

steaming quicksilver, flicking through the images it conjured there. Scenes of war. All the realms were in uproar with the coming of Sigmar. From time to time, it stopped to examine this hero or that, emitting a gentle purr of satisfaction when it saw one worthy of note, clucking in annoyance at those who disrupted its carefully placed webs of cause and effect. Once it had toyed with individuals of this type for its own ends. The Many-Eyed Servant had spent long lifetimes of men twisting the threads of fate into pleasing patterns – but no longer.

There was a tightness around its spindly limbs, chains of fate that were not of its making. Once it had been merely the Many-Eyed, but then Archaon had learned its one true name, and forced upon it the role of servant. Now it was bound to the Everchosen's purpose, along with all its siblings.

The facets of the Many-Eyed Servant's lair darkened along with its mood. Displayed by sorcerous means in panes of crystal were images of its eight counterparts. A few worked in their own dens, each a sanity-testing place conjured by the architect's ineffable whims. Others were abroad in the realms, doing the bidding of their master. Wherever they were, they looked up as one at the Many-Eyed Servant's pique and scolded him, wary lest Archaon's attention be directed toward them. The Many-Eyed Servant hunched its shoulders and turned its back upon them. The others were overly concerned by Archaon. If Tzeentch learned of their bending to the Everchosen's will, the displeasure of the Changer of the Ways would make Archaon's worst wraths seem as nothing. Nevertheless, although the Many-Eyed Servant would not admit it was afraid of their current lord, it returned to its scryings, compelled by dread and duty.

Archaon demanded champions, and so the Many-Eyed Servant looked for them in every realm.

In the Realm of Beasts, there was a prairie of such extent it had no single name, a landscape that a man could not cross in the space of a single life. Stretching for thousands of leagues, the plains encompassed mountains and seas, forests and mighty canyons, but for the most part they comprised grassland of rich and infinite variety. Great beasts walked there, their horns as high as the crowns of trees. Men hunted them, as bewildering in the profusion of race and tribe as the beasts themselves were in variety.

The Bloodbloom Fields were found on these plains. The grasses were red, and its flowers crimson. The partly fossilised ribcages of animals of impossible size studded the scarlet, higher than cathedrals, their breastbones covered in patches of woodland that trailed long creepers earthward. Their eyeless skulls were osseous mesas, the phalanges of their paws greying crags.

At the time of the Bloodbloom's breeding, when the wind blew just so, the flowers opened and spat their pollen to be carried far and wide. The flowers sang for days during this season. Individually, the voices of the flowers were almost too quiet to be heard, but the sound of millions together created a musical sighing that gave the Bloodbloom Fields its other name, the Singing Steppes.

These were rich lands, well populated with beasts and tribes. Even at the close of the Age of Chaos when Sigmar's warriors rained down from the heavens with wrath in their hearts and lightning in their hands, there remained free people of the plains who had survived the terrible centuries. They were hunted because of it, for the gods loathe freedom above all else, but they survived.

It was to this place that the Many-Eyed Servant's attention was drawn. Its restless fingers paused in their fretful dibbling, the ripples on the silver stilled. The image sharpened, and it leaned in closer.

Upon the Bloodbloom Fields was assembled a host of men. These were the Bloodslaves, the horde of Lord Kalaz the Hewer. The name came to the Many-Eyed Servant immediately. In ordinary times they moved restlessly across the plains, cutting a swathe across grass, herd and nation alike. Not today. Rank after rank of blood warriors and bloodreavers were arranged in a hollow circle atop a hill of stacked, gargantuan bones. To the north, the greying faces of the bones made cliffs twenty yards high; to the south, the hill sloped down gently to the plain. Atop this plateau, black and bronze armour gleamed in a sultry morning hazed by pollen.

Around the hill, the scorched marks of the Bloodslaves' hundred campfires pitted the red with black. A broad road of crushed flowers stretched over the horizon, marking their passage to this place of battle. A trampled field of torn earth and dark bloody stains bore silent witness to the great slaughter that had been done there the prior day. Eight cairns of fresh skulls, still pink from flensing, ringed the site, all that remained of the Heyeran people.

The Heyeran's horses' bones charred in fires made with the shattered timbers of the defeated tribe's chariots. A hundred of the tribesmen lived on, but in body only. Given the choice between the dark feast and death, they had opted to consume the hearts of their comrades. Already their old existence slipped from minds clouded with Khorne's rage.

All present desired fresh slaughter, and none more than the once-Heyeran, but all was still. The horde waited in silence. Their eyes were upon the open space at the centre of the ring of flesh and brass they made. Save for the moaning of chained khorgoraths and the snap of banners in the wind, silence reigned.

The extermination of the Heyeran had been a costly victory. Lord Kalaz the Hewer was dead, cut down at the height of the battle, the last bold act of the War King of the Heyeran.

Five of the tribe's Gorechosen remained. The slaughterpriest Orto, the bloodstoker Danavan Vuul, the skullgrinder Kordos and the tribe's two exalted deathbringers. There to the south of the ring was the one who called himself Mathror, horned and proud. The other was the voiceless Ushkar Mir. The ranks of the Bloodslaves were a quarter reduced, the three other Gorechosen among the slain. It did not matter, for Khorne cared nothing for the deaths of his followers, only that death had been done, and the Heyeran had been worthy foes.

The banner of the tribe's dead bloodsecrator spiked the earth. The hum of wrathful energy demanded a new bearer, but it and all other things must wait. Before aspirants could attempt acceptance to the circle of eight, the Bloodslaves required a new lord.

Ushkar Mir and Mathror glared at one another. They had fought for many years together, but such things counted for nothing among the worshippers of the Blood God. Barely contained fury radiated from both.

Mathror was a hulking brute, muscles swollen by the dark energies of chaos. A pair of brazen horns sprouted from his temples. He wore the Blood Armour, a spiked set of plates that completely enclosed his body from his cloven feet to his eyes. A bevor encased the lower part of his face, but he had no need of a helmet. His horns were as much a part of that dread panoply as any other piece, offering protection to his head. From above the bevor glared a pair of bloodshot eyes, yellow irised, trapped within a perpetual glower and overhung by brows tense with the need for violence. He bore a huge sword the weight of two men, finned and spined the length of its bloody blade. Old gore caked its runnels, but the edges glinted bright steel and were sharp enough to draw a cry from the wind. On his other arm he carried a tower shield, dark red, embossed with the runes of Khorne and the holy eight-pointed symbol of Chaos.

Ushkar Mir was taller. He too retained a general human shape, but was also grossly swollen with unholy power. An unbeliever would have seen him as a giant, although like all the Bloodslaves he had once been an ordinary man, untouched by divinity. About his face, Khorne's whims were clearly exhibited. Mir's lips had withered away, leaving his teeth exposed to the root in a perpetual snarl. Around his eyes was bound a brass ring, riveted to the bone of his skull with iron. The brass was stamped deep with runes. Dark now, they glowed hot in battle. Ushkar Mir's head was consequently a mass of twisted tissue haloed by thin wisps of brittle hair, for the runes' heat tormented him, driving him to greater rage, which in turn made them burn hotter.

Mir disdained armour, preferring speed and fury to a coward's shell of metal. Beneath his simple leather harness his scars were clear to see, raised welts all across his back and chest. Unlike his mutilated head, these made coherent imagery – Khorne's skull rune, Chaos' eight-pointed star, and the four-base tally marks of his many slaughtered foes.

Mir's twin axes Skullthief and Bloodspite lay crossed upon his back, their querulous heads muzzled by their sheaths. One was black, the other red, gifts from Mir's master. His fists were clenched, the brass bands around his knuckles buckled with the expression of his great and furious strength. His chest heaved in and out, muscles flexing with every bullish breath. Mir's snorting was a provocation, an invitation to violence. The noise of it dominated the hilltop.

Orto looked between the two once-men facing each other across the circle.

'So?' he said. A single word, loud as a bell and as clear as a trumpet call, carried on breath that reeked of blood. The Bloodslaves shifted at its uttering, movement rippling through the crowd's mass. Fire kindled in their hearts after their rare minutes of inaction. However the day was to end, its beginnings were sown then, in that moment, in that one word.

Orto had drunk of the slaughtergruel the day before, a tincture of boiling heartblood tainted by daemon gore and powdered warpstone. Khorne had deemed him worthy once again, for he lived still, and he had been granted yet more power. His skin was taut with new muscle and his terse words carried the authority of the great Skull Lord himself. Power shone through him from Khorne's own throne.

'Mir is not worthy,' said Mathror. 'It should be I who leads.'

'See!' said Orto. He strode to Mir's side on legs grown unnaturally long. He pinched at Mir's muscles, rapped huge knuckles against Mir's brass blind, caressed the raised scarring on his massive chest. 'The gifts of Khorne.'

'Gifts for the unworthy,' said Mathror.

Orto touched the black and red axes of Mir fleetingly, so as not to rouse the daemons sleeping within.

'Twin axes he bears, daemon-kin from Khorne's own legions. These are not the marks of the worthy?' Orto barked a laugh. 'You deny Khorne's judgement. Your skull shall be his.' Orto gripped his double-handed axe meaningfully. It was a cruel thing, toothed with black spikes.

'I do not deny the judgment of the Skull Lord,' said Mathror. He raised his hand, and Orto paused. For all his monstrous appearance and the fire of rage that burned in him, he spoke evenly. His voice was no ragged war-shout, but a silken thing, suggestive and deadly, a weapon in its own right. 'Instead it is you, Orto, who denies his sense of humour!' Scattered guffaws came from the horde. 'Khorne laughs at Mir, and that is well. You mistake amusement for favour. Ushkar Mir will not lead us. He lacks faith.'

'You think you should lead? Ha!' said Orto.

'I will not follow you,' said Danavan Vuul. Kordos the smith, as ever, said nothing.

A blood warrior stepped forward from the horde. He was smaller than many present, close in size to the city dweller he had once been. Tight black armour clad him, while his tall-crested helmet he carried under one arm, leaving his face free. His skin was pale blue, marbled with bloodmarks. His eyes were the same colour, so that they were hard to distinguish from the rest of his face. He looked a living sculpture carved from exotic marble. Even so, the intelligence in those eyes could not be missed. Skull was cunning, a master of intrigue in a herd of killers, and that made him dangerous on and off the field of war.

'Skull!' Orto spat. The priest despised Skull's temerity, most especially in his taking of a holy name. 'What do you want here?'

'I speak for Mir,' said Skull. His voice was high, insinuating.

'You have no business here.'

'Lord Khorne saw fit to deprive the Great Ushkar Mir of his voice, and then Lord Khorne saw fit to provide him with the service of Skull.' He bowed to the slaughterpriest. 'Skull speaks for Mir. Skull always speaks for Mir.'

Orto growled and snapped his teeth.

'You dislike my name, I know,' said Skull. 'Must we have this dance every time we meet? If you would slay me, do so!'

'You have no right to it,' said Orto. 'You will die for your blasphemy.'

'You may challenge Mir to dispute my right,' said Skull. 'I am under his protection.'

Mir growled, the first sound other than his bellows-breath he had made since the gathering began.

'Let the Court of Blades decide the matter. Then you may present your complaint directly to the brass throne,' said Skull.

Blood rage flushed Orto's skin, but he restrained himself. He had no desire to fight Mir – it was not a contest he could win.

'Speak then, insolent wretch!' he said.

Skull inclined his head in mock deference to the slaughter-priest. 'I shall, and I say this – Mir is worthy.'

'And why would you not say Mir is worthy?' scoffed Mathror. 'Your word means nothing! You are his thing, his creature. You live because of his patronage. How dare you address your betters – get out of my sight! When this is settled, I will come for you and scrape the flesh from your living bones. Run now, and you may survive a little longer.'

A smile flitted across Skull's face. He adjusted the grip on his sheathed longsword. Mathror exaggerated. Mir was not his sole guarantor of safety – Skull was a talented warrior himself. He thought often on his own and Mathror's relative might. Perhaps Skull's skill was greater, though his strength was undeniably lesser. Khorne's servants were not known for their consideration, but for those like Skull who could hold back the fury and fight with head and heart, life was full of such assessments.

'Mir is worthy,' said Skull again. 'None fight better or harder for the Blood God than he.'

'Fight harder? Maybe. I fight better,' said Mathror, clanging his shield against his breast. 'And however he fights, he does not fight for the Blood God.'

'No?' said Skull. He cocked one silver eyebrow. 'Then who does he fight for?'

'Ushkar Mir fights for himself,' said Mathror, and his contempt revealed itself fully.

'Your proof, my lord Mathror?' said Skull.

'His words are his proof. All heard them. His own prayer condemns him. "By each skull I pave the road to your throne, by each step I come closer to vengeance."' He quoted the prayer of Mir, one the champion had uttered quietly in every battle before Lord Khorne took his words forever. 'Who else but a faithless servant would say that? And a fool to whit – none may fight the Lord of Skulls!'

'Khorne took away his voice. There is nothing to hear,' said Skull. 'Khorne respects bravery. Mir is brave, not a fool. Khorne enjoys defiance, not the cringing obeisance you offer.'

'Khorne took his voice to protect his toy so that none could hear his blasphemy! I am no toy. I am worthy, he is not!' bellowed Mathror. 'I will lead the tribe!' He held up his shield and sword, and the larger portion of the Bloodslaves chanted his name.

Mathror sneered at his opponent in satisfaction.

'Silence!' shouted Orto, and his voice was the crack of Khorne's own whip. The chanting of Mathror's name faltered. 'Mir is worthy,' said Orto. 'It is you who blaspheme. Mir reaps skulls and lives. They go to Khorne, as will Mir, his skull for the skull throne. You also fight for yourself. Your ambition to lead is clear. A true servant fights not for his own glory, but for Khorne's.'

'I am for Mir,' said Danavan Vuul. He walked to stand by Skull and Mir, his well-fleshed body wobbling as he walked. 'Khorne has use for all murder, no matter the cause or the manner of death. This is our creed. Mir is a greater deathbringer than you, Mathror.'

'You are a coward who hides behind your whip, making others do your killing!'

'My whip and blade bite deep,' Vuul hissed through crooked,

yellow teeth. 'By their application I slay more than even you, mighty Mathror. Khorne cares not as long as the blood flows.'

'Mir is a test!' roared Mathror. 'Many of us fell in the fight with the Heyeran. Khorne tests us with this blasphemer, rewarding him to see our reaction when we come close to failure time after time. He is displeased – that is why Kalaz fell. It is plain!'

The agitation of the horde was growing. A split formed across the mass of warriors. Men glanced at one another. Minds clouded again with Khorne's red vision and the distinction between friend and foe became blurred, irrelevant.

'Khorne is not a subtle god,' said Skull. 'Do we not follow him for his directness? Do we not revel in his rage? He has no time for petty intrigues. Skulls and blood are his demands, and Mir delivers no matter his own intent. That is why he is rewarded.'

'This one is the proof of my argument,' said Mathror, gesturing at Skull. 'A weasel's tongue in a serpent's mouth.'

Mir growled again.

'Venerated Skullgrinder Kordos,' asked Skull. 'Where will you throw your lot, with Mir or with Mathror?'

The warrior smith did not reply, nor did he move, his chained, burning anvil scorching the flattened red grasses. His masked face gave nothing away. Skull shrugged. Skullgrinder Kordos served Khorne alone. He had no loyalty to any man, and few words for them. 'And what does the slaughterpriest say? You speak for Khorne, give us his judgement!'

Orto's eyes flicked back and forth between the deathbringers, weighing them against each other. His black tongue wormed along scarred lips as he hesitated. 'Khorne does not speak. Khorne is displeased we do not fight, but talk like weaklings. There is one way to settle this. Skull invoked the Court of Blades, so let the test of arms settle it.'

'You will not name a favourite? You are unsure who will win,' said Mathror. 'You do not wish to take sides. Who can respect such cravenness? You display your weakness this day, Orto.'

The slaughterpriest puffed himself up and snarled. There was truth to Mathror's words.

'Does any of this matter?' said Skull. 'Mir is the best warrior. None is as mighty as Mir. No one has a higher tally in skulls and blood. Whether Mir reaps skulls for Khorne or Mir reaps skulls for revenge, it does not matter. All death is worship, however given. Khorne does not care from whence the blood flows.'

Mathror smiled evilly. 'Now you see my point exactly.' He drew his sword and leapt at Mir.

The horde bisected itself, swift as the surging sea parts on a reef. A faultline of animosity that had existed for many weeks yawned wide, those for Mir on one side, those for Mathror on the other. It was telling that Mathror's followers outnumbered Mir's by a third again.

Mir did not speak, but Mir could hear. Mir looked like an insensate monster, but Mir could think.

Here is what he thought as he unsheathed the axes Bloodspite and Skullthief: *Mathror is right. I have no faith. I have only hatred for Khorne.*

Khorne did not care. Khorne was amused, Mathror was right in that too.

Bloodspite and Skullthief cried out with joy at their release.

'Blood for the Blood God!' screamed Bloodspite, the red axe.

'Skulls for the Skull Throne!' replied Skullthief, the black axe.

'I shall spill more blood than you,' said Bloodspite.

'And I shall take more skulls!' rejoined the other.

The axes laughed metallically as Mir swung them. Several blood warriors were ambitious enough to chance their lives against Ushkar Mir, and flooded into the space between he and

Mathror. None were his match, and all died quickly. Skullthief and Bloodspite drank the life fluids into their uncanny alloys. Their gleaming surfaces were never marred by the death they wrought.

The two parts of the horde crashed together with a tumult of bloodthirsty roaring. The singing of the Bloodbloom flowers was eclipsed by the clash of arms as the sides met. None were taken by surprise as their fellows fell upon them; these were warriors of Khorne, and they were ever ready for the spilling of blood and the red harvest of skulls. Men who had fought together and shared the flesh of the slain Heyeran around fires yesterday gladly buried their swords in each other's guts today. Axes lopped heads from shoulders. Blood sprayed from severed arteries as limbs were cleaved from bodies.

'Khorne! Khorne! Khorne!' they roared. 'Blood for the Blood God! Skulls for the skull throne! Let the red votive flow!'

Within minutes, a battle that began as two rough sides degenerated into a formless melee. The flowers sang mindlessly and on the hill skulls watched disinterestedly as the warriors of the Blood God butchered each other. Sights like these were common occurrences in those dark times.

Kordos stood motionless amid the turmoil, awaiting some signal known solely to him. Orto roared his praises to Khorne as he fought, but was careful not to seem to help either Mir or Mathror. The melee would be done eventually, and his instinct for self-preservation stayed sharp even as the deep rage came on him. Skull protected his master's back, his sword quick enough to best any but those of the Gorechosen.

In the centre of the battle, Mathror and Mir fought. They were well matched. Mathror was methodical, in control of every movement and action. Mir was rage and fury, his daemon axes screaming exultantly as he leapt and twisted through the air. Neither gained advantage. Mathror's shield turned Skullthief and Bloodspite aside, and they caught Mathror's blows in return. The air around the deathbringers was misty with smoke shocked from their weapons' blades. Blinding, multi-coloured sparks erupted from them as they met. Bloodspite and Skullthief howled in anger. They were bloodletters of the legions, and they did not recognise defeat. No mortal weapon could stand before them, but Mathror's was no ordinary blade. A mighty sword, heavy with blood-magic, this also was a gift of Khorne. The Lord of Slaughter was generous with his boons, for he liked to see them pitted against one another.

Mathror shoved Mir backwards with a combined push of blade and shield. 'You cannot win, Mir. You lack the proper regard for Khorne. Only I am worthy of leading the Bloodslaves. Lay down your arms and acknowledge me as lord and you shall live.'

Mir made a curious growling and came in for another attack. Words he could not speak ran through his mind. *I hate you, Mathror. I hate you all. I look upon what I have become, this monster of rage and anger, and I hate myself. But above all things I hate Khorne, and I will not rest until I have trodden the red road to its very end and stand before his brazen throne with my axes in my hands. You will not stand in my way, you will fall before me.*

Khorne had rendered Mir dumb, and so his words went unsaid, but Khorne heard. In response to Mir's treacherous thoughts the runes in the band that blinded his mortal eyes glowed with growing fire.

Searing pain built in Mir's head. The furnace heat of the ensorcelled brass cooked his skin, transmitted down the iron nails into the bone of his skull where it gnawed and spread and baked his brain. The Bloodslaves saw the ring as a great blessing, but it was not. Khorne allowed Mir to live, but he punished him often and hard for his blasphemy. Pain became agony. Thought became impossible. Mir surrendered himself to his killing rage. The shades of red that coloured his vision grew deeper, until the world around him was clouded by a gory murk. Far away he heard the roaring howl of Khorne, ever hungry, demanding more skulls, more blood, more war.

'Interesting,' murmured the Many-Eyed Servant, watching from its crystal donjon. It was party to the secrets of men, being able to peer into their minds. The brass ring about Mir's head was resistant to sorcery and stymied some of this ability, but the Many-Eyed Servant saw enough of Mir's thoughts to intrigue him.

'Here is a man who defies his own god, even while he serves him,' it whispered. 'Here is a man who is dedicated to Chaos, but to serve his own ends.' The Many-Eyed Servant made a hideous sound which served it for laughter. 'How Archaon will adore this one! How alike they are!'

More had to be done before the Many-Eyed Servant was convinced. The Bloodslaves were a lesser horde – their dead master had been no Khul or Baudrax. Kalaz the Hewer's name was unknown beyond the rolling steppe. And who had sung the name of Ushkar Mir in either praise or fear? Few, if any.

'A test, a test, I must set a test!' hissed the Many-Eyed Servant.

It searched a while through the Realm of Beasts, a thousand scenes of strife and horror passing beneath its hands. In a land far away, it found what it sought. The ogor followers of Skargut burned to avenge the death of their master at the hands of Baudrax. They massed around their cook-priests, who at that very moment offered up the choicest offal to their hungry god, beseeching him to guide them to their foe.

Maw-portals opened, red and glistening as gullets. The ogors screamed out their desire for revenge and poured through.

For one such as the Many-Eyed Servant, it was a small matter to manipulate such simple magic and send the ogors where it willed.

Somewhere far away in the Realm of Chaos, the Many-Eyed Servant heard an angry, brutish bellowing, but it paid the complaints no heed. The Ravenous One was feeble. Tzeentch was not.

It seemed to the Bloodslaves that Khorne grew bored with their squabble. Around the battleground where Mathror and Mir duelled, several shimmers took hold of the air. The stink of magic flooded the plain. A foetid wind blew, ripe with the smell of spoiling meat, rank sweat and old food. As it rippled the grasses, the Bloodbloom's song wavered. Discharges of energy crackled from the centre of the shimmerings.

'Look! Look!' bellowed Orto, severing the head from a screaming bloodreaver. 'A new foe comes! Khorne blesses us! Khorne hears our war! Skulls! Skulls! Skulls!'

At first the magical storms stabbed lightning out randomly, earthing in the wargear of the dead. But the jags of power concentrated themselves, gathered up by magic into a double row of crackling, interlocking dagger shapes. Only when the skittering light blinked out were these revealed to be teeth – fangs in a mouth like Mir's, bare of lips and dripping with drool.

With a roar, the first of these mouths opened into a gaping circular maw. The quivering skin of a realmgate was held between, delicate as a meniscus of saliva.

Through this stepped a huge ogor, then another and another. More gates opened, all around the horde and within it. A whole tribe of ogors charged into the brawling horde, knocking men flying with their huge guts and striking down those who raised their weapons against them with great clubs and mauls.

'Khorne favours us! A true foe!' shouted Orto ecstatically. 'To war, to war!'

The battle between the Bloodslaves ceased immediately. Men stepped back from one another and unlocked their blades. Their prior enmity was forgotten.

'Blood for the Blood God!' they roared, and attacked the ogors gathering on the field.

'Another time perhaps, Mir,' said Mathror. He disentangled his sword from Bloodspite, but kept his guard up in case Mir had ideas other than a truce.

Through the fog of pain and rage, Mir recognised the greater threat and the opportunity it presented. Here were many skulls for his road, large cobbles on the route to revenge. He nodded to Mathror, and they stood side by side.

'For Khorne! Skulls for Khorne!' shouted Mathror.

Mir roared out his wordless self-hatred, and together they ran at the ogors gathering on the plain.

There were at least two hundred ogors, and they attacked with a cunning that defied their brutish appearance. The first wave threw themselves on their foe as the greater part organised. The ogors in the centre comprised their best fighters, far bigger than the biggest of the Bloodslaves, and heavily armoured. Large iron plates covered their guts and arms, and they carried long falxes which cleaved warriors in two with a single blow. The ogor vanguard, more lightly armoured, halted their advance into the horde. Mir saw that they awaited their fellows still pouring through the realmgates. The heavier ogors were forming themselves into a hollow arrowhead that new arrivals quickly filled in.

Skull jogged at Mir's side. 'We must crush them quickly, my lord, before their wedge is completed.'

Mir nodded. He understood this. Once he had been a general of note, and was greatly frustrated that he could not communicate his intentions. Tactics that he could not speak crowded his boiling head.

But Skull seemed to infer them somehow, and was able speak Mir's own thoughts back to him.

'My lord, should I call upon your authority? I can order the men by your name, tell them to form squares to oppose the ogor rush, when it comes. Mathror is no use. Look at how he howls after glory, trailing those bloodreavers behind him in no formation. They will break on the wall of the ogors!'

Mir grunted a laugh. It was true. He nodded at his follower. Skull peeled away from his side and bounded up the spongy, weather-worn surface of an ancient bone to the top of a knoll higher than the rest of the hilltop. Shortly afterwards a horn winded, and Skull's voice cut across the battle, shouting orders to chieftains and champions.

'Control your fury, warriors of Khorne! Meet the ogors together, do not throw your lives away piecemeal. Do not disappoint Khorne! As a wall of flesh and steel shall we throw them back! I speak for the Lord Mir. It is he commands you now! Form up!'

Men stopped to shake the rage from their minds, looking back to Skull. A small group of warriors already gathered themselves around him. Mir strode to Skull's side atop the knoll, and the trickle grew to a flood, scores of men ranking up into tight blocks about the bony knoll. Mir roared out and men looked to him. He gestured with his axes, and they understood, deploying themselves to his intent without error. Soon five hundred well-blooded warriors stood in readiness. A score of skullreapers came to Mir's side, all slick with gore. Their skullseeker leader saluted Mir, and they gathered as a bodyguard around him. Then came Orto and Kordos, and the deathbringer's battle line was complete.

But many of the Bloodslaves did not heed Mir and instead followed Mathror.

The wedge of ogors was two hundred yards from Mir's position. Mathror's men had broken through their skirmish screen and seethed around the ogor arrowhead. Ogor weapons scythed them down, sickle blades hacking them into bloody chunks. Mathror fared well, slaying all who came against him, but there were always more to replace those felled, and the ogors required great effort to kill.

Mir looked to the flanks of the horde. The ogors continued to display their cunning. Large beasts were coming through the gates, arraying themselves into battle lines either side of the wedge. Bellowing at their shaggy mounts, the ogors goaded them so that the lines became oblique, facing in towards the leading edges of the wedge.

'They mean to trap Mathror's warriors between their skilled centre and the beasts,' said Skull. 'Should we aid them?'

The shake of Mir's head was decisive. Mathror would live or die on his own. Those men that had chosen Mathror could die beside him. They were caught up in battle lust and remained ignorant of the approaching danger.

Mir's attention was fixed on a massive ogor at the heart of the wedge. Bigger and even fatter than his followers, he stood a head over the next largest. His thick armour was decorated with gaping mouths inlaid in precious metals, and he carried a massive, two-ended bludgeon whose heads were huge ingots of spiked iron. Mir marked him. This gutlord would fall to his axes, he resolved, a fitting tribute to the god he would eventually slay.

The last of the ogor elite strode through the portal. The

wedge was complete. A number of ogors lifted their hands to their mouths and let out a tremendous hallooing, strangely musical after a fashion, and the others drew themselves up.

'Skargut!' roared their warlord.

'Skargut! Skargut! Skargut!' they replied.

'We kill for Skargut! Revenge!'

That was a sentiment Mir could understand.

The ogors marched. The rest of Mathror's supporters were shoved aside as easily as children.

A second vocal trumpet hooted from the left flank, a third from the right, and the ogor war-beasts lurched into motion, braying loudly, their heavy tread making the ground shake. The war animals broke into a ponderous trot. Shouting their war-cries, the riders guided the warbeasts to smash into the horde either side of the wedge, decimating the Bloodslaves. Mathror was confronted by a rearing monster sporting a wide sweep of stony horns, and disappeared under its feet.

Mir grunted at this with a hint of satisfaction, and turned his attention to the closing ogor elite. He stared at their leader until their eyes met. Mir saluted with his axes. The ogor inclined its head in recognition. The challenge had been accepted. The ogors picked up speed. They came on, guts swaying, shouting deafeningly. As they neared, they raised their weapons over their heads.

'Brace, O bloody men of Khorne!' shouted Skull. 'Cast them back!'

'Blood! Blood for Khorne!' screamed Orto, and brandished his axe over his head.

Kordos silently wrapped one more loop of chain about his hand and gripped it tightly.

The ogors' charge was slow, almost sedate, but when it hit the Bloodslaves' line it was devastating. With a roaring cry louder than the falling of city walls, the ogors thundered into Mir's men. Return shouts of 'Khorne! Khorne! Khorne!' were cut short as the first ranks of Mir's Bloodslaves were crushed or knocked flying to land on those behind them. There was a rolling clatter emanating from the point of impact, followed by a second as the ogors' long hook blades fell, lopping limbs and heads.

The men of the Bloodslaves were encircled, but they did not fall. Leaning into their adversaries, they pushed back against the great scrum of ogors. Their feet ploughed furrows in the blood-sodden earth as they were forced backward. Men threw themselves at other men's backs, pushing hard until all the horde strained against the enemy. The ogor wedge penetrated only a little into the massed Bloodslaves. Their line flattened against that of the Chaos warband, and their charge was arrested. Hooked weapons whistled through the air, cutting down three men at a time, and the line buckled, but still the ogors could not force their way through to the bony knoll at the Bloodslaves' centre. Men leapt up from the rear ranks, lightly armed bloodreavers running along the armoured backs of blood warriors. They screamed dark praise to their bloody god and hurled themselves forward, axes swinging for ogor heads. Dozens fell, split by the ogors' massive blades, but more came through, planting their axes into piggy faces, or scrambling onto shoulders and stabbing down with serrated knives into the tough muscle of the ogors' necks. Others leapt for the ogors' arms, preventing them striking with their weapons. Their fellow warriors saw their chance, and pushed their blades up to the hilt in the ogors' fleshy bodies.

With terrible screams and crashes, the ogors began to fall. The Bloodslaves' horns let out a brazen call, and they surged forward.

From their vantage upon the bony knoll, Mir, Orto and the rest watched the battle shift. The ogors surrounded them in a long bow. Their war-beasts had done with Mathror's men and were coming to the aid of the others, but the ogor elite barred their way, and the beasts milled about uselessly behind the main line. The time was right. Mir raised his axes.

'Forward for the glory of Khorne!' screamed Skull.

'Skulls for the skull throne!' shouted Skullthief.

'Blood for the Blood God!' shouted Bloodspite.

Mir leapt from the knoll, sailing with supernatural might over the heads of his warriors to smash into an ogor. The giant warrior was rocked off his feet by the impact, gaping in surprise at the power of one so small.

Its face was still wearing that expression when Skullthief swept off its head.

Mir ploughed on into the ogor elite. Now they were in disarray, not the solid wall Mathror had encountered, and he hacked his way through them. Where they pressed too thickly he leapt at them, pushing off their thick limbs and stout bodies with his legs. Every swing of his twin daemon axes killed another. By his efforts alone he opened a wide gap in the ogor tribe, and his skullreapers came behind him. Massive, mutated men whose Khorne-given strength was a match even for that of the ogors, they widened the gap in the line. Lesser Bloodslaves came in their wake, advancing over a carpet of ogor fat and muscle.

Mir fought forwards, seeking out the ogor lord. All the while, his open challenge to Khorne played in his head: *By each skull I pave the road to your throne, by each step I come closer to vengeance.*

The runes in his punishment band glowed with hellish fire. His flesh sizzled, but he did not stop his blasphemous prayer.

The last of the ogors between Mir and his target fell, and the ogor lord was before him.

'You! Little man!' roared the tyrant, pointing a finger fat as a man's arm. Gobbets of saliva flew from his red mouth. 'You I kill now.'

Mir raised his axes to attack. The ogor tyrant swept round his double-ended maul, catching Mir in the chest and slamming him backwards. The ogor's smile of triumph turned to a snarl as Mir shook off the blow, though his ribs glowed with a swirl of bruises, and blood ran from a deep gouge that showed bone. The tyrant advanced on him.

'I don't know who you are, twisted one. The Great Maw sent us to you, and not to he who slew Skargut, but you will do as an appetiser. Your god killed Skargut the Great, Prophet of the Maw, so we kill you!' grunted the ogor chieftain. 'We smash you puny men down, then we eat your livers while you watch.'

The tyrant spun his maul around with astonishing speed, turning the iron heads into blurs of grey. Mir dodged one, then the second, but the third crashed into his face. Nails tore at his skull as his punishment band took the brunt of the blow. His head reeled, and he went down onto one knee.

'Now you die. I ain't one for pretty speeches, but I'll tell you, I'll kill every one of your bloody kind I see. I should have started long ago. Your god will learn to fear the followers of Skargut!' The tyrant lifted up his maul, and brought it down towards Mir's head with a force that would have pulverised the skull of a juggernaut.

Inches before the impact, Mir swept Skullthief and Bloodspite together onto the bludgeon, shattering it into a thousand spinning fragments of iron that glowed with magical heat. They hissed as they landed on the combatants' flesh. The ogor roared, overbalanced by the sudden shift in the weight of his weapon.

Mir's unholy vitality drove back the pain of his wounds, and he stepped aside as the ogor stumbled forward. The chief half recovered before Skullthief took his leg off at the knee, and he collapsed to the ground. A hand he raised to protect himself was similarly removed by Bloodspite, who cackled madly as he drank the blood coursing over his blade. Great hot spurts of life fluid pumped from the tyrant's wrist to drench Mir.

'A curse on you and all your murdering kind,' spat the ogor chief, before Mir ended him. The deathbringer stooped, picking up the sodden mass of the tyrant's ruined head, and held it aloft. Its face twitched as Mir roared his incoherent defiance at his divine master.

The ogors quailed to see their mightiest warrior cut down. The end had begun for them.

Mir fought his way onwards, butchering ogors wherever he met them. Kordos barged past him, flaming anvil whooshing through the air, each ogor it hit engulfed and flung backwards. They wailed as their copious body fat ignited with the sorcerous fire, turning them into living candles. Danavan Vuul's barbed whip whirled around his head to strike the Bloodslaves and drive them on, provoking them to greater savagery.

Many ogors were fleeing back to their gates. The Bloodslaves gave chase. A war-beast, its riders hanging dead in their harnesses upon its back, reared up against Ushkar Mir, threatening to pound him flat. A mad cry answered from the left, and the Bloodslaves' two khorgoraths leapt at the monster. The beast fell. Mir did not stop to watch as one of the khorgoraths bit the beast's head off, shattering its great horns in its powerful jaws, and swallowed it whole.

He ran on. Bodies large and small carpeted the field once more. He fought down his exultation at the slaughter. That way led to true damnation. He clung to the kernel of his own will that still survived. He cut down a fleeing ogor, then another. The maw gates shone redly not far away. And then there was Mathror, coming toward him, sword held high.

Mir abandoned his pursuit, and readied himself to continue his duel.

Skull grabbed his next trophy's hair and yanked upward, preparing to cut his skull free so that he might add it to the growing cairns.

The man moaned and opened his eyes, and Skull let his head drop. He rolled the man onto his back. The warrior, a bloodreaver, blinked eyes that were free of rage and newly filled with fear.

'Where am I? Where is this place?' he said. He looked down his chest to inspect the deep wounds in his torso and saw the thick muscle, the crude tattoos, the spiked harness he wore as clothing. His eyes widened. 'What has happened to me? What have I become?'

'Ah,' said Skull. 'The fury has fled you.'

'Fury? Who are you? Where am I?'

'I am Skull,' Skull said. He squatted next to the bloodreaver and drove his long knife into the turf. 'Tell me, why do men fight?'

The man's face creased in puzzlement.

'I am dying, and you pose me riddles? Help me!'

'I am helping you. Answer the question, and you will have some idea of where you are.'

The man gasped. His breaths were coming in short bursts, pink blood frothing at his lips. 'A man fights to protect his land and his family. Or for money.'

'And when those things are gone?'

'A man fights to survive.'

'Very good. So did you,' said Skull.

The man's face took on a look of horrible realisation.

'Old gods! I remember... What have I done? What have I done! The redness has gone from my vision. I see, I see!'

'Shhh,' said Skull, and knelt by the warrior. He smoothed hair wet with sweat and thick with blood. The man's skin was slick, his beard caked and filthy. His face was disfigured by tattoos like those on his body, but what looked out from behind the savage mask was pure anguish.

'The red rage has left you. Khorne has no more use for you. He abandons you.'

The man wept. 'I killed them all... My friends. I ate their *hearts*.'

'And why did you do this?' asked Skull. 'You did it to survive.'

He looked over to where Mir and Mathror still battled. In the gathering evening the men fought, neither besting the other. The ogors were dead or gone, and the Bloodslaves had ceased their own struggles. Those handful who were left sank exhausted to their knees, dumbly watching the deathbringers. A few of them made their offerings to Khorne. Wandering the battlefield they hewed the heads from the fallen and piled them onto the cairns from yesterday's battle. One of these had grown higher than the rest, and had been lit. Open jaws and eye sockets glowed with fire.

'I shall tell you a story,' said Skull softly. 'There was once a land, with a glorious city named Mir at its heart. It had kings both just and kind, whose reigns were held to be exemplary. Mir had many armies, with fine warriors and knights mounted upon fabulous beasts, and a talent for battle. Hundreds of mages were theirs to call to war, and the peoples of its towns were master wrights. They were peaceable, but they turned their talents to the construction of engines of death readily enough once the gods abandoned the realms. By these means they remained free while the nations of their neighbours fell to Chaos, either destroyed or seduced one by one, until only the land of Mir was left, all alone in a sea of darkness.

'For long years Mir persisted, a beacon in a dark age of blood. Refugees from other lands flooded the streets, but Mir took them in without complaint. Diversity became their strength.'

Skull sighed. 'There is but one story Chaos tells, and that is of defeat. Fast or slow, it comes to all who defy the Four. Every year saw the borders of Mir shrink. A duchy here, an island there. Sometimes the land of Mir fought back and retook the lands it had lost. Every victory was tainted with sorrow, so many dead in return for territory made barren by the power of Chaos. Seas turned to blood, forests became hellish groves of screaming bone trees, farmland withered to dusty plains where phantom armies fought every night. Very little taken back could be made use of, and Mir died, one bloody bite at a time, until only the city remained.

'Ushkar Mir...' gasped the man. 'He was the king?'

Skull shook his head. 'No. Mir was not the king, but he was the champion of his age, blessed with an ability at arms to rival Sigmar himself, and a command of strategy not seen since the Age of Myth.' Skull smiled at the futility of it. 'But he could not win. Then came the inevitable night when Mir's walls were assailed a final time. The full might of Khorne's armies were brought to bear on this one last city, for Mir's continued defiance had become an affront to the Lord of War. They could not hope to win. But Mir, he was... he is... a singular being. He looked out upon that endless horde of brass and steel, and he did not despair. He could not win, not on that battlefield, so he chose another. That is why Mir wished to survive, to find a ground better suited to victory. He was offered the Dark

Feast by Korghos Khul himself, it is said. He accepted without complaint.'

'So did I, so did I! I am sorry, so sorry.' The man choked. 'So sorry.'

'Do not ask for forgiveness!' snapped Skull. He pointed to the duelling deathbringers. 'That is Ushkar Mir! His wish to live is no petty desire to preserve a worthless life. Mir plots revenge! By dedicating himself utterly to Khorne's red road, he hopes to ascend to the heights of daemonhood, and challenge the gods themselves. Do you not see my friend? In a sane world, a man achieves immortality through his children or through his works. But this is no longer a sane world. Children are slaughtered and works cast down. If the great powers of the universe take family and achievement away, a man is left only one means to gain immortality – to survive, and to exceed his master. Of course, the Lord of Skulls knows of Mir's desire, but I think the Blood God takes some pleasure in his defiance. Maybe Mir shall succeed, maybe hubris is the gods' only weakness. Maybe... well, who knows?'

Skull looked down at the bloodreaver. Sightless eyes stared out of his face, the light gone from them. Horror remained on his dead face. 'This is what I have learned, this is what Mir taught me.'

Skull stood. 'Skulls for the Skull throne!' he whispered, and severed the man's head with a quick downward strike of his sword. He retrieved his knife, took the head up and carried it to a pile where he tossed it high, then went to the next dead man to repeat the grisly ritual.

All around the battlefield, the skull cairns grew.

Finally, as night drew in, Mathror fell. The two deathbringers were exhausted, their bodies sporting dozens of cuts and

Mathror's armour in tatters. Blood stained their skin from head to foot. Mathror's ankle turned on the horned helmet of a dead blood warrior, and he went down, driving the point of his nameless weapon into the warrior to steady himself. Were he fresh, he might have sprung back to his feet with alacrity.

Were he fresh.

Bloodspite swept across Mathror's blade. With a chilling scream it cut straight through the metal. The magic left Mathror's blade with a mighty bang, and the halves turned to granular dust that pattered down onto the ground.

'Wait!' said Mathror.

Skullthief was Mir's answer to that plea. The daemon weapon lived up to its name, its edge so sharp it cut through the flesh and bone of Mathror's neck without leaving a mark. For a second Mathror gaped and gurgled, his eyes rolling, then blood welled up through his mouth and along the line of the razor cut. Only then did the head topple to the floor. Mathror's severed head lived just long enough to feel itself lifted from the ground in Mir's brass-bound fingers.

When Mathror's skull was laid upon the highest cairn, a silky, diabolical laugh rolled over the Bloodbloom Fields. It grew louder and louder, until it became a clarion ringing in the distance. Mir looked that way, toward the sound's eminence far out over the Bloodbloom Fields. The stars swam and became eyes looking down upon him on the slaughter ground. A faceless creature, spread thin over the night sky regarded him. Man or daemon or both, Mir could not tell. Its body was tall and thin, its head oddly shaped with many eyes upon it. Its robe too was made all of eyes, millions of them, greater in number than the stars.

'You hear the call, Ushkar Mir. Heed the horns of Chaos.'

Who are you? thought Mir, and the apparition heard him.

'No one, and someone. I am the herald of Archaon. Go to him, fight for him. He will reward you. You hate the Lord of War. This is your chance to fight for something greater than a god.'

I desire only revenge, thought Mir. *I fight to live, so that I might become great in the eyes of Khorne and come into his presence. There I will offer up true worship, I will smite him down.*

'As you wish, Ushkar Mir. Go to Archaon, in Shyish he awaits! Go toward the rising sun, there you shall find a gate amid the Arman Forests. It will take you to the Realm of Death! Go!'

The figure faded. The eyes closed, becoming stars again.

Mir felt rage unending, but his thirst for revenge outweighed it. He clung to this tiny pebble of himself. The core of who he once was grew smaller with every passing year, but it was not gone, not quite.

The Bloodslaves had a new master. There were but an eighth of the number that had been present that morning, but they were the strongest, the fastest, the most skilled. They gathered behind their new lord and awaited his command.

Ushkar Mir, Warlord of the Bloodslaves, threw back his head and roared at the sky.

KNIGHT OF CORRUPTION

David Annandale

The daemon considered the nature of vision. It was his power, it was his goal and it was his frustration. Through vision, the Many-Eyed served Archaon. In serving, he saw more and more. The more he saw, the more distant the moment of great revelation became. That sight, lost to him except in blurs and fragments, was his eternal torment and goad.

No accumulation of knowledge came close to what had been. It must never stop. His vision must reach further and further, embracing more and more. Piece by piece, he would construct infinity.

The Many-Eyed Servant thought about the eyes of a fly, of the mosaic of a single insect's vision, limited in distance yet all-encompassing in the immediate. Sight compounded then compounded again by the multiplicity of a swarm. So many pieces coming together, creating clarity.

For those with eyes to see.

How well does he answer the call? The voice came, as deep

with power and with the thunder of Chaos as if the speaker were present. It was the voice of the sorcerer's master, the voice of Archaon, reaching across the realms.

'He hears,' the Many-Eyed said. 'He strives. He lacks clarity.'

He is aware of his shortcoming?

'He is, Everchosen. He seeks to know what he must do.'

Then the trial continues.

'As you command.' Standing in the empty throne room, the Many-Eyed Servant looked beyond its walls. He received the vision of the swarm.

The flies were speaking to Copsys Bule again. They burrowed into his scalp, took his blood and laid their eggs in his lank, dripping strands of hair. Their buzzing was music that had accompanied him for years. It was the sound of Grandfather Nurgle's growing garden, the melody of blessed corruption. Now, though, it had become something else. It sounded very close to whispers. The drone of insects, growing louder and softer as the nimbus circled him, had a shape just beyond his ability to perceive. He wondered if that shape would match the apparition that had spoken to him. The drone was urgent. It was commanding. It pulled, but he could not discern the direction of the tug. Since the retreat from the seraphon, the call had become both more insistent and more vague. He had a duty to fulfil, one different from any he had known until now.

He seeks a champion, the apparition had said. And then, with meaningful symmetry: *Seek him, champion.*

And Fistula, deep in fever, speaking unconsciously, had said *Archaon.*

And there were other duties too. A portion of the garden had been uprooted. Nurgle's blessings had been rejected. There were reparations to be made.

So Fistula was quick to remind him.

'We should go back,' said Fistula. He marched beside Bule. His words were for the commander's ears alone, but he did not temper their volume as much as he should have.

Bule did not know if any of the other Rotbringers heard. He thought not. But Fistula's anger was clear. His tone was on the verge of a challenge.

'You would have us return to annihilation?' Bule asked.

'No, for vengeance. For Grandfather.'

'Your zeal is sound. Your judgement is not. We cannot go back. What makes you think the gate would return us to our point of departure? Do you even know what realm this is?'

'No,' Fistula admitted.

'We are fortunate to have emerged where we have,' said Bule. 'Grandfather Nurgle still blesses us.'

The realm was blighted; the Plaguefather's gifts were everywhere. The warband moved through a diseased forest. The gate was far behind but Bule wanted it further yet. He didn't think pursuit was likely, but until his diminished warband had recovered some of its strength, it was better not to risk another clash with the seraphon. He had lost his trident in the most recent clash and now carried a pock-marked axe. He looked back at his warriors. They had been bloodied. Their numbers were reduced and the shame of retreat hung over them. This portion of Nurgle's following had withered, and it needed to blossom once more.

'There is no glory in luck,' Fistula said. His bald head reddened with anger. The white spots of emerging blisters appeared. They gave him no joy. 'And we are still retreating.'

Bule did not argue. Whether an enemy pursued or not, the effect was the same. The march had begun as desperate flight. Nothing had changed that initial impulse. Bule needed to turn the retreat into an advance. There was still strength in his warriors, and there was strength all around them. For the day and the night since their arrival, they had been surrounded by the glorious blight. The garden was flourishing. There was cause to rejoice even as there was work to do.

The terrain was rolling and gaining altitude. A river flowed on Bule's left. The water was brown and grey and gelid, despite a fast current, and soft, rotting shapes tumbled through it. Black-crusted foam burbled around rocks, leaving a patina of slime. On both sides of the river, the forest quivered. Pendulous fungi hung from trees. There were no leaves. Huge colonies of mould covered the branches, the growths thicker than the trunks. They hauled the branches down toward the ground. The loam was thick, a festering carpet of decomposition. It rippled with feasting insects.

'Children of the Plaguefather!' Bule shouted. Phlegm thickened his voice, and he revelled in the wet, crackling pain at the back of his throat. 'We turn our backs on sorrow, and march towards the ecstasy of blight. Enough of retreat! Now we hunt!'

'What is our prey?' Fistula asked.

Bule smiled. 'It must be found. That is the first stage of a hunt, is it not?' His chest expanded with an eager hope.

Bule's optimism found its reward after they had marched less than another league. To the east, deep in the forest, a huge shadow lurked. Its form was suggestive, and Bule turned off the path to investigate. He found himself standing before the crumbled remains of a vast monument. Much of what had once been was gone, but the angle of the exterior sides of the foundation stones suggested an obelisk. If that were so, it would have towered many times the height of the tallest trees. The shattered base extended far into the forest, wide enough to have supported an entire keep. The ruins were overgrown with black, glistening lichen. At the top of the stones, the growth had been scraped away, revealing naked rock.

Bule walked the length of the monument, his boots squelching and sinking deep into the toxic mulch. Disturbed by his footsteps, swarms and stench rose in waves. All around Bule, life erupted in the celebration of abundance and decay.

'There has been work done here,' Bule said. 'Someone has been building something.' The monument had fallen long ago, but it had been disturbed recently. Though the rot had spread over it again quickly, he could see the marks of tools. Stones had been removed. Beyond the wall, the diseased vegetation had been flattened as the scavenged masonry had been dragged away. The stones that remained were so huge it would have been impossible for anything less than an army of slaves to move them.

The flies buzzed in Bule's ears. The whine was excited. He grinned, ripping open the pustules on his lips. He had the scent of prey.

And there, the words of the flies became a little clearer. Here was purpose. Here was destiny. If he hunted *this* prey, he would find what he had been told to seek. And he would serve…

He blinked, surprised and puzzled.

A conviction formed. He would be in service to a being who was neither Nurgle nor one of his champions. Yet he was equally certain this allegiance would not in any way be contrary to the Plaguefather's wishes. The paradox confused him. His need to answer the call was clear. It was his paramount duty. He was summoned. But the source of the call was lost in the insect miasma. He did not know how he was to answer.

He looked again at the wide swathe of drag marks in the putrefying vegetation. There was his direction. The marks were a clear sign. Whatever answer he must make, he would be propagating the garden, and clarity lay ahead.

Clarity and prey.

Exhilaration drove away the shame of defeat. His laugh was loud, long and braying. It turned into a generous cough, spraying yellow phlegm before him. The sputum hit the ruined wall. At its touch, the sickened, spreading lichen convulsed, bursting into sudden, accelerated, tumorous growth before dying. The lichen decomposed into a corrosive acid, pitting and crumbling the stone beneath. But as the lichen liquefied, it revealed a portion of an engraving. Bule paused. He used the edge of his axe to scrape more away, revealing the head of a hammer. Decayed as the stone was, the skill of the ancient work was clear. The majesty of the weapon shone through the grime. Bule growled and struck the wall, smashing the engraving and erasing the memory.

He turned to Fistula. He wondered if the other Rotbringer could see the triumph in his eyes.

'I have the scent,' he said. He raised his voice for the warband to hear. 'Feasting lies before us!'

He lurched off, cutting through the suppurating woods in the direction of the drag marks. His vigour spread over his followers, a joyful contagion. After a few minutes, they reached another, wider path. It showed signs of recent use, and of the ferrying of heavy loads. Bule charged along the route, his hunger and eagerness growing together. The ground rose. The forest thinned, withering to a bubbling sludge at the peak of a hill. There, Bule saw his goal.

Below the hill was a wide valley. A river, much larger and even more polluted than the one the Rotbringers had left behind, flowed in from the west. It had once irrigated agricultural land. Even now, long after its conquest by Nurgle's children, the valley's former character could be seen in the grotesque parody it had become. The fields waved with tall, ergot-covered stalks and undulated with squirming decay. At their edge, heaps of fungi multiplied, each the parasite of the one beneath, their accumulation rising many feet into the air. A ruined city rotted in the centre of the valley. Black water filled the open foundations. The ramparts were gone, lost beneath fungal mounds. The roads were broken, collapsing into the banks of foetid canals. None of the original buildings stood; they had all crumbled into piles of shattered stone and brick.

But not everything had fallen. There were statues here, colossi hundreds of feet high, bestriding the valley. An army could pass between the huge columns of their legs. The statues had been defaced. Some heads were shattered half-moons. Others were missing altogether, and monstrous faces had been carved into the torsos. None had any hands, their arms ending in jagged stumps. Their shapes, once heroic, had been eaten away until their proportions were skeletal. They were corpses now.

And they moved.

Arms rose, coming together for absent hands to clasp in prayer before absent faces, then fell again. The western-most statue, closest to the entrance to the valley, bowed and straightened again and again, filling the air with the slow grinding of rock. Creations of wonder and majesty had been reduced to immense, meaningless, idiot gestures. A great city had been razed to nothing but a mockery.

In its place, something new had risen.

A tower had been built using the ruins of a hundred other structures. Its construction was crude. Even from this distance Bule could see the mismatched stonework, each block marked by the fragments of ancient carvings. It was a rough, scavenged construct. There was no artistry in its design. It was blocky, almost as wide as it was tall. Speed and resilience had governed its making. But it was big – its crenellated peak soared higher than the Rotbringers' position on the ridge. Where it rose, the glorious ruin and bounty of Nurgle's generosity ended. Around the base of the tower and spreading eastward to the valley's mouth, the ground was barren. The temple was order reformed from chaos. Its stones, irregular and damaged, had been forced into something coherent. And clean. The walls had been scoured. There was no growth, no celebration of convulsed life on its surface. Though it was heavily fortified, it was not merely a keep, it was a site of worship. The walls had been carved to suggest armoured visages of a sort Bule had never seen before. He guessed what they represented: a myth he still refused to credit with any validity.

Further to the east, the land dipped towards a barren plain. Bule saw no life there, either. There was only the evidence of a terrible cleansing, the ground scorched by lightning. Worse still, it held the potential for new growth, unblessed by the Plaguefather. Less than a league from the temple, Nurgle's blight ended. The meaning was clear. The land beyond was the site of another defeat. There was no way to guess what enemy had scraped the land clean of blight, but that a foe had done so was beyond doubt. For a moment, Bule wondered if the inhabitants of the tower were responsible for this tragedy. No, he decided. They had built this high edifice, but only from the wreckage of what had been before. The scoured earth did not begin at the tower. Rather, a finger of purifying fire had reached this far into the valley from the battlefield. What had happened beyond the valley must have been the inspiration for the construction of the temple, and for the noise that came from within and from the roof.

The temple rang with human voices.

'What's that sound?' Fistula asked.

'You don't recognise it?'

'No.'

Of course he didn't. Such a young warrior. So inexperienced. He had not known the great wars of the past. He had not been formed by those struggles. He had not witnessed the fall of empires. He had not witnessed the extinction of what had suddenly dared to be reborn.

'That,' Bule said, 'is song. It is hope.'

The song travelled to them on the humid air in snatches. It was, Bule thought, uncertain. It was spontaneous, but unled.

'*Hope.*' Fistula's breath wheezed with the intensity of his anger.

Bule shared his underling's rage at the blasphemy. But he also celebrated. Here was a prey whose destruction and *instruction* would be satisfying. The annihilation of hope was a pleasure to be savoured. The Rotbringers would hurl the temple down. All within would experience the gifts of Nurgle and know true apotheosis in the exquisite opulence of disease. An easy victory for the warband, but rich in satisfaction.

His flies buzzed in growing excitement. The pull was much stronger. The longer he stared at the temple, the closer to clarity he drew. The fall of the temple became of crucial importance. The defeat by the seraphon was suddenly trivial, merely one battle among many. Somewhere in the temple, destiny awaited.

'Sound the horns,' Bule commanded.

To raise his voice in praise was a strange sensation. All his life, the very idea of song had been inconceivable. He only knew what song was because of the monstrous chants of the dark warhosts. Song was the triumph of Chaos. Song was the announcement of doom. It was the liquid, burbling, discordant, cackling sound that presaged slaughter. There was no song in the lives of the people struggling to survive under the reign of night and plague.

No song until that moment when Brennus witnessed the deeds of the beings that blasted down from the heavens. Beings of light, beings of fury, their coming had illuminated the landscape with fire and routed the armies of disease. He and his fellows had watched the battle from a distance. The waves of the war had lapped at the edge of the valley while they had hidden and sought what refuge they could in the remains of the city whose name had been lost long ago. A purging sliver of fire had reached into the valley, and that holy blaze was surely the promise of more.

The destruction had been pure. The blight was gone. The emptiness to the east was sacred, and so was the sear in the valley. It was the sign of healing to come. Of the return of dawn.

And so they had built the temple and built it as high as the dead-but-restless statues. The inhabitants of the valley had numbered only a few score at the beginning. But the battle had been witnessed by many more, scattered through the hills and the forest. The activity of construction had become a beacon. Before long, hundreds had joined in the act of worship. Then thousands. They were all ragged, hungry, ill. Many were maddened by pain and grief, yet they were able to complete the simple tasks of hauling stone, even as they babbled and shrieked their horror. But even the most feral also had hope, and they were strong with it. A following formed. And those who began the building, those who led by example, and so were expected to continue to lead, were the priests.

Brennus was among their number. He knew what he had become. He accepted the calling. He was proud of it and humbled by it, as were the others who had been called to wear the robes of their new office. To their rags they added pieces of scavenged armour and fragments of robes, vestments that bore marks which resonated with their spirits, even if they did not know the meaning of the signs. And now they sang their strength. They sang their praise.

On the roof of the temple, the celebrants had erected their altar of war. Brennus himself had found its largest piece, half-buried in the ancient foundations upon which the temple would be built. It was a portion of an ornate crimson anvil, larger than a man. The beings of light had great hammers. Surely the anvil had some connection to their divinity. At the entrance to the valley, a black helmet framed by a golden halo had been found. Its visage was as unforgiving as it was blessed. The priests had placed it on the altar and it had given focus to their praise, and to their determination. They would pray here, and when the time came, they would take up the hammer to fight for their lives and their still-inchoate faith.

A large fire pit was next to the altar. A massive cauldron sat over the flames, its contents boiling. Around the cauldron was a large group of the most damaged of the faithful. Most could barely speak, and they mortified their own flesh with their fervour. They were no longer victims. Now they were flagellants, and their wasted bodies were kept alive by the fury. On all sides of the temple, sentinels stood at the crenellations, keeping watch at all hours, vigilant for signs of evil or of deliverance.

And around the altar, around the fire, around the ramparts, Brennus and his comrades sang.

The song was a patchwork, constructed of bits and pieces dredged from the collective memories of the worshippers. The people combined melodies and words passed down from generation to generation, eroded and forgotten as the centuries of darkness passed. They took the fragments, many of them devoid of any meaning save the impulse to praise itself, and put them together in the same manner they had built the temple. The result was irregular, a thing of awkward rhythms and strange halts, but it was powerful. It gave voice to the soul. Brennus sang his thanks, even though he did not know who he thanked. The hymn was raised to unnamed gods. The objects of praise were the warriors who had brought the light. Whoever they were, they had broken the forces of the Dark Gods, so they must be divine.

The worshippers sang for the warriors seen only from a distance, offering thanks for the miracle already performed, and calling upon them to return.

'Movement,' Kalfer shouted.

The worshippers kept singing. Brennus and four others detached themselves from the circle and joined Kalfer at the ramparts. Silhouettes gathered on the summit of the hill to the south. Soon they covered the slope. The forms were bloated, twisted. Torsos and limbs were malformed. Some were swollen. Others were too long, tentacles instead of arms. The air, foul and choking as ever, became fouler yet. Brennus' throat began to feel tight and raw just from looking at the hulking, pestilential shapes.

And then there was music, the terrible music, a jangling discordant sound in celebration of corruption.

All along the lines of the assembled host, horns were raised. They sounded. Their blast reverberated across the valley. The noise was huge. It ratcheted like lungs filling with fluid. It buzzed with the wings of millions of insects. It echoed, it squirmed.

Brennus was sure the light in the valley began to fail more quickly, as if sickened by the sound. The air grew still worse. Brennus swallowed, and he felt the tickle of legs crawling at the back of his mouth and down into his chest.

'Our trial has come,' Kalfer said. He sounded determined, but Brennus could hear the fear just beneath the surface.

'We are prepared,' said Brennus.

'I had hoped...' Kalfer trailed off as the warband began to march down the hill.

'For what?' Heccam asked. 'To be left alone?' He had already picked up a double-headed flail from the stacks of weapons lining the ramparts. Its handle was long enough to be used as a staff. He held it up like an icon.

'No,' said Kalfer, already sounding stronger. He touched his forehead, where he wore a tight band of studded metal.

'Good.' Jessina was arming herself too. 'Our duty is not to hide and hope for deliverance.'

'It is not,' Brennus agreed. 'We will give praise in struggle. And if we die, we must die with pride and with hope. Then victory will be ours, no matter what.'

The horns sounded again. The army of Rotbringers was midway down the slope and moving fast. Laughter and shouts followed the second blast. Voices thickened by the flow of pus and the pressure of tumours mocked the celebrants. At the head of the host was a massive warrior. His helmet was terrifying in the blankness of its features – it had just three holes drilled into the front, which suggested an unnatural configuration of eyes. A single horn curved out and down from the right side. He raised his right arm, pointing a gigantic, pitted battle axe.

'Grandfather Nurgle summons you to the celebration!' he roared. His voice was thunder, and beneath it was the hum of a million insects. It came from a throat raw and suppurating and powerful. Its invitation should not be refused.

The celebrants of the tower refused it.

They loosed volleys of arrows at the Rotbringers. Untrained, they did so too soon. Most of the arrows fell short. The few that reached the warband did so only because the corrupted warriors advanced into the hail of shafts. Their shambling gait was surprisingly fast. The diseases cratering their skin and twisting their forms gave them strength, and they charged with the fervour of zealots. They too gave praise, and they came to spread the contagion of their faith.

Brennus looked back toward the centre of the roof. 'Hurry!' he called. A group of flagellants dragged the cauldron toward the north rampart. Brennus helped lift a curved length of metal. It was the first and only product of the temple's forge, ten feet long and widened at one end to better receive the contents of the cauldron. The priests fastened the chute into place with rope and a wooden framework. The larger group hauled the cauldron up. As they did, disease-ridden ungors loosed a volley of arrows against the temple walls. The plague warriors laughed. The attack was simple mockery. Even so, a number of arrows whistled through the crenellations. One struck Kalfer through the throat. He staggered back, eyes wide, his mouth open in silent shock. His hands clutched at the shaft. They came away slimy. The arrow was dark with filth. The fletchings looked as if they were made from feathers, but the vanes were coiled and wiry, and they released a small cloud of spores as Kalfer stumbled and the arrow shook. One step away from him, Loressa began to cough. Kalfer fell, twitching. Retching blood, Loressa pulled his body away to the north end of the roof. She managed to reach a wall before slumping over the corpse.

'Ready!' Jessina called. The cauldron was in position. At the same moment, Brennus heard the clash of weapons far below against the metal door that was the sole entrance to the temple.

'Burn them! Burn them!' Heccam shouted.

Many hands tilted the cauldron. The boiling water poured

into the chute. Brennus ran to the next aperture and looked down.

He wished they had oil, but there was only water, collected from a clean and pure stream that ran through the edge of the scoured region. Hauling the water back over those leagues had been a task almost as painstaking as the construction of the temple. Now, kept in stone reservoirs, was enough good water to last for months. And enough to hurl at the enemy.

Steaming, the boiling embodiment of resurrected faith and hope, the water fell upon the Rotbringers.

Bule had his axe raised to strike the door of the temple when the scalding rain came down. It took a few moments for the water to work its way through his armour. He ignored the pain at first, but then it became ferocious. The warriors on either side of him howled, recoiling from the burn. Bule snarled. Simple water should not hurt like that. It should turn to muck on contact with him, more irrigation for Nurgle's garden. Instead, it dug deeper into his flesh with flashing agony. One warrior fell to the ground, the skin of his skull and his left arm sloughing off, dissolving into sludge.

This water had been transformed. It burned with noxious purity. When it touched the ground, it scoured again, eating the diseased plant life and leaving bare stone.

Bule had expected sport in killing the inhabitants of the temple. Now he encountered blasphemy. He would permit no portion of Grandfather's garden to wither. He roared, dismissing the pain. Where his skin deliquesced, pus ran over the surface, overrunning the purity with a wealth of illness. Beside him, Fistula also stood his ground, his scalp an oozing mass of open blisters. They exchanged a look. In this moment, Bule shared the blightlord's rage. Fistula pulled back, giving Bule the space he needed. Heedless of the searing rain, he raised his axe again, and brought it down against the door. The iron barrier shuddered in its frame. The blade left a gouge two feet long and as deep as his hand. Rust spread from the lips of the wound. The disease of metal cracked the face of the door. A prayer to the Plaguefather on his lips, Bule smashed the door again.

It buckled.

Brennus rushed down the uneven stairs of the temple. His spirit was fired by what he had witnessed. The temple worshippers had struck a true blow against the Rotbringers. He had believed they could be defeated after seeing the beings of light. Now he believed they could be defeated even by forces that were not divine. He did not dare hope that defeat would come at his hands and those of his fellows. But he would fight as if it could.

On the ground floor, there were no windows. There was only the door. In the vast hall, the worshippers in their thousands stood armed with old axes and blades. The people waited as another terrible blow battered the door. They were ragged, but they were an army, and they were ready to fight.

Brennus stopped on a landing at the top of the hall.

'No!' he cried as he saw some movement towards the entrance. 'We'll keep them out yet! Block the door!' In a direct confrontation, he knew the Rotbringers' strength would be overwhelming.

One of the men nearest the door turned around. 'But we'll be trapping ourselves.'

'If they get in, they will win quickly,' Brennus said. 'Keep them out, and we continue to hurt them. Do it now!'

The man began to object again, but at both sides of the door other congregants rushed to release a cluster of ropes. Freed, the ropes swept up toward the ground floor's ceiling, passing through a large iron hook. On the other end, massive blocks, the heaviest the people had been able to find and move, fell from their suspended position just above the doorway. They hit the floor with a booming *crack*. The door to the temple became meaningless. Now there were only walls.

'Take to the stairs!' Brennus called. 'Strike the enemy from above.' There were hundreds of arrow slits in the tower. The faithful would fight until the end.

Iron tore and crumbled before Bule. The door fell. Behind it was solid stone. Bule laughed, his good humour returning. He walked away from the blocked entrance. More scalding purity fell on him. The pain meant nothing. The bounteous rot of Nurgle surged into the wounds, infecting and swelling his flesh with new toxic gifts. He gathered his warband a few yards from the base of the temple wall, out of range of the water, but well within reach of the archers. He and his warriors laughed at the poorly aimed volleys. Arrows bounced off armour or sank into putrefying flesh, doing little more than release floods of larvae to the air.

'Why hide yourselves away?' he asked the mortals. 'Why refuse Grandfather Nurgle's generosity? His garden is a riot of delights. If you will not revel in the garden out here, we will send the garden to you.' He faced his warriors. 'They send us purity. We should answer in kind.'

The warband constructed a bonfire from the diseased branches of trees standing twisted and putrefying in the ruins. They filled copper vessels with the thickened water of the river. Within minutes, as the horns sounded again, a thick, damp smoke filled the air. It embraced the temple. The breath of Nurgle wafted into the tower's apertures.

When he heard the first sounds of distress emerge from the interior, Bule said, 'Thus the Garden grows.'

There was satisfaction in the lesson being taught, but even as he spoke, he knew it was not enough. His warriors would not content themselves with victory at one remove. It was a poor substitute for the direct mortification of the enemy's flesh. And there was more. The goal that called to him was not the simple extermination of this false hope. His destiny waited inside those walls. The flies about his head flew in a concentrated swarm at the temple again and again. The call, now so tantalizingly close to clarity, was just beyond his reach.

He must find a way to pass through those walls, or shatter them.

Brennus returned to the roof of the temple. The Rotbringers' smoke came for the priests and flagellants. He felt his chest hitch and his throat tighten in anticipation in the moment before the coiling tendrils enveloped the tower. He coughed. The stench was foul. It was rotten meat and writhing flesh. It was as dry as hollowed-out bones, yet it was as clammy as a damp fist. Heccam was among those at the ramparts and the first to breathe in the poison. The defenders dropped their bows and collapsed. Heccam clutched his head, weeping and choking.

'We can't,' he moaned.

'Stand up,' said Brennus. He breathed through his mouth. The air felt thick enough to chew. It was furry with legs. It sank into his body. It tried to sink into his soul. It weighed him down, whispering the death of hope.

He refused to listen. With weeping lesions on his arms, he hauled Heccam upright. 'Do not surrender,' he exhorted. 'Keep fighting!'

'For what?' Heccam muttered. Thick, yellow saliva dribbled from the corner of his mouth. Sores appeared on his face, clustering and bursting.

Brennus let go of him. He picked up his weapon instead. He turned to the wall and loosed an arrow into the spongy air. He was not alone. Others acted with him, and when one priest fell back, another stepped forward. They fought, though Brennus knew their arrows were futile against the warband, and though he heard the bubbling laughter of the Rotbringers. Each time he drew the bow string, Brennus struggled against the despair that sought to erode him from the inside out. And each time he released the bow string, he struck a blow against the despair. His eyes were watering. He felt the lesions spreading over his skin. But he would not surrender. Hope had returned to the world, and he held it fast.

The valley dimmed with the murk of floating plague and the coming of a darker night. Yet there was light. Brennus felt it in his soul. It was his strength. He saw it behind his eyes, and it guided his shots.

And then the light was real. It slashed through the gloom from above. Lightning slammed into the ground at the base of the temple. It struck the edges of the ramparts, and for a moment the temple had a dome of thunder. Priests threw themselves to the side. The light faded. Brennus' eyes cleared, and he saw the divine warriors.

The largest part of their number had appeared outside. The blast of their arrival forced the Rotbringers back. It banished the evil smoke. On the roof, Brennus gazed upon the leader of the gods. He was a towering figure in cloaked armour. He was flanked by archers. Above, winged warriors alighted for a moment on the edge of the broken roof before taking off once more.

Holy terror assailed Brennus. He joined his fellow priests in falling to his knees. These gods were forbidding in aspect, clad in obsidian, and the cold visages of their helmets were ominous. They were beings of metal forged from the night itself. Yet there was nobility here, reflected in flashes of gold amid the black. It rimmed the shoulders. It shone from the hammer icon of the shields. And it was there in the halo that framed the helms.

The leader spoke. 'I am Merennus. We come to bring justice to the darkness. You have fought well in the defence of the gate.'

'Gate?' Brennus said. But his voice emerged as a croaked whisper, and the warriors had already turned to the needs of the battle. They moved to the wall facing the Rotbringers. They towered over the ramparts. They raised magnificent bows whose strings were of searing blue light. They drew their weapons and awaited the command.

'Judicators,' Merennus said, 'pronounce your judgement.'

As one, the Anvils of the Heldenhammer visited destruction on the bearers of plague.

The light. The thunder. The sudden host of warriors, their armour black yet gleaming with ghastly purity, sterile, an affront to the carnival of decay and life.

No, Bule thought.

He knew what he saw. He knew what these beings called themselves. They were Stormcast Eternals, and they were a rumour. He had heard of the struggles against them. He had dismissed the reports as lies. The gods of Chaos were triumphant. Sigmar was beaten, hiding behind his walls, trembling before the spread of the garden. The Stormcasts were lies propagated by Nurgle's rivals and by warbands who refused to acknowledge the shame of their own defeats.

The Stormcast Eternals did not exist. This he had believed. This he had declared.

And now the myths attacked.

On the roof of the temple, armoured figures drew bows, but the arrows they loosed turned into lightning. The blasts incinerated tumour-bloated barbarians. Bule took a hit in the shoulder. It knocked him back. He snarled at the flames that shook his body. They burned brightly, attacking him with the purity that he strove to destroy with his every act, with his every breath.

'Decimators to the fore!' came a voice of doom from the tower. 'Tear out the heart of the enemy! Liberators, lock shields! You are the marching wall! Crush all before you! Prosecutors, strike from the east and west! Teach the enemy to fear the skies and the wrath of Sigmar!'

And from ahead and from above, war as he had never known fell on Bule and his legion of plagues.

The lightning arrows continued to rain down. In the midst of the fury, Bule exchanged a look with Fistula. The blight-lord's eyes blazed. He nodded to Bule. They were united. The Rotbringers had fled one defeat, and now, still weakened, they faced an enemy fresh to the battlefield. This new war began with the odds against them. This was not the prey Bule had brought his band to hunt. This was a formidable opponent.

So be it.

There would be no retreat. Bule had seen, beyond the valley, the desert that came when Nurgle's garden was uprooted. He would die to preserve the Grandfather's gifts. And he would smash through any barrier, be it stone or metal or flesh, that stood between him and the call of his destiny.

He raised his axe high. He defied the lightning. He roared his joy of service to Nurgle, and of the fight for the glory of the garden. The warband echoed his cry. Barbarian marauders and knights of Chaos, vassals and lords, mortals and things transformed into shambling infections, all of them charged with the Lord of Plagues.

The enemy lines clashed, Bule's mob of pestilence hurling itself against the perfect, shield-locked line of the warriors of light. Phalanxes of Stormcasts wielding huge thunderaxes cut into the mass of the Rotbringers. Bule hit the Stormcast before him with the full force of his bulk. The impact brought his enemy to a halt. The warrior swung his two-handed axe into Bule's exposed flank. The blade cut deep through fat and muscle. Polyps burst. Rot surged through Bule's flesh. It did not weaken him. It purged his body of the light. It gave him the strength of contagion. He laughed at the wound. He leaned into it, trapping the axe blade in the folds of his body. He brought his own axe down, shattering halo and helm. Beneath the metal face was a visage just as noble, but animated, snarling with its own fury. The Stormcast yanked his weapon free. Before he could strike again, Bule, still laughing, swung his axe sideways into his foe's jaw. He cut the knight's face in half. The warrior fell.

And then he and Grandfather Nurgle were robbed. He should have seen the body burst open with maggots and worms. It should have blackened with the proliferation of life, become a new mound for the garden. Instead, the corpse vanished, transformed into a blast of light. It shot from the ground. It cut through the clouds, and was gone.

These beings would not even die properly.

The falling night rang with the clash of blades and the shouts of combatants. Bule took down more Stormcasts, but their line remained unbroken. They tightened their ranks with each loss, and held the Rotbringers back from the temple's foundations.

The bowmen sent volleys of lightning into the rear ranks. Winged Stormcasts swooped out of the sky, their hammer bolts smashing into the flanks of the warband.

'Break them!' Bule shouted. 'Loose the maggoth!'

The ground shook as, from the rear, the beast thundered forward, a huge mass of festering muscle and horns. It stamped into the Stormcasts with legs thick as tree trunks. Its arms were longer than its legs and batted the foes aside with broad claws. Its multi-forked tongue lashed out from a circular maw, grasping warriors in an armour-crushing grip. It lumbered into the line of Liberators, and broke the formation.

A Stormcast with a skull-faced helm cried out to the skies, and they answered. Lightning stabbed down at his command in a night-shattering, blinding maelstrom. The maggoth vanished, burned out of existence, and across the wide swatch of scorched earth, the Stormcasts surged forward once more, trampling Bule's Rotbringers into the dead stone.

'There is no retreat!' Bule shouted. 'There is only victory for Grandfather Nurgle!' He wielded his axe with one hand. He spread his arms wide and grabbed two Stormcasts by the neck, yanking them from their shield formation. He used his massive bulk to immobilize them. He reached deep into the Plaguefather's blessings. His strength was more than physical. He was disease made flesh. To see him was to sicken. To approach him was to die. He roared, and his voice was the vortex of contagion. His reach was enormous. He embraced his warband. He embraced the enemy. He grasped the length and breadth of the temple. In the ecstasy of his decay, he turned the air into a roiling mass of death.

His roar became the lead voice of a choir. It was joined by the shouts of his fellow Rotbringers, the ratcheting, coughing, gurgling cry of plague at war. The warband fought with greater ferocity. Each warrior's own manifestations of disease blossomed, polluting the air even further. From inside the temple came the cries of the prey. The men and women who had been singing in praise now fell to coughing and spluttering. He could not reach their souls as his forces had with their earlier attack, but his grasp eroded their bodies. Skin turned slick. Lungs filled with fluid. Bones softened.

His assault hit the Stormcasts too. They shouted in defiance, but those near him weakened. They coughed. They staggered. The two he clutched sagged. When he released them, they clawed at their helms. Their movements were slowed, clumsy. One of them managed to pull his helm off. He gasped for air. His face was cratered. His tongue, swollen by layers of sores, filled his mouth. He could not breathe. Bule left him to suffocate. The prolonged death gave the Lord of Plagues the satisfaction of seeing a Stormcast rot before returning to the sky in that hateful light. He decapitated the other before wading in against the next, slamming his axe left and right, and at last he broke through the line.

The temple wall was only a few yards away, sealed and featureless. The route to his destiny was still blocked. The momentary triumph brought him no closer to his goal. A swarm of flies whined about him, calling and urging, but clarity eluded him.

In the moment of Bule's hesitation, the leader of the Stormcasts leapt from the upper floor of the temple. His leap took him over his own men, and he fell to earth like a meteor. He broke the spine of a barbarian as he landed, causing the swollen marauder to burst open in a spray of pus. The Stormcast Eternal wielded a rune-marked blade and a hammer. He tore his way through the Rotbringers, gutting, severing heads, and chopping warriors down with a single blow. Three knights of Chaos charged him at once. The ground shook with their heavy steps. Their swollen, suppurating muscles expanded through the gaps in their spiked, filth-encrusted armour. They came in with halberds, axes and blades gripped in both hands. They swung with strength that had felled trees and infected entire cities.

Their blows never landed.

The Stormcast made a sweeping gesture. His cloak billowed as if caught in a wind of its own creation. Lightning and shadows clashed within. In a storm of gold as bright as the Lord-Celestant's fury, a hail of spell hammers slammed into the knights. Amour exploded into fragments. The hammers pulverized limbs. They reduced torsos to jellied pulp. They punched through the skull of one knight and his body took two confused steps before the fact of its death sank in, and it collapsed.

Bule saw the tide of the battle turn again. The Stormcasts reformed their lines and moved to join their leader. They brought ruin to the Rotbringers between them. When the warriors met, their wedge would cut the warband in half.

The hammers of lighting came in volleys from above. The winged Stormcasts were besieging the Rotbringers, always beyond reach, beyond revenge.

Bule snarled. As the Stormcasts nearest him pulled back in order to create a more powerful formation, a fist to smash his forces, he started to pursue. But more of the enemy leapt from the upper floor of the temple to engage him. Three were on him. He welcomed them with rage. Let them gaze upon the three-eyed blankness of his helm. Let them see the mark of the fly, the mark of the Plaguefather.

And let them die.

He turned to drive his spiked pauldron up through a Stormcast's gorget. The spike was as long as Bule's forearm. The warrior choked, impaled through the throat, then up into the brain. Bule turned his gaze from the glare of the Stormcast's dying light. He used his anger at the purifying burn to power his axe swing into the next warrior. He cut an enemy's sword arm off at the shoulder. The third stabbed him in the gaping sore in his belly. The corruption of his organs hissed against the steel. This was no common blade. It burned him with a god's anger, but his own god's blessing reacted against the assault, keeping him alive on a foundation of plague. He slammed his axe into the Stormcast's chest plate, hurling the warrior back. The sword slid out of his body. He pressed his advantage, blinded by pain, furious with determination. This battle was more than a struggle between two hosts. It was a war between gods.

Bule was willing to die for the glory of the garden. No matter the numbers of the Stormcasts, he would fight them, ripping them asunder with his bare hands if need be. If this was his final battle for Nurgle, he would make it a brutal one.

But no, not here. The conviction was too strong. The buzzing call was deafening. His duty was not to make a final stand. He must answer.

The call was not just coming from inside the temple. It was coming from below.

Bule looked beyond the Stormcast with which he wrestled to the left of the temple wall, at the polluted river. It flowed behind the temple, but part of the structure's base extended into the water.

Flies clustered at that corner. The swarm took on a shape. There was the suggestion of robes. A hint of a hoe-shaped head with many eyes. A long, clawed hand pointed down, to where the river flowed beneath the tower.

Bule ran at the Stormcast. He wished the warrior could see

his smile behind his helm. It was the smile of revelation. He collided with the Stormcast. The thunder of their impact shattered the air. The ebon-armoured knight drew his arm back and stabbed Bule again. Bule moved forward on the blade. His axe shattered the Stormcast's mask. Corruption spread over the warrior's face. Bule struck again, cleaving the hated visage in two. The Stormcast fell. Bule pulled the sword from his own gut. Steam rose from the blade and he hurled it into the night.

The path was clear to the river. Most of the combat had moved to Bule's right as the Rotbringers sought to mob the Stormcasts' wedge.

'Hold them!' Bule shouted to his army. 'Destroy their illusions!' He pointed to a group of knights and marauders nearest to him. 'With me,' he cried. 'We go below!'

He ran for the river. It was blacker than the coming night. It was the sanctuary of life's final degradation, unspoiled by the repulsive purity of the Stormcasts. Insects and worms squirmed in their millions over its surface. Its depths promised worse. They welcomed Bule as he plunged into them, closing over his head in a foetid embrace.

The water was thick with chunks of rotting matter. Its textures washed over him as he sank. It flooded his wounds with new parasites and infections. As he fell into the dark, he discovered it was not absolute. The glow of decomposition lit his way. In the wavering strands of green, he could just make out the black mass of the temple's foundations.

He touched bottom, Fistula and the others following a few moments later. Already his lungs were straining. He took slow, heavy steps toward the wall. His boots disturbed the muck of decay. Bones, rags and heavy putrescence floated upward, wreathing him in a nimbus of greater filth. The sounds of battle filtered down through the water in muffled echoes.

Bule neared the wall, and it was all he could do to hold his breath, to not shout in exultation. There was an archway before him. He tried to run. Destiny was open to him. The call was so intense, he thought he could hear the buzzing of the flies underwater.

And even now, he did not know what called. He did not know what answer he must give.

He entered the archway. Now the darkness was complete. He was blind, yet his steps were sure. There was only one direction now. There were no barriers.

His lungs cried out for air. His head filled with the sounds of his body: the strange beats of his pulse, the bubbling in his blood, the wet rustling of flesh disintegrating and reforming in distorted configurations. The slowness of his movements turned the expectation of triumph into agony.

Then he found steps. He mounted them, rising into a sickly green aura again. At last he broke the surface. He drew the air into his lungs. It was close, stale and thick with spores. Bule found himself on the edge of a wide dais in the middle of a domed chamber. The curved walls and the dais dripped with fungi and lichen, which were the source of the glow. They were green-black, bulbous with disease and formed a carpet thick enough to distort the lines of the masonry. At the centre of the dais stood a high archway.

A gate. Bule approached it. He stared at it while Fistula and the others gathered on the dais. Flies circled it endlessly. The call had brought him here. This was his goal. But the gate was inert. There was no passage here. The buzz of whispers was the most insistent it had ever been, but even now they were not clear. He had no answer. Revelation was withheld.

'Why have you brought us here?' Fistula snarled. 'There is no way up. All we have done is ensure our defeat.'

'Destiny has brought us here,' Bule said. 'This was commanded.'

'By whom?'

Bule didn't answer. He didn't know. Again, he felt that paradox: the command was not Nurgle's, but if he served the master who called, he would not be betraying the Plaguefather. He might even be pleasing Nurgle.

There was no way through the confusion except forward.

Fistula was correct, though. There were no other exits from the chamber. There was no way of moving upward into the temple and turning the tide of the battle from the interior.

Yet this was where Bule was supposed to be. He examined the growths on the archway. They looked different from the rest. They were a pure, glistening black. No glow came from them. He reached out and his hand sank deep into their moist, fleshy texture. They were not fungi. They were naked tumours. They were the material of disease itself. The pure, unfiltered gifts of Nurgle.

They were inspiration.

New strands of pestilence ate into his flesh. They turned his blood to slime. He became their master. He was a Lord of Plagues, and he commanded his vassals to multiply.

To spread.

To march.

The garden of Nurgle exploded into voracious life. The black growths of the archway infected those on the dais, remaking them. Darkness poured from the gate. It spread over the waters. It rose up the walls. The green glow fell into the devouring corruption.

So did stone.

This concentration of disease was so virulent that its hunger surpassed flesh. Whatever could be eroded fell into its jaws. Bule willed it into the mortar. He sent it gnawing into the fissures in the stone, widening them, destroying structural integrity. His soul was a thing of uncounted hungers, and he would eat the temple.

Sigmar, Brennus thought. That was the name the divine warriors called out as they fought. They were not gods, as much as they appeared to be. They served Sigmar, and how resplendent must be his glory if these beings were his servants.

'*Sigmar!*' the warriors shouted as they cut into the Rotbringers with light and sword.

'Sigmar!' Brennus called too, and his fellows joined him. Many could not shout. They were too weak. Brennus could barely stand, but he leaned at the edge of the ramparts and he used his bow. Heccam was further gone, but with the coming of the Anvils of the Heldenhammer, he had recovered his will to fight. He slumped against the wall. He could barely draw his bow. But he fought. And he whispered, 'Sigmar.'

Disease wracked Brennus' body, but he had hope. He believed in the defeat of the plague. When a portion of the Rotbringers had broken off and disappeared into the river, the struggle shifted decisively in favour of the Anvils. The evil would be vanquished. The land would be purged of the foulness. So would his body.

'Sigmar!' he called, and drew his bow.

The roof cracked. The tower trembled.

Brennus stumbled, his arrow flying wild. He clutched at the crenellation to keep from being pitched out to the ground below. Darkness seeped up. Tendrils of multiplying growths spread over the roof like talons. Dust burst from the walls. The sounds of breaking stone became deafening. The tower shook harder. It groaned. The temple was diseased, and it was dying.

The blackness shrouded Brennus in a cloud of jagged flakes. His throat and eyes were on fire. Breathing felt like drowning.

The Anvils of the Heldenhammer remained in their positions. They unleashed their lightning on the Rotbringers. But their bolts dimmed. The darkness spread up their legs, the black of corruption seeking to cover the gleaming black of retribution.

Tendrils became talons. Talons became tentacles. They uncoiled from the tower and reached into the land. Perfect putrescence covered the battlefield. The Rotbringers rejoiced. They fell upon the Anvils with renewed fervour, propelled by the wave of unleashed plague.

'Sigmar,' Brennus croaked. He had found his light in the darkness. He would not release it. He would have this victory until the end.

The temple shuddered. It swayed. The blackness closed its fist completely around the tower. All that remained was for the grasp to close, and crush everything.

'Sigmar.' A desperate whisper against the night.

But then a great shout...

'SIGMAR!' The Anvils of the Heldenhammer roared at the night, and though Brennus could see nothing, he could hear a still more ferocious clash of arms.

And he knew that where the Anvils fought, the monsters could be defeated.

He was fuelled by a power far beyond his own. Bule felt the tower and the land contained in his hands. They were his to turn into the most perfect flowering. He had tended Nurgle's Garden faithfully, and now he would make it bloom through the heart and bones of the enemy. The strength of a thousand plagues was his. He *was* the plague.

The dark was complete. The light was gone from the temple. His power reached its apex. And in that moment of completion, something else was accomplished.

The gate sprang to life.

The centre flashed. It twisted and coiled. Paths opened before him. He saw them with the myriad eyes of insects, a compound vision of choices. One choice dominated all others. It came into being with the activation of the gate. The power he held had opened the way, and now he must pass through or bring the temple down.

Behind him, the other Rotbringers were shouting victory as the walls shuddered.

'Drop the walls!' Fistula shouted. 'Crush the lightning men!'

But Bule heard the call again, and it came from the other side of the gate. Archaon awaited.

'What are you waiting for?' Fistula demanded.

'Archaon...' Bule whispered. Louder, he said, 'We pass through the gate.'

'And leave the field again?' Fistula was outraged.

Yes, Bule thought. They would leave. 'Yes!' he shouted. 'Archaon calls!'

He stared at the path through the gate. It flickered. It led into a grey void. A cold wind blew in Bule's face. It felt like emptiness, like the wail of the tomb. There was no garden at the end of this path. There would be nothing to cultivate. The call demanded he step away from any recognisable trace of Grandfather Nurgle's dominion.

He made his decision. I will go, he thought.

The passage exploded with swarms of hungry flies. A welcome.

Bule looked back at Fistula and the rest of his warriors. His chosen few, he saw now, much as he had been chosen. 'We do not abandon the field,' he said. 'We march to a grander one. A magnificent flowering.'

He entered the gate, abandoning the temple to its illusion of hope. Let the Stormcast Eternals triumph here. How meaning-less that victory would be. How bitter it would taste for them when he returned.

When they and all their kind would learn what he had become.

THE TRIAL OF THE CHOSEN

Guy Haley

Under purple skies flickering with far-away storms brooded a vast desert the horizon could not contain.

Its sands appeared coarse, greyish in colour, but closer inspection revealed them not to be sand at all, but crushed bone. In some of the smaller pieces the delicate lattice of desiccated marrow was visible, clinging to sharp-edged shards. The larger fragments were recognisable as the knobbed heads of femurs or curved portions of skull, like pebbles and stones. Few people ever saw the desert and fewer still lived to tell the tale. The realm of Shyish abounds with lands that do not take kindly to the presence of the living. The Bone Sands were among them.

Unlike in a mortal desert, there were no traces of any living creature; no mummified plants awaiting the next rain, no tracks in the rough sand to hint at small creatures eking out a life. There was bone, and more bone, and nothing else, for league after league until the purple sky and grey sand touched at the edge of sight.

But the Bone Sands were not quite empty.

At the very centre was a monumental archway. Though huge, it cast no shadow in the directionless gloom. Two giant plinths stood either side, as tall as towers, their sides covered in bas reliefs depicting the bloodless wars of the dead, still crisp after aeons in the changeless desert. Atop the plinths waited a pair of giant necrosphinxes, facing each other across the broken bones cluttering the ground. The statues were massive beasts of stone and metal with men's torsos atop lions' bodies, barbed scorpions' tails, outstretched wings and twin blade shields on their arms. The statues held their bladed limbs forward to point at one another, forming a lesser arch under which a traveller had to pass on entering or exiting the greater.

The sphinxes were huge, but the gate was bigger. Stacked vertebrae threaded onto green copper rods made the posts of the archway, curving together like monstrous tusks. The bones at the base of the columns were the size of buildings. Those at the apex were tiny, stolen from dead animals of the fields and hedgerows of distant lands. Many of the bones had crumbled. The left column leaned a little because of this erosion, but the structure held and the distortion robbed the edifice of none of its power.

The desert around the gate had a vital tension entirely lacking from the rest. The feeling of magic was strong there, and perhaps it was for this reason that the arch was surrounded by generous heaps of skeletons. All lay face down, their outstretched arms reaching for the arch. They were piled around the base of the plinths, and cluttered the span of the gateway three deep. Examples of all the strange races of the Eight Realms could be found, for all things that die find their way to the underworlds of Shyish in the end.

Pitted weapons were tangled with bones. Brittle cloth was

draped over fleshless limbs, ready to vanish into threads and dust at the slightest touch of the desert's rare winds. Banners were planted in the ground, leaning drunkenly, all colour leached from their blazons. Shields of every conceivable kind hid their designs under the bones of their bearers.

A thing walked out of thin air, growing from ethereality to solidity in the space of five long steps. It was a curious creature, with arms and legs so thin it should not have had the strength to move, but it walked with energetic purpose, its staff clacking down onto the bones with every decisive step. Its long cloak of fluttering eyes stirred the dust into lazy whorls that settled slowly.

This was the Many-Eyed Servant, agent of Tzeentch, but now unwilling vassal of Archaon.

It came to a halt fifty yards before the arch. The aura surrounding everything there – bones, gate and guardians – revealed itself to the sorcerer's supernatural vision as a deep purple. Very rarely was one colour of magic so clearly presented, and the sorcerer stopped to admire its patterns. The creature remained in contemplation until the weight of its enslavement became palpable, invisible chains of sorcery binding it to the Everchosen's will. The Many-Eyed Servant became uncomfortable. Archaon saw all, and he was impatient. If the Many-Eyed Servant was not swift, it would be punished.

The Many-Eyed Servant set to work. With keen magesight it pinpointed the parts of the gate that had to be charged with magic. This realmgate had long been dormant, locked and barred by parties unknown through the long centuries of the Age of Chaos.

The Many-Eyed Servant gripped its staff with reedy fingers and raised it over its hoe-shaped head. The line of eyes that crested its face closed in concentration. It began to chant.

It was a powerful sorcerer, and so its magic took effect rapidly. Power blazed from the ends of its staff in braided torrents that unfurled into individual tendrils of lightning, each striking at the gate columns' vertebrae. They skittered about, probing for the points the Many-Eyed Servant's magic required. Finding them, the lightning rooted itself in the bone, joining gate to sorcerer. The space between was quickly filled with jumping, arcing currents of yellow, blue and purple. The gateway vertebrae shifted on their copper supports, flexing like trees in a storm. Hidden runes carved into the bone revealed themselves in blazing colours.

The gate glimmered, the air framed by the arch growing thick with light, blurring the vista behind it, then turning opaque.

The Many-Eyed Servant cried out in pain from the magic coursing through it and in exhilaration of its mastery over the energy. Slamming its staff down, it uttered a deafening word of power. The lightning ceased. A blast of energy emanated from the base of the staff, sending a shock wave out across the plain that whipped up an expanding circle of dust and sent it racing towards every horizon. The Bone Sands moaned, a sound akin to the last breath expelled from the lungs of a corpse.

The staff remained embedded in the bony ground, quivering with potency. The Many-Eyed Servant lifted its hands, placed them back to back, and pushed them wide as if it were parting a curtain.

With a silken tearing sound, the realmgate opened onto another world. Some difference in the atmospheres caused an imbalance in the wind, and a gust of tomb-dry air blasted out from the desert, exchanged for the brief, moist scents of leaf mould and animals. The Many-Eyed Servant looked through onto a broad rise of forested mountains somewhere in the realm of Ghur. Men knelt on the other side, two hundred huge

killers warped by the power of Khorne, a pair of chained khorgoraths in their midst. The Bloodslaves had been praying to
their god to open the way, but as the gate opened they stood.
They hefted their weapons and looked suspiciously through
into the world beyond. The slaughterpriest Orto, the blood
warrior Skull, Danavan Vuul the bloodstoker and the taciturn
skullgrinder Kordos, smith of Khorne, who rarely deigned to
speak to mortal men, all looked on. These were the leaders of
the Bloodslaves, and they gathered around their lord, Ushkar
Mir, another silent killer, although unlike Kordos his silence
was not by choice. Mir was taller than a man ever should be,
massively muscled, his burn-scarred head bound with a tight
ring of brass that covered his eyes. The runes stamped into the
band were dark for the moment.

'The way is open! Khorne gives to those who take! Onwards
to battle,' shouted their priest. The Many-Eyed Servant winced
at his bellowing. So obnoxious, the priests of Khorne. It pained
the sorcerer to make use of such crude pawns.

Ignorant of the sorcerer that had opened the way, Orto lifted his
double-handed axe in one fist and pointed it into the bone desert.

The Bloodslaves moved forward with a rattling of armour.
They stank of blood and sweat, their beards were stiff with
gore, and their filed teeth were yellow. Eyes wild with rage
and desperation looked right at the Many-Eyed Servant, but
they did not see it. The Many-Eyed Servant was visible only
to those it allowed to see.

Mir rumbled a soundless warning and held his hand up.
His men stopped.

'See, my lord!' said Skull eagerly. His blood-and-blue marbled face was full of triumph. One day this warrior might be
a danger, thought the Many-Eyed Servant, but that was a concern for another time. 'Why do we wait? Khorne has provided!'

Ushkar Mir stared into the Realm of Death. In his head the call of Archaon rang loud. The Many-Eyed Servant could hear it too. For each of the champions it was different; for Mir it was the brazen blare of harsh trumpets and the cries of angry daemons.

The Bloodslaves looked to Ushkar Mir expectantly. For five minutes he stood, before moving without warning straight towards the gate. The Bloodslaves followed unhesitatingly.

They stepped from lush turf to dusty plain in a single step, leaving one realm for another, their boots crunching on shattered bones as they passed into Shyish.

'Is this the land of Khorne?' asked one. He kicked a skull from the shoulders of a skeleton. 'There are many skulls here.'

The khorgoraths sniffed at the bones, but quickly withdrew and mewled. Crumbling bone had no interest for them, and they were hungry.

To the Many-Eyed Servant, the Bloodslaves' disappointment was obvious. They were wary. This was not the warrior's welcome they expected Archaon to lavish on them.

'No,' growled Orto. 'Fool! This is Shyish, the Realm of Death. These are bones stolen by the Lord of Death from the Lord of Fury. This is an unholy place.'

'But where in Shyish?' asked Skull thoughtfully.

'Who knows?' said Orto. His nostrils flared, sniffing at the wind. 'Shyish is a million underworlds, with ten deaths for every mortal in each.' He snorted and spat bloody phlegm onto the bones. 'Khorne will rule it all. It is his right. This is the start.'

Such confidence, such naivety, thought the Many-Eyed Servant.

It was then that the sorcerer chose to be seen, although not in its favoured form. It drew the shape of another over its being and manifested. The champion's test had begun.

* * *

A stirring of dust fifty feet from the gate caught Skull's eye. He patted Mir's massive bicep and pointed as the disturbance grew to a tiny whirlwind. Mir looked with his Khorne-given blindsight and saw fragments of bone leaping up from the ground. To Mir's eyeless vision, the maelstrom was surrounded by flickering fires of magic. He growled and drew the axes Bloodspite and Skullthief. They howled, eager to prove themselves against weakling sorcery.

The whirl of dust grew until a column writhed before Mir. Then it abruptly stilled, what little fragments were carried on its currents pattering to the floor. In its stead stood the skeleton of a man, garbed in the ancient panoply of war, a spiked helmet on its skull, a visor covering its face and ragged robes about its legs. A dull steel sword hung at its side.

Skull took a step. Orto moved forward, axe up. Mir stayed them with the flats of his axes.

The skeletal warrior lifted up its hands to its head and removed the helm, revealing a bony face set with five eye sockets. In each one a lidless eye glistened.

'What is this?' asked Skull. He loosened his sword in his scabbard. The Bloodslaves drew around their leader, fear tainting their divine fury.

'Ushkar Mir hears the call of the Grand Marshal of Ruin!' pronounced Orto. 'He comes to serve him!'

The skeleton remained silent.

'Who are you?' said Skull. 'Answer, or I will add your malformed head to Khorne's bone piles.'

'It is a test,' growled Kordos, speaking for the first time in weeks. 'One does not walk into the camp of Archaon. Mir must prove himself worthy.'

'Where is he? What do you know of Archaon?' demanded Skull. But Kordos said no more.

'Ushkar Mir is worthy,' said Orto. He clacked his sharpened teeth at the skeleton in challenge.

'None are worthy until they have proven themselves,' said Danavan Vuul. 'A simple truth.'

'Pah! Let us cut this corpse thing down,' said Orto. 'Let us gather fresh skulls for Khorne. Who cares for the glory of Archaon, when Khorne's hunger is never sated?'

'Khorne's fires are not what Mir desires,' said Skull.

Orto looked at Mir uncertainly. He was still not comfortable with Mir's blasphemous desire to challenge Khorne, and yet his might was indisputable, as was Khorne's favour of him.

'Kordos spoke of tests. Who will set them?' asked Skull. 'This creature?'

'Khorne sets all tests for Mir,' said Orto.

'Archaon serves all the four powers,' said Vuul. 'We must be wary.'

'A test of the gods then,' said Skull. 'Four in number.'

'We should attack! Kill it again.' Orto advanced. Mir motioned again for him to hold. Orto did so reluctantly.

That will be the way, thought Mir. The creature sports many eyes, as did the herald I saw in the sky. He struggled to keep his thoughts straight against the rage of Khorne. The red haze in him thickened daily. He must not forget who he was. Four tests it would be – one for each of the gods. To serve Archaon will aid me, he thought. I will brave these tests. No matter the outcome, there will be bloodletting, and that will take me closer toward my vengeance.

Mir nodded to the skeleton. It inclined its head in response.

'Mir has accepted the challenge,' said Orto. 'Praise be to Khorne.'

'Stand ready!' said Skull. He drew his sword and the warriors of the Bloodslaves raised their weapons in response.

Ushkar Mir saw. In his blindsight he saw a dread purple glow creeping across the desert ground, gathering about the skeletons lying there. It was strongest around the great statues guarding the gate.

The first test begins, he thought.

A creak of metal, so loud in that endless silence, made the Bloodslaves start.

The purple light of death magic was strong enough now to be seen by mortal eyes, glowing from every skull. Suddenly the Bloodslaves began slashing downward, smashing bony hands that were stretching out to grasp their ankles and stamping ancient skulls to fragments.

A great host of the dead was clambering up all around them. A bloodreaver went down, bellowing out glory to Khorne as he was torn to pieces by raking fingers.

The worst was yet to come. Mir pointed and growled a warning. The eyes of the necrosphinxes glared with amethyst magic. With the grinding of stone muscles, they turned their heads to look upon the trespassers. At their awakening, the skeletal warriors presented arms, adopting attack positions. The dust of ages poured off the statues as they stepped down from their plinths, revealing skin of black stone and the dull bronze of their mighty weapons. The ring of dead warriors surrounding the Bloodslaves parted noisily to let the sphinxes through, closing ranks once the beasts had trodden heavily past. The Bloodslaves waited uncertainly, brandishing their axes and cursing the silent dead.

Mir did not wait for the attack. Roaring loudly, he shoved his way through his own men and ploughed into the skeleton horde.

'Skulls! Skulls for Khorne!' yelled Orto, and the Bloodslaves followed their master.

Sightless eyes tracked axe swings. Skeletons dodged and parried with all the alacrity of the living. This was the Realm of Death, and its servants were strong there. The Bloodslaves roared out their cries to Khorne, but the skeletons fought soundlessly, having no voices with which to speak. They moved mechanically fast, their ancient weapons ringing from dark iron, bones clacking a rapid tattoo.

The Bloodslaves split, each of them heading into a different part of the undead army – all save Skull, who was ever by Mir's side. Orto went at the head of a phalanx of blood warriors, sweeping his giant axe through brittle ribcages. Kordos strode on alone, his flaming anvil roaring through the air on its chains as he swung it around his head. Every pass decimated the skeletons, shattering them into burning flinders of bone.

Mir made straight for the sphinxes and attacked one head on while the other ploughed into the body of his warband. Though huge and fashioned from stone, they too moved quickly, slicing their arm-blades through the air at such speed that they blurred. The wind of their passing stirred Mir's fire-scorched hair. He leaned backward, barely evading the cutting edge. Mir swung Skullthief at the living statue's leg, seeking to cripple it, but the great blade attached to its left fist swept the blow aside and its scorpion tail stabbed down, the gems on it glowing with evil magic.

Mir dodged the sting, and the tail smashed into the carpet of bones on the ground. He swung Bloodspite around with all his considerable might. The daemon axe crashed through the enchanted stone of the tail. The tip came away, and the tail whipped back. The face of the sphinx was an expressionless mask, but it reared up in response to the wound. Its broad lion's feet pawed at the air before stamping down in an attempt to crush the life from the Chaos warlord. He spun aside, axes whipping round. Bloodspite shrilled in excitement as it bit a chunk of onyx from the left foreleg. Cracks spread from the impact. Mir followed with a hit from Skullthief, and the cracks widened. Splinters of stone sprayed outward and the leg came free, falling to the ground and smashing more of the bones there. The sphinx staggered back, its remaining forepaw thumping down heavily. It limped around on three legs, the veins of minerals in its shattered limb bleeding magic.

Mir attacked again. Deflecting the axe unbalanced the sphinx, and Mir leapt high over the construct's sweeping blades, twisting his back and body to clear them by inches. He landed on the other side. The crippled necrosphinx staggered around, but Ushkar Mir was already clambering up the decorative bronze-work studding its hide. The creature's human torso twisted around, but it could not bring its arms, bound as they were into its blades, to bear on Mir.

Howling madly, Mir drew both axes back to his right and swung them together at the creature's neck. Their supernatural blades cut through the bronze like paper, and clove deep into the stone.

The necrosphinx went rigid and its head toppled from its shoulders. Mir leapt from its back as it fell over onto its side, now only a defaced statue, metal bending and stone limbs cracking free as it crashed down.

The second necrosphinx was in the thick of Mir's warriors. They attacked from all sides, their weapons marking its smoothly polished hide with chalky scratches, but they could not bring it down. Seeing an opening, Vuul whipped the khorgoraths into the attack. Both took long, deep wounds from the animated statue's blades, but they did not fall. Driven to greater heights of fury by the bloodstoker's expert goading, they grappled with the sphinx, holding its arms in place while the rest of the warband laid about it with their weapons. Orto hacked at its back leg, taking chips from the stone with his two-handed axe.

One of the khorgoraths roared, wrenching off the blades from the construct's stone arm with a squeal of rending metal. The sphinx lashed out with its fist, slashing the khorgorath's hide with the twisted remnants of its weapon. The khorgorath bit down hard, shattering its own teeth on the arm, but crushing stone nevertheless, and the arm came away.

Mir moved in for the kill, pounding through the swirling melee. He smashed into the side of the necrosphinx, battering at its side with his daemon axes. He howled as his rage was stoked higher by Khorne and the runes in his punishment band burned. Stone chips flew and cracks ran all over the statue's sides. His followers joined him, jabbing weapons into the crevices Bloodspite and Skullthief had opened up and levering them wider.

Vuul goaded the khorgoraths, manoeuvring one into position on the far side of the statue to Mir while the other hung off the sphinx's remaining arm. The poisonous tail of the necrosphinx stabbed down, the bronze barb plunging deep into the khorgorath's back. The crystal bulb on the tail pulsed, and the poison drained away, pumping into the twisted Khornate beast. Bellowing, the khorgorath raised its fists and pummelled at the statue's back, ripping open its own skin on spined armour as it tore it from its mounts, exposing the fixing pins beneath. Three times the khorgorath's fists pounded down, each blow weaker than the last. Mir and the Bloodslaves hacked away at the living stone on the other side. Then the khorgorath's fists descended a final time, and the statue shattered into two pieces joined only by twisted trails of wire.

Its unnatural life left it instantly.

Around the gate the battle was nearly done. The last few

skeletons fell under heavy axe blades. Silence returned to the Bone Sands.

The five-eyed skeleton alone remained. Its glistening eyeballs rolled in their sockets in different directions as it took in the aftermath of battle.

Skull leaned panting on his sword hilt not far from Mir. 'The first test. Fury for Khorne. What is the nature of the second?'

The skeleton raised one hand and pointed. Whether north, east, west or south had any meaning in this realm was unknown to the Bloodslaves, but the purple glow of the sky was brighter in that direction.

The skeleton herald collapsed into the bone carpeting the floor.

Skull turned over its head with a foot, revealing five eye sockets full of dripping ooze. 'I don't trust this,' he said.

Mir grunted. A soft wind whispered over newly shattered bone. Behind him, the poisoned khorgorath was choking out its last painful breaths. The other plodded around the field, stuffing dry skulls into its maw and lowing mournfully, perhaps for the lack of meat to savour, perhaps in sadness for its companion.

'Ushkar Mir brings us victory!' shouted Orto. His loud voice was immediately swallowed by the dry vastness of the desert, and the slaughterpriest looked dismayed for a moment.

'A hard victory,' said Vuul. He looked at the dying beast. With a last rattling moan, it expired.

Many Bloodslaves had died on the march to the gate. Two dozen at least had fallen to ancient blades here. There had been two thousand Bloodslaves only months ago. Less than a tenth remained.

'Mir leads us. What does Mir command?' asked Skull.

Ushkar Mir grunted and pointed with his chin to the lighter patch of sky.

'Onward, then,' said Skull. He plucked his sword from the dry earth, and sheathed it. 'More skulls await, though precious little blood in this dusty place.'

If a sun shone over the Bone Sands, it was forever hidden by louring clouds. There was a day and a night of sorts, but the cycle played inconstantly. A day might last ten hours, or one. The land never grew any brighter than when they had first arrived, and the nights were utterly black, starless and frigid. The Bloodslaves' lips blued and they shivered in the chill. They had nothing to burn and nothing to hunt. Each man carried only scanty provisions. There was no change to the relentless landscape. Horizons receded before their march to reveal yet more endless flat land, its featurelessness broken only by isolated skulls or ribcages that had escaped the attentions of time.

All save Kordos felt the punishments of thirst and hunger. The skullgrinder was sustained by the unholy fires of his chained altar.

By the end of the third day, their meat and drink had been exhausted.

The Bloodslaves' confident march became halting. They dragged their weapons through the dust, leaving wavering trails behind them.

On the fifth night, the Bloodslaves fell on the weakest among them.

Darkness came suddenly. They huddled together as close as they dared as the temperature plummeted. Some instinct took a sole bloodreaver away from the rest. One too many hungry glances in his direction, maybe. He sat crosslegged, his hands on his weapons, but he could not defeat sleep. He had had no rest for days. No power can keep man from rest forever, unless he is highly favoured by the Four.

Three men attacked as soon as the drowsy bloodreaver's head nodded onto his chest. He was up quickly at the sound of their approach. He desperately dispatched one of his attackers, but if he had hoped that this provision of unlooked for meat would save his life, he had been mistaken. He had been marked for death, and in that realm death did not relent.

Skull, Vuul, Mir, Orto and Kordos watched as the bloodreaver was killed. The warrior's axe halted a blow aimed overhand for the crown of his head, but he had nothing to stop the knife that one of his erstwhile comrades plunged up under his ribs, piercing his heart. He fell dead instantly – a mercy. The Blood-slaves were not above eating their victims alive.

'Fresh meat!' rumbled Orto. The brassiness of his god-voice was diminished by thirst, and the desert was quicker to steal it the further they went into it.

'Aye,' said Skull. 'We eat, but there are fewer of us.'

'The weak perish,' hissed Vuul. His lips dripped at thought of the feast. He wiped them on the back of his arm.

'That they do,' said Skull. 'But there can only be one who is strongest. Do we devour each other until he remains, then starves himself?' He half drew his sword, then slammed it back into its scabbard.

The rest of the band gathered around the corpses of the bloodreaver and his felled killer. They waited, glassy-eyed with hunger, as the bodies were stripped. Two skullreapers hoisted the slain bloodreaver up by his ankles. A third crouched and slit the throat. Life fluid drained from the cut neck, splatter-ing on the dust.

'Meat for us, blood for Khorne,' said Orto, his voice grow-ing stronger at the sight of the blood.

'Meat! Khorne provides!' responded the others.

They cut their dead comrade's head free.

'Skulls for Khorne!' shouted Orto.

'Skulls! Skulls! Skulls!' howled the others.

'*No,*' a voice boomed across the desert. The Bloodslaves looked around fearfully.

'Look!' cried one. He pointed at the ground, and they all stepped back. Where the blood wetted the bone dust it bubbled and hissed.

They readied their weapons. A figure rose from the ground, slathered in blood at first, but the fluid froze and cracked away to reveal a greenly glowing phantom within. Its ghostly eyes were blank orbs and its face bore no expression, but its mouth jerked to a will not its own.

'This land belongs to Lord Nagash. All who perish are his,' spoke the phantom.

Spectres arose from the ground all around the Bloodslaves and flew over to spiral around the first, making a terrible shrieking that had the Bloodslaves clapping their hands over their ears.

'No!' shouted Orto. 'These skulls are Khorne's! Begone!'

Three skullreapers lunged for the spirit. Their twin blades slashed the air, cutting nothing. The spirits moved around them like weeds disturbed in water, swirling about but never snagging. Their eyes grew brighter and they shrieked, diving down on the Bloodslaves. Their touch was death. Ethereal claws slid into chests and men's eyes bulged as their hearts stopped. The Bloodslaves were brave and fired by the righteous wrath of Khorne, but against a foe that no weapon could touch they began to waver. The remaining khorgorath moaned, batting at the untouchable spirits as their hands caressed its warped flesh, leaving blackened trails of necrotic tissue in their wake. One swooped low, scooping up the half-flayed head of the slain bloodreaver, and started to retreat.

Mir had no fear of the spirit host. His men drew strength from his example, forming up as best they could around him as he strode into the thick of the spirits. Skullthief and Bloodspite hissed through the air. The daemons within whined at the touch of the dead, for they were of fire and hate and the coldness of the grave was unpleasant to them, but Mir forced them to strike. Wherever the axes fell, the spirits dissipated into shreds of vapour that were sucked screaming into the blades. They tried to flee, what little was left of their mortal souls terrified of the deathbringer's axes, but they all fell to Mir and were consumed. He pursued the last, that which had stolen the skull of the bloodreaver, and hewed it from the air. Orto plucked the head from the dust and brandished it triumphantly.

Only the first phantom remained. It turned doleful white eyes on the deathbringer. Once again, its mouth seemed puppeted by some distant, malign entity.

'You shall suffer for this insult. These are the lands of death!'

With a mighty cry it departed, shooting skyward as a pillar of green light. Where it hit the clouds above there was a flaring, and a single peal of thunder boomed across the sky. It echoed across the desert for an age.

'Khorne's meat! Khorne's blood!' shouted Orto.

There were many corpses now, thanks to the spirits' attack.

'We feast! To victory! To Mir!' bellowed Orto.

'Ushkar Mir! Khorne! Blood and flesh!' The Bloodslaves cheered and drew their knives, advancing hungrily on their dead.

From nowhere, a sudden wind blew, dry but laden with the scent of slow putrefaction, whipping hair into eyes and choking the men with whirling dust. The Bloodslaves' looks of anticipation turned to horror and woe, for the corpses withered in front of their eyes. Skin turned grey and flesh wizened. Lips drew back in hideous black grins. The bodies of the fallen dried to husks in an instant. Their skeletons collapsed to the ground where they fell into brittle pieces, as ancient in appearance as the bones they joined. Most were reduced to a powder that was carried away by the fell wind.

A few corpses held together, scraps of dried flesh adhering to their bones. Two bloodreavers, one desperate in his hunger, the other disdainful of the magic of the dead, tore off strips of this matter. It was tough, leathery as jerky. They worked their mouths on it hard, the hungry man fearful, the other laughing in his boldness.

They died choking on the flesh of their fallen brethren. Black lines ran over their skin, a map of corruption depicted by tainted veins. They fell, fingers scrabbling at the ground.

The Bloodslaves watched nervously. The wind did not return, and the bodies remained whole, but they did not eat these last casualties. Nor did they attempt to slaughter one of their own again. The servants of Khorne had learned wary respect for Nagash's domain.

'Onward,' croaked Skull.

The Bloodslaves' ranks thinned further as they succumbed to thirst. At first those falling listlessly were the weaker bloodreavers, but it was not long before the blood warriors started to drop, then even the mighty skullreapers, whose Khorne-given might availed them not against the harshness of the desert. Still the Bloodslaves followed Mir, who was fixed single-mindedly on the call of Archaon. Always it sounded in his ears, sometimes so faint he had to strain to hear it, at other times blaring so loudly in the night that all his followers heard it. Orto exhorted them to go on, while Skull whispered terror into their ears. Kordos said nothing.

One pale morning, the last khorgorath left them. As the Bloodslaves twitched awake from dreams of corpse banquets, the beast consumed the skulls of four warriors dead of thirst in the night. Ordinarily the creature would have continued its snuffling after fresh skulls to devour, whimpering at the endless pain that dogged it. Not this time.

The last skull eaten, the khorgorath stood erect, head held high and eyes wide. It came out of some stupor, for it gazed around the warband as if seeing it for the first time. It took up the chains that hobbled it in paws that had mutated into snapping mouths. Weighing them for a moment, it tugged hard, then wrenched, until it had split them asunder.

'The beast!' hissed Skull, kicking the bloodstoker, Vuul. 'It is loose! Use your whip! Do something!'

Vuul looked up, startled.

'Catch it!' roared Orto. 'Stop it from escaping!'

Several warriors advanced on it, grabbing at its manacles, but the khorgorath was indifferent to their efforts. It walked away, dragging the men that would not let go behind it and swatting at those who attempted to bar its progress.

Ushkar Mir reached for his axes, but the pudgy, calloused hands of Danavan Vuul stopped him.

'No my lord, it cannot be stopped,' he said. 'Orto! Skull! Do not stand in its way.'

The others faltered, looking to Mir. Mir nodded that they should obey. The men got out of the beast's path.

'It has eaten its fill of skulls,' explained Vuul. 'Now it must return to the Lord Khorne and vomit them at his feet. Later it will return to the Mortal Realms. Maybe it will come back to us, maybe not.'

'Let us hope,' said Skull, rejoining his lord.

Orto stood at the edge of the crowd and watched the

khorgorath go, then his long, mutated legs brought him back to the side of the deathbringer and bloodstoker. 'It is true. It is the sacrament of beasts. As we smash skulls upon Kordos' anvil, or stack them into cairns so that they might be taken up by Khorne, the khorgorath has its own way of honouring the Blood God.'

'You should have prevented it from feasting!' said Skull. 'That is a sore loss.'

Vuul shrugged. 'I kept watch upon it and my whip kept it from consuming too many skulls. Who else took upon themselves this duty? I am no beastmaster. If it is time for it to depart, then that is as Khorne wishes. The khorgoraths are his creatures.'

'It is the will of Khorne,' agreed Orto. 'Do not question it.'

They watched the Khorgorath plod away from the warband. The desert air was clear, and even after they took up their march again in the opposite direction, the khorgorath could be seen as a dark shape far away, until a flash of fiery light carried it away from the Bone Sands and the realm of Shyish.

'It is still a sore loss,' spat Skull.

The twelfth day came. Armoured corpses marked the Bloodslaves' trail as far as the horizon, lonely metal islands in the bone dust. Above, the clouds cleared a little, finally revealing glimpses of a dim, purple sun. When it shone, the desert turned violet and made their eyes ache. There was no change to the desert until Skull stopped and raised his hand to shield his eyes against the glaring sky. He caught Mir's wrist.

'My lord! Look!'

Some distance away there was an irregularity on the horizon. The Bloodslaves picked up their pace, staggering and half dead though they were, desperate for something other than ceaseless dust and bone to look upon.

Giant stone skulls were set in a circle facing outward. The spaces between them were tangled with a thicket of black-leaved thorns. As they grew nearer, the tell-tale glint of water shone.

'An oasis!' they cried. 'Water!'

They jogged toward the oasis, many abandoning their weapons and throwing themselves at the bushes to get at the pool they guarded. Thumb-sized spikes of wood tore at their skin as they fought their way through. Others, more circumspect, hacked at the branches with axe and sword.

Mir marched up and swung Bloodspite at the bush.

'I am no woodsman's axe, to cut back the weeds!' protested the weapon. 'I am the chosen killer of Khorne!'

Down Bloodspite came anyway, forced to do Mir's will. Where it cut into the tangle, the thorn bushes curled back, shrinking away like paper from fire. In a moment, the way was clear and the Bloodslaves were through. A silver-grey pool awaited, as still as a mirror. Mir's men bounced from his back as they struggled past him, throwing themselves at the water. Mir watched them.

'Stop! Stop!' shouted Orto, his commanding voice ruined by thirst. He went to the men and pulled them from the water's edge, but those there did not heed him and drank deeply. 'This land is cursed!'

The men started to cry out. Those not yet at the water backed away cautiously as several of their comrades were afflicted by wracking pain. They splashed around in the water, crying for mercy and gripping at their heads.

Flesh convulsed and warped, limbs withered, and new ones sprang in profusion from backs bent into fantastical shapes. One man screamed as his bones tore themselves from his skin, the bloody skeleton running laughing into the desert, leaving the man's soft parts behind as a heaving mess. Another lit up with blue flames that did not consume him as they burned, and the bloodreaver writhed and screamed until Orto cut off his head. The rest mutated rapidly, dying as their hearts gave out under the strain.

Orto pointed into the oily water. Green light pulsed in the depths.

'Warpstone. This oasis is poisoned.'

There was a crack of thunder and a smell of brimstone. Over the water the messenger of Archaon appeared.

It was the same being as before, but in a different form, one assembled from other remains. The eyes were the same, nestling moistly in a skull ten thousand years dry, but the skull was different, as were the clothes and the rest.

'New bones for our examiner,' croaked Skull. 'Why does it show itself now? Is it another test?'

'I say Mir has completed three,' said Orto. 'Fury for Khorne, endurance for Nurgle,' he looked at the shivering remains of the mutated Bloodslaves, 'and restraint for the Dark Prince.'

'You guess. These tests could go on forever,' said Vuul.

Skull scowled at him. 'You were vocal in your support for Lord Ushkar Mir.'

'That was then, this is now. This gambit offers no reward. The call of Archaon could be false.'

'It is not false.' Skull pointed back at the desert. 'If you are unhappy, leave. My lord is ready for the fourth test,' said Skull.

'Then what is it?' snapped Vuul.

The skeleton responded by pointing to the water.

Now Skull felt doubt. 'No, no! The water offers only death.' He drew his sword and waved it at Archaon's herald.

The skeleton gestured and the sword flew from Skull's hand. Another gesture stayed his attack, freezing him in place, and a third lifted him into the air. Skull made a strangled noise.

'Maybe, maybe,' murmured Orto. 'To drink deeply of this oasis is to die as you have seen. But to take one drop – could it bring power, visions, wisdom?'

'It will kill him,' said Vuul.

'I drink of the slaughtergruel. That is deadly, if one is unworthy. Mir is worthy.' Orto addressed Ushkar Mir. 'You, Ushkar Mir, must face this trial and triumph, or the way to Archaon will be closed to you and we will all die.'

'How can you know?' said Vuul.

'Khorne whispers in my ear. He must drink but a single drop!'

'It is his choice, not yours, slaughterpriest. What will Lord Mir do?' asked Vuul.

Orto grunted. 'Cowardice is not Khorne's way!'

Ushkar Mir was already kneeling by the pool. He extended one huge finger to the surface, and touched the water. The mirror surface broke but slightly, rings of ripples chasing each other and fading fast.

Skull fell to the ground with a clatter.

'I do not see we have much choice,' he said.

'Nevertheless, it is our lord's choice,' said Orto. 'It is not ours. He is the chosen of Khorne!' He held his axe aloft in his hand and the remaining Bloodslaves fell to their knees.

Raising the finger to his exposed teeth, Ushkar Mir looked at the herald of Archaon. Its five eyes stared back.

'But one drop!' warned Orto.

Mir extended his crimson tongue, and licked the tip of his finger.

Immediately, the world went black.

Ushkar Mir fell through darkness. Wind rushed past him, but even its roaring could not subdue the far-away bellows of

Khorne, demanding more blood and war. The call of Archaon he heard also, a trumpet blast that went on and on, unvarying in pitch and volume.

Then it was over and he was upon solid ground. Rain hammered off his head. It revived him, washed the dust from him. He licked at it, running his tongue over his arms and his chin to catch the moisture and moaned at the relief it brought from days of thirst. Noise of a different sort came to his ears – the sounds of battle. A wall of rough stone met his hands, and he scrabbled at it ineffectually. Shakily, he got to his feet, alarmed at the weakness in him, but it quickly passed. His sight returned and he found himself leaning upon a parapet looking down into a cauldron of war. Daemons and mortal followers of Khorne seethed around the base of mighty city walls, as numerous as ants.

Towering bloodthirsters whipped on lesser daemons and humans alike as they pushed at the bases of brass siege towers, two hundred feet tall. There were dozens of towers, absurd in scale. They should not have moved at all. But Chaos has no respect for the natural laws of Mortal Realms, and move they did. Gargants and other, less recognisable things strained in harnesses at the towers' fronts. As Mir watched, one was speared by nine long bolts hurled by war machines from the wall, and fell howling. It did not matter. Its traces were cut, its body hauled aside by dog-faced beastmen, and the siege tower ground forward. The towers moved slowly, but were indomitable. Boulders rattled off their thick plating. The fire from magical artillery fizzled harmlessly from their spell wards. Every hit that was turned aside marked another dozen feet moved toward the wall.

Lightning boomed in stormy skies. The churning clouds were black, patterned with bright blue lightning. The wall on which Mir stood was deserted by the living, and choked with the dead. Proud knights and humble soldiers lay contorted in the positions of final agony, commoner and lord intertwined. Death holds no regard for rank.

The rain pouring out of the gargoyle spouts set into the wall's outer face was coloured red with blood washed from the wall-walk. Mir knew, remembered, that soon the skies would send down not water but blood. A great tear would open in the very stuff of the realm, and the kingdom of Khorne would send forth its mightiest daemon legion. Already three of the five bastions he could see from his position had fallen, and the wall was riven with cracks. It would not be long now.

He looked again on the last day of Mir, and his last hours as a mortal.

'I should kill you where you stand, traitor,' said a voice behind him.

Mir turned suddenly, taken unawares for the first time in decades.

A tall, powerfully built man stood there. He wore a lamellae coat of iron plates enamelled red and gold, and a tall helmet with a horse hair plume. In his hands he held twin axes of blue steel.

'And yet why do I not?' asked the man curiously.

Ushkar Mir gaped, the rain running into his lipless mouth.

'Ushkar Mir,' he said, discovering to his amazement that he could speak once more. The words were clumsy, his lack of lips hindering his ability to talk, although less than it should. The man before him was Mir as he had been, before that terrible choice. A choice that, the Mir of the future realised, must soon be made again.

'That I am. General of this city, and until hours ago bearer of its last hopes. But hope has deserted me.' He looked hard at Mir. 'How came you here to the top of this wall? None of the Blood God's servants have surmounted it alive. Are you an assassin, come to kill me before the final attack? I did not think that your lord's way, but then, we have irked him for some time.' He smiled sorrowfully. 'Tell me, before I kill you, what is your name?'

'Ushkar Mir,' said the future Ushkar Mir.

The Mir of the past shifted back in alarm. 'What?' He searched Mir's face for any recognisable feature. 'That may be so. I have fought too long against the madness of Chaos to discount anything. That time is not free from the perversion of the Four surprises me not at all. But if it is the case, then I am much changed.'

'Khorne,' said Mir. 'He... Argh!'

This latest test was the worst of all. Pain attacked Mir from every angle. His punishment band glowed with heat, his heart thudded with anger fit to burst, his blinded eyes ached. Worst was the pain in his soul. All the rest was imposed from without, but this pain came from deep within and tormented him mercilessly.

'Look at you grovel. How could I become such a thing? No doubt I am offered the choice of the Dark Feast.'

Mir nodded.

'And I fail?' said the Mir of the past.

'Not failure!' gasped Mir. He pitted his will against his punishment band, pushing back the heat. He managed with effort, a feat he had not accomplished before. Perhaps this was some effect of his journey through time, or perhaps he was strengthened by the presence of his purer self.

'Revenge?' said the Mir of the past.

Mir nodded. 'I fight in his wars, but I have but one goal. I will stand before him and spit in his face, and bury my axes in his head.'

The Mir of the past laughed. 'That does sound like me.' His laughter deserted him. 'How many innocents have you slaughtered to further your vengeance?'

'Thousands,' said Mir. 'They would have died anyway, and for ignoble ends. There is nothing good left. Better a quick death for the weak. After Mir falls, there is only Chaos. Revenge is all there is.'

'Revenge that can never be achieved!' said Mir of the past. 'They say Khorne is as tall as a mountain and as mighty as the sun! Nothing can fight him. No man or daemon can kill the Blood God.'

'Gods die,' said Mir.

'By the hand of the likes of us?' Mir frowned. 'Impossible. The realms are large and not all the free people will fall. I still harbour hopes of that. Better to kill as many of these filth as I can, and die with honour.'

'I once thought so, but all kingdoms fall, one by one,' said the Mir of the future bitterly. 'To serve Chaos is your only chance at survival, and the only path to revenge.' He shook his head. 'This cannot be. This is an illusion. I have not been as you are for five hundred years.'

The Mir of the past silently contemplated their situation. 'If it is an illusion, then you are the illusion, not I – one last torture before I die. The Chaos Gods are boundless in their cruelty.' But then he closed his eyes. 'No. This is real. I feel it.'

The Mir of the future felt it too. He felt his memories change. He recalled this meeting from the other side, many years ago. Within a minute, he could not remember ever having not recalled it.

They watched as magical fire shot in a giant plume to engulf one of the towers, burning so hot the metal of its superstructure glowed red and ignited. Screams of pain and outrage sounded from that quarter, as showers of burning brass mingled with the rain fell among the warriors of Khorne.

'If you are myself from some distant time, tell me what befalls me,' said the Mir of the past. 'How do I go from this to you.'

'In but a short time, the rain will turn to blood. The Lord of Skulls will open the gates to his own realm, and the worst of his hellish legions will come out. The city will fall. You will fight every step of the way while everything you care for and love is destroyed. Finally, in despair you will be taken, alive, at the steps of the Old Palace, and given the choice by Korghos Khul himself.'

'You said yes to this choice.'

'With my voice I did. With my heart, I did not,' said Mir. 'I say no every day. Khorne took my voice for defying him. He put this band upon me to torment me. But I amuse him, I think. He keeps me alive. That will be his mistake.'

The Mir of the past looked at his twisted future in disgust. 'Then I thank you for showing me the consequences of revenge. I shall make sure to choose differently.'

'No!' shouted Mir. But his earlier self had brought his axes up with blurring speed. Mir's arm was cut deep.

'Stop! Wait!' he shouted.

'I will slay you first. You have become what I most fear, all for a coward's moment of weakness. Death is preferable to this.'

The steel axes came at Mir's head. But the Mir of the past stopped suddenly, his eyes wide with surprise. His axes fell from nerveless hands.

Mir of the future wrenched Skullthief out of his earlier self's chest. The Mir of old had been a mighty hero, but the Mir of the Bloodslaves was blessed by Khorne. No normal man could best him.

'No!' screamed Ushkar Mir. 'No!'

Then a most curious thing happened. A lightning bolt smote the wall-walk where Ushkar Mir had died. The Mir of the future was thrown back, dazed. When he recovered his wits, his earlier self had gone.

Ushkar Mir had no time to ponder this new development. The first of the siege towers hit the wall. Its brazen drawbridge clashed down onto the parapet and the warriors of the Blood God streamed across.

Very well, if his earlier self was not here to fight, then Mir would take his place. Mir ran forward to engage them, to spill their blood again and try vainly to save his home. But the wall dissolved beneath his feet, and the battle's noise vanished. He wheeled his arms as he fell back into blackness, helplessly falling.

Ushkar Mir's body convulsed. He sat bolt upright, coughing hard. Black sludge poured from his mouth. When he reached his hand up to wipe it away his arm twinged with pain. Looking down, he saw the gash inflicted by the Ushkar Mir of the past, and marvelled at it.

'You have succeeded,' said a voice from the sky. The skeleton fell apart, splashing into the pool. The sky wobbled, and a huge skull set with five eyes shimmered into being in the heavens. The sky convulsed again, and the daemon-thing that Mir had seen in the Bloodbloom Fields revealed itself to all the Bloodslaves.

'The way is open!' said the Many-Eyed Servant. Its voice sounded loudly, from everywhere, and the Bloodslaves shrank back from it. 'I judge you worthy. Go to Archaon and submit your pledge. The final decision rests with him. You will find him elsewhere in Shyish. Beware, for others come also.'

'Do we fight them?' shouted Skull.

'That is up to Mir,' said the herald.

The vision, Mir tried to say. Was it real? All that came from his mouth was animal moaning. The herald understood.

'All choices carry consequences, Ushkar Mir. Choose wisely!'

A crackle of magic ran from horizon to horizon. The bushes withered to nothing and the pool was sucked away into the ground, leaving no trace of its existence. The skulls pulled themselves under the ground. Endless desert once again greeted the Bloodslaves, and they wailed in despair.

'A trick!' hissed Vuul.

'Wait,' said Orto.

A light shone over the place where the pool had been. A bright star as large as a fist flared into being before Mir's face, rays of hard light stabbing out from it. The desert wavered through its light. The star burst outwards. A shower of sparkling motes hit the ground and a way opened up.

The Bloodslaves looked through the portal and saw a new land where a kinder sun shone. Dark against the horizon was a range of low hills covered in sere grasses. The tiny dots of birds wheeled in the sky. It was arid, but a paradise in comparison to the Bone Sands. Warm wind blew through the gate.

The horns of Archaon blared again. Ushkar Mir stood. He probed the wound he had taken in his vision, uncertain what it meant. Was what had happened real or illusory, or both?

Skull sniffed at the wind. 'I smell decay.'

Orto pointed through the gate. On the faraway hills a line of marching figures went along a ridge. The faint strains of cheerful music reached their ears along with the foetid reek.

'The servants of pestilence. Filth-eaters,' said Orto.

'The others the herald spoke of,' said Vuul.

'Some. There will be more,' said Orto. 'We will slay them all.'

Mir was not listening. He put the vision from his mind. There was only blood and skulls, and the distant possibility of vengeance. Nothing else mattered.

He sheathed his axes, and set out towards his destiny.

IN THE LANDS
OF THE BLIND

Rob Sanders

The Many-Eyed Servant, whose many eyes were everywhere at once, blinked his way across the Mortal Realms. Sights. Scenes. The serenity of horror observed but not experienced.

A banquet for the eyes. The daemon drank in the multiplicity of the realms, and of existences beyond that.

Life, death and everything in between played out before him like an unpleasant fiction. Children were born, their cries echoing those of their mothers just moments before. Men roared their rage, groaned in agony and spoke their secret and most desperate thoughts to themselves. Kings and beggars ached for what they couldn't have, while the beasts that roamed the realms around them knew only the living moment. Here in the lands of the blind, where mortal wretches understood nothing more than the immediacy of their world and their miserable place in it, the Many-Eyed Servant was all-seeing, all-knowing.

The daemon's gaze focused. In a blink it was drawn back to a story unfinished and a tale untold. Orphaeo Zuvius, the

Prince of Embers, was near. A fellow disciple of fate's dread architect, the god Tzeentch, and a sorcerous champion of darkness, it was he who would find a place in the ranks of the Varanguard – those ushers of the apocalypse, those knights of almighty Chaos selected by the Everchosen to serve the Ruinous Pantheon by his side.

The prince had come far since the Many-Eyed Servant had first seen him. He who had been far was now nearing. He had already faced great trials but he had to be tested anew, for the Everchosen was exacting. Only those of the blackest soul and darkest talents would fight in the company of living doom.

It was for that reason that the Many-Eyed Servant kept his eternal watch. He was Archaon's terrible gaze cast far across the realms, but here he found an aspirant before their gates.

The Great Spoilage. A rotten wasteland.

Death, as far as the eye could see. Bodies carpeted the land, lying as deep as a lake or shallow sea. Mouldering. Putrefying. Liquefying. Whatever cataclysmic event had been responsible for such devastation was lost to time. Thousands, perhaps millions, had died or been dumped there. Had it been a battle to end all battles? There were plenty of butchered warriors rotting there, but it could just as likely have been a genocidal slaughter, a grand suicide pact or some unnatural disaster that had visited its elemental wrath upon the masses, with corpses raining from the sky.

Orphaeo Zuvius, the Prince of Embers, negotiated the cadavers with difficulty. From the Beaten Path, Zuvius had followed the crows. He had followed them as they moved from battlefield to common butchery. He had followed them as they feasted upon lone travellers and slaughtered armies alike. He had followed them to the Great Spoilage, where it seemed every other crow in the realms was enjoying a scavenger's bounty.

Like harsh, hilly terrain or the crests of powerful waves, the Great Spoilage was an undulating landscape of cankered flesh and bone. Ribs gave, soiled cloth tore and rotting meat turned to maggot-choked, watery mush about Zuvius' boots. However, while the land reeked of death, the place was very much alive. Blankets of fat flies smothered the sea of carcasses, filling both the ear and mind with their incessant drone. Rats swarmed through the dead, gnawing, tunnelling and expanding their rancid nests. Crows feasted on both flesh and flies, hopping, swooping and wheeling about Zuvius and his warband as the Tzeentchians made their way across the corpselands. So great was the plague of carrion birds that they blacked out the horizon ahead. Larger pot-bellied scavengers scrambled up and down the fleshmounds, tearing yellowing flesh from bodies and crunching the marrow from bones.

Zuvius held the ragged edge of his cloak over his mouth. The web of melted skin that stretched across the rawness of his scorched face squirmed with revulsion. This place was undoubtedly sacred to the Great Lord of Decay. Its stench saturated the blue straggles of the prince's hair. Its rank taste was on his smeared lips and silver tongue. Zuvius detested it but in truth could think of no more suitable test or obstacle to place between a servant of the Great Changer and his goal than an expanse of stagnant rot.

The bird Mallofax circled their progress, riding on the rising stench, watching for potential threats. The warband had come across few. Small nests of ghouls picked over the bounty in places, while nomadic looters crossed the corpselands, neither interested in Orphaeo Zuvius or where he was headed. Even Zuvius had doubts about that. Archaon, Everchosen of Chaos and Exalted Grand Marshal of the Apocalypse, had called for him. Zuvius had followed the signs, followed the crows, but they had led him to a carrion paradise, a mouldering land of dead flesh that undoubtedly attracted every bird in the realm.

Behind the Prince of Embers, Sir Abriel followed. The groaning knight had once been the captain of the royal guard. What remained of that band was now the Hexenguard. They trudged through the spoilage in silence, dark knights of Tzeentch whose plate glowed with enchantments. In their footsteps followed the Unseeing – Zuvius' coven of blind sorcerers. The wretches staggered and tripped through the dead, one gnarled hand laid upon the shoulder of the sorcerer in front. They looked ancient and helpless, but their appearance belied their true power. With a gesture, the sorcerers could re-craft the flesh of nearby foes into representations of their twisted visions.

Using the sorcerous glaive A'cuitas to cut a path, Zuvius waded through the morass of breaking bones and sloughing flesh. Hauling himself up onto the corpse of a festering gargant, the prince knelt and rested, putting the raw skin of his forehead against his weapon's haft. As Sir Abriel, the Hexenguard and Zuvius' wretch-sorcerers climbed up onto the monstrous cadaver beside him, Mallofax returned, perching on the bill-hook of the glaive's crowning blade.

Zuvius tapped the pommel of the glaive on the gargant's hide. It was hard, waxy and mummified. Fungi bloomed across the giant carcass. Looking out across the corpse mounds, the prince watched as crows spooked by other scavengers took to the skies, wheeling about in rancid formations before settling once more. He tried to catch his breath but it was difficult. Every lungful of air was concentrated corruption that closed the throat and heaved the stomach. Mallofax flapped. The Hexenguard stood like warped, knightly statues. The Unseeing broke up and spread out across the gargant's chest, feeling their way across jutting bone.

'The Varanspire,' Zuvius said. 'Where is the damned thing?'

'Everywhere and nowhere, my prince,' the reptilian bird told him in a series of hisses and squawks. 'It exists in the Realm of Chaos. It is here but also there. Near but impossibly far.'

'Enough with the riddles,' Zuvius warned.

'I speak only truth,' Mallofax said.

'Well, you're bad at it,' Zuvius told him. 'You should stick to lies, they're more convincing. I'm beginning to think that we are going to end up the same way as these miserable souls.'

'My lord?'

'Perhaps they all set out for this palace of Chaos,' Zuvius mused, 'and died on the journ–'

Zuvius felt a quake through the soles of his armoured boots.

'What is it?' Mallofax squawked.

Zuvius stood, looking down at the yellowing flesh of the gargant. The quake turned into a series of thrashing tremors that shook the colossal carcass. The Unseeing froze while Sir Abriel and his malformed knights drew the notched blades of their longswords. In front of them, a sorcerer of the Unseeing suddenly disappeared. One moment he stood there in his rag-robes, the next he had been swallowed by the cadaver.

Disappearing into a pit of chewed flesh, the sorcerer screamed his way to death. The gargant's corpse bucked as a terrible creature erupted from it. Feeding quietly on the underside of the great carcass, a horrific maggoth had smelled their freshness. Chewing up through the rot with the shredding teeth of its maw, the thing erupted from the gargant like a monster of the deep. Its arms and legs were but stunted remnants used to propel it through the dead, and its skin was sticky with spoilage. It held there for a moment before blasting a stream of half-digested rot back at the sky.

As Mallofax took off, Sir Abriel and the Hexenguard came forward with swords presented to protect their master. The maggoth went under once more, wriggling itself loose of the carcass. The Unseeing grasped for one another while the Hexenguard pulled Zuvius back from where the giant corpse met the sea of bodies. Cadavers twitched and death-stiff limbs moved as the monstrous maggoth swam and ate its way through the corpses. Zuvius turned A'cuitas about in his gauntlets and pursed his lips in disgust. Not only did the prince have to wade through the Great Lord of Decay's detritus, he now had to suffer the attentions of some Nurglesque monstrosity stalking them through the killing fields.

Zuvius felt the cadaver buck beneath them again as the maggoth rose once more. Chewing up through the body, it exploded from the gargant king's gut. Another sorcerer of the Unseeing fell back into the pit of shearing teeth and rotting mulch. As he instinctively reached out, a member of the Hexenguard grabbed for him.

'No!' Zuvius called.

As the sorcerer thrust out his hand blindly, the tattooed symbols on his bony palm burned with fear. The Hexenguard knight, already a twisted, god-pleasing thing, clutched his chest, his screams joining the sorcerer's own. His plate screeched as he began to contort and change shape, becoming the frightful vision of terror that flashed through the sorcerer's mind during his last moments.

Toppling forward, the monstrosity knocked into another member of the Hexenguard. The knight slipped, his armoured boots scrabbling down the pit of rotting flesh. His dark blue steel sword bounced behind him, down into the maggoth's great trap of teeth. Zuvius lunged and grabbed the knight by the arms. Surging once more, the maggoth clamped its obscene jaws about the knight and thrashed its teeth. Cutting the warrior of Chaos almost in half, the creature tugged, dragging Zuvius over the ragged lip of the pit. Sir Abriel reached for his master. Zuvius scrambled away from the great maggoth but his boots and gauntlets slipped through the slime of the gargant's entrails.

The Unseeing moaned in their blindness. Mallofax squawked overhead. Zuvius kicked and turned, freeing himself of Sir Abriel's ghoulish grip. The maggoth's jaws gaped open and a black pool of digestive rot rose up from within. A warty tongue shot out of the pool like a serpent, wrapping itself around the prince's leg. As Zuvius kicked and slid towards his doom, the muscular tongue retracted, hauling him to the edge of the maggoth's fang-lined jaws.

From above, Zuvius heard Mallofax's half-stifled squawk. The bird was flapping his wings with effort, trying to stay above the cadaverous pit while clutching the metal shaft of A'cuitas in his scaly talons. As the weapon dropped, Zuvius watched the glaive tumble blade over pommel. Both the prince and his weapon were heading for the same place – the maggoth's foetid mouth.

Zuvius snatched the daemon-forged glaive out of the rank air. Spinning the weapon around, he cut through the monster's scabrous tongue with one sweep of the heavy blade. It did not stop the beast. Turning A'cuitas about, he aimed the pommel of the weapon down the creature's cavernous throat. The eye at the end of the glaive's shaft opened and a stream of lightning leapt from the weapon. Lighting up the darkness of the doom within, the lightning caused the maggoth to retract, tremble, boil, and finally explode.

Zuvius held his position through the black tempest of rot that erupted about him. As a putrescent mist drifted back down, Zuvius used the glaive to climb out of the gargant-corpse's abdomen. Reaching down, Sir Abriel hauled his master up. With the exception of Mallofax, who circled above, the whole warband dripped with stinking corruption.

'We are being tested,' Zuvius said through gritted teeth. Spitting rot from his lips, he once more descended into the sea of the dead and set forth, leading the warband onwards.

'Where is it?' the Prince of Embers demanded. They had been walking for days, the rankness of rot and death coating them like a blanket. There had been no sign of the dark citadel that Zuvius had seen in his vision or the gateway leading to it. The Great Spoilage seemed to extend forever, in all directions. The flocks of crows blacked out the sky, the cacophony of their incessant cawing an invitation to insanity.

'We shall find it, my lord,' Mallofax assured him.

'Will we indeed?' Zuvius roared. 'Will that be before or after we join the fallen at our feet?'

He turned A'cuitas on the bird, whose cryptic explanations were almost as infuriating as the endless horizon of crow-pecked corpses, and unleashed a blast of lightning that arced across the mouldering landscape and scalded the stench about it. Narrowly missing Mallofax, the stream of energy sent the bird flapping and squawking for the safety of the sky.

He wasn't the only one. Disturbed by the sudden crack of lightning, the crows carpeting the wasteland ahead of the warband took to the air in a storm of black feathers. As the flock lifted and cleared the path before the Prince of Embers, a fortress was revealed. The colossal castle reached into the skies with clawed turrets, citadels and towers of brick and blade. It was an abominate construction, its concentric walls an unbreachable barrier of dark stone and iron, each more towering than the last. They surrounded a central spire that pierced the heavens and resembled a spiked gauntlet punching victoriously at the sky.

The infernal architecture of the place was as disturbing as it was impressive, a fortress-shrine to Chaos, blasphemous in sculpture and indomitable in design. Its very presence brought forth storms that tore the sky asunder. Daemonic furies perched amongst the spires and circled in furious unnatural squalls. Elevated walkways of blood-stained stone spanned the fields of perpetual flame that raged about the castle and its moat, while its gargantuan gates were lined with monstrous metal teeth.

'The Varanspire,' the Prince of Embers said.

'What else could it be?' Mallofax agreed, coming in to land on his master's glaive.

'Let's find out,' Zuvius said.

The corpselands, though they had sapped the vigour of the warband with their stench, their marshy putrefaction and their bone traps, were now nothing to the Tzeentchians. Every crunching, squelching, spore-cloud-disturbing step took them closer to the dark majesty of the Varanspire – the fortress of Archaon, the Destroyer of Worlds.

As the cadavers began to thin and Zuvius' boots found the blasted black grit of the solid ground that lay beyond the corpse marshes, the prince noticed other groups moving towards the fortress. Some were armoured and rode on horseback, while others moved in great barbarian hordes. Champions of Chaos and their doomed followers. The Blood God's butchers. Slaaneshi deviants. Other sorcerers of Tzeentch, and the diseased of the Great Lord of Decay. He shouldn't have been surprised at the sight, and yet he was. These were other warriors who had fought their way to this dark place from across the Mortal Realms, intent on impressing unholy Archaon with their dark talents and commitment.

Grit became shattered stone and shattered stone the blood-polished marble of an elevated walkway. It trembled with the killing taking place there. Zuvius became part of the madness. Perhaps it was the infectious doom of the place, or perhaps it was the collective insanity of ruinous champions who had fought through so much to be there. In reality, Zuvius knew that the servants of the Chaos pantheon did not really need a reason to fight. Like territorial predators, it was in their nature to kill their competition. Through such unnatural selection did the forces of ruin grow ever more powerful. The weak were sacrificed for the Chaos Gods on the dark altar of the strong.

Warriors of Chaos threw themselves at the prince and his warband. Battle cries and all manner of damned weaponry cut through the air. It was a bloody free-for-all, an unspoken quest to be the last champion standing on the bridge. Zuvius became one with the slaughter. He needed no invitation. With his Hexenguard fighting behind him and the sorcerers of the Unseeing casting nearby champions into horrific new forms, Zuvius fought his way across the bridge. In the shadow of the Varanspire and with, he hoped, the gaze of the Three-Eyed King upon him, Zuvius killed for his new master, for his place in the ranks of the Varanguard. For the Everchosen's entertainment and for his own murderous whim.

Zuvius moved through the dread butchery. Khornate savages jangled with teeth and skulls while swinging serrated axe blades at sorcerers who smouldered with unnatural powers. Slaaneshi hedonists gutted Nurgle's children, who were already one with their own agonies. The diseased, in turn, seemed desperate to spread their suffering to all. The greatest hostility seemed to erupt between champions of the same patron. Blood knights on horseback hacked their way through barbarian hordes pledged to Khorne, while the witchbreeds and warriors of the Great Changer couldn't take their eyes off one another for fear of the treachery they all too well knew existed in the hearts of their compatriots. Mouthing dark enchantments and blasting Tzeentchian flame at one another, they created a spectacular firestorm of mutually assured death and damnation. No champion of Chaos wished to show their weakness before Archaon and his monstrous shrine-fortress, especially not the Prince of Embers.

Zuvius stabbed and skewered servants of the Dark Prince, who moaned their ecstasies while impaled on the daemon-forged weapon. The infected spilled pus and entrails before his boots. Monstrous knights in bone-lined armour stained their plate with their own gore as Zuvius passed his heavy blade through their throats. He stove in the skulls of warrior-enchanters like himself before the cursed incantations that resided there could reach blue Tzeentchian lips.

As Zuvius fought up the walkway, with unnatural flame roaring about him from the broad, infernal moat, he noticed the daemonic furies thunderbolting from the sky. Bringing their leathery wings in close, the fiends snatched warriors from the many walkways leading up to the great iron gates and portcullises of the castle. Tearing horses apart and tossing the remains of Chaos warriors between them like rag dolls, the flocks of furies seem to delight in their sport. Champions screamed as they were dropped from the storm-wracked skies and knocked into the roaring inferno that surrounded the Varanspire.

As the warriors of Chaos killed each other, the daemons thinned out their number, further, protecting the Varanspire from those who would threaten it. Zuvius tried to remain calm as the champions he was fighting were torn from the walkway about him and savaged by the flying monsters. A ragged fury landed on one of the Hexenguard and proceeded to snap his head from his shoulders and feast on his warped flesh. Zuvius heard Sir Abriel issue the low groan of an order. The Hexenguard brought up their battered shields.

Striding on towards the fortress, buried in the shadow of the Varanspire's mighty walls, the Prince of Embers held his nerve. The raw stench of death was intoxicating. He drank it in, uncaring of the daemons that swooped by. The furies' attacks became ever more savage and indiscriminate. A muscle-bound barbarian of the Blood God, as broad as he was tall, was knocked from the walkway and into the flames below. A bloated knight of Nurgle exploded with the rank gases of decomposition as a daemon sank its talons into him, while a smooth-skinned marauder screamed in pleasure as he was dragged up into the sky and shredded.

Zuvius tried not to flinch as another of his Hexenguard was snatched from the walkway and his flesh stretched between winged monstrosities trying to tear him apart. A moaning sorcerer of the Unseeing was next, and then another, the wretches never setting eyes upon the horrors that were their end.

Zuvius felt the blood-bead eyes of some plummeting beast upon him. It was a thing unknowing of the Prince of Embers' destiny. Zuvius' gauntlets tightened about the shaft of his glaive. He killed the Khornate crusader before him, knowing the fury was sweeping down towards him. With savage beats of its wings it surged, claws and talons ready for the kill.

The prince held on for as long as he could. As he turned the glaive to present it to the beast, however, the thing's infernal reflexes saved it. Crashing down onto the walkway, it skidded and hauled its head back. Zuvius swung the glaive about him with a devastating reach, but it was not enough. The arc of the blade should have passed straight through the monster's ugly skull but instead whistled past it, incensing the beast. Screeching its rage, it drew others from the sky and away from their slaughter. Zuvius felt a throng of furies, all enraged by the champion's challenge, swoop down towards him.

Like some hellish hound, the fury on the walkway snapped and shot forward. Jabbing with the glaive, Zuvius held the creature's blood-stained jaws at bay. Pretending that he hadn't seen another fury dropping down at him with outstretched talons, the Tzeentchian kept his focus on the beast in front of him before bringing the weapon up suddenly. Skewering the airborne monster with the force of its own momentum, Zuvius heaved it aside, smashing it into the stone of the walkway. As the first daemon surged, it found the thrash of wing and claw and the spear-point of Zuvius' glaive. Holding tightly onto the weapon as the thing impaled itself, the champion leaned back out of the snapping, spitting death-rattle of the beasts.

As a third landed behind the sorcerer, cracking the stone, Zuvius unleashed the sorcerous power of the glaive. With the weapon still skewered through the daemons, he blasted the newcomer off the walkway with a stream of lightning. As scraps of the creature and a mist of infernal blood hissed across the surface of the flames below, more furies swooped in on Zuvius. Putting his boot against daemonflesh, he freed his glaive from the bodies of the impaled creatures. Behind him, the Unseeing moaned their blind fear and the Hexenguard stood with shields raised.

'Protect your prince,' Zuvius ordered, prompting the Tzeentchian knights to run forward and surround him. Beasts smashed their horned heads against the blue steel and tried to push their snaggle-toothed jaws between the shields. Sir

Abriel put his ghastly form between Zuvius and an attacking fury, distracting the creature while the Prince of Embers thrust his glaive over the knight's shoulder and into the daemon's open mouth. Retracting the polearm and pulling half the monster's warped skull out of its jaws with it, Zuvius turned to find another fury almost on top of him.

The beast reared and brought up a wicked claw, aiming to rip down through the Tzeentchian champion. Its eye bulged suddenly and its jaws chomped in surprise as its flesh suddenly rebelled against it. Bones broke within it and leathery skin stretched over the new form it was taking. As it fell to one side, Zuvius could see a sorcerer of the Unseeing behind, visiting the damnation of his dark magic on the thing.

It suddenly came at Zuvius, morphing into something warped, ungainly and even more terrifying than before. The prince ducked a pair of jaws within jaws and rolled between the spawn's erupting legs. As it turned to reacquire him, the wretch-sorcerer visited his dark visions upon the daemon once more – twisting and sculpting the monster into ever more horrific forms. As a second head and a pincer ruptured from the body, Zuvius batted them aside with the pommel of his glaive. Aiming the opening metal eye of the weapon at the abomination, he prepared to blast it to shreds, but the transformation inflicted upon it by the Unseeing finally – horribly – wrung the life out of the creature.

As Orphaeo Zuvius and his warband fought their way towards the fortress, other warriors of Chaos kept their distance. Some even watched with bitter amusement as daemons rained from the sky to attack their competition. Zuvius spat. He would kill them all. Flicking infernal ichor from his glaive, Zuvius turned around and then around again. Up until now there had always been some winged thing behind him ready to pounce. Suddenly there was not. Looking up, he saw that rather than hauling off or losing interest, small throngs of furies were simply hovering, flapping their bat-like wings. They were waiting for something.

The fortress before him shimmered in shadow and heat. Zuvius looked about. Something was not right. In fact, everything seemed wrong. The flames around them seemed higher.

'Mallofax,' the prince called, catching his breath.

'My lord?' the bird squawked, swooping in to land on the warrior's shoulder.

'Fly on ahead,' Zuvius ordered. 'I want to know what we're walking into.'

Zuvius could see now a tidal wave of fire rising through the flames surrounding the fortress. It was a doom conjured by Archaon's fell sorcerers. Roaring its way around the Varanspire, the wave would engulf the elevated walkway. That was why the furies had taken to the skies. Zuvius would be damned before he let himself be seared free of the Varanspire like an insignificant insect.

'Hexenguard,' the Prince of Embers called. 'Form up and lock shields.'

Sir Abriel and his Tzeentchian knights moved to create a shell of battered blue steel. Bringing in the Unseeing behind the shield wall, Zuvius watched for warriors of Chaos attempting to take advantage of their distraction. A mounted Slaaneshi warlord in immaculate plate looked down his nose at Zuvius. Khornate killers bedecked in spikes and horned helms fought on towards the Varanspire.

A nearby figure stood regarding Zuvius and the shield wall with suspicion. The champion was a Tzeentchian warrior whose ensorcelled blade crackled with dark energies. He held out the weapon between Zuvius and himself as a warning, slipping off his helmet. A nest of tentacles that had been squirming within dribbled down his breastplate like a beard. The change-blessed warrior regarded Zuvius with dead, deep-sea eyes, before considering the apocalyptic tsunami of flame rolling towards them. Shouting to his cerulean-skinned followers, the champion of Tzeentch and his horde of warrior witchbreeds took cover behind the shield wall of the Hexenguard.

A chain reaction was initiated along the stone walkway. Champions and the servants of Chaos behind Zuvius saw what was happening and saw the blaze encroaching with their own eyes. Some emulated the Hexenguard, locking shields if they had them to present a unified front against the wall of flame. Others abandoned their warped steeds, skidding and scrabbling down behind blue steel.

Zuvius watched as a hulking warrior of Nurgle ran towards him, slimy, pale rolls of fat spilling out of his rusted chainmail. The warrior shook the stone beneath Zuvius' feet with his determined steps, grubs, maggots and leeches raining from his blight-festered flesh as he ran. Ducking down beneath the shield wall Zuvius waited for the blast wave. The Tzeentchian smiled to himself. He cared nothing for the followers of other fell gods, disciples of his own or champions of Chaos competing with him for the Everchosen's favour. He only cared for what might be achieved through saving their lives in the undoubted challenges to come.

Zuvius heard the boom of the inferno against the shield wall and felt the shudder of the stone walkway. He watched the Lord of Decay's monstrous warrior disappear in a rush of flame. Slaaneshi swordsmen on steaming horseback lost their race with the firestorm, while there was little the blades, muscle and fury of the Blood God's brutes could do to save them in the face of such fiery destruction.

The Prince of Embers felt his hair burn and his flesh blister. The raging flame boomed about him – and then it was gone. The Hexenguard unlocked their shields and the Chaos warriors that had sheltered behind them brought up their heads. They watched the bank of flame roll away.

Zuvius heard the flapping of wings. Mallofax was back. He had flown above the fire and scouted out the fortress approach, its portcullis gate and defences.

'The gate?' Zuvius asked as the bird landed on the blade of the glaive.

'Carnage, my lord,' Mallofax told him. 'The gate stands firm against all assaults. Archaon's warriors wait within.'

'And the wall itself?'

'Sheer,' Mallofax told him. 'There's no way in.'

'There's always a way in,' Zuvius growled. 'There has to be. All those who stand in service of Archaon within once stood beyond the fortress walls.'

Zuvius knew he had to keep pressing forward. He wasn't going to wait for the infernal wave to come back around. He wasn't going to wait for the furies to attack again. He had saved the warriors of Chaos on the walkway. If he could just get them and others into range of the fortress' warped defences, a retaliatory assault on the Varanspire might be able to achieve some momentum. He would lead by example, down a doomed path the warriors of Chaos had already chosen.

Zuvius ran. The bridge between him and the Varanspire was all but clear of warriors. Only those champions already close to the Varanspire's walls had managed to find shelter from the bank of flame and, hiding in the architectural flourishes of the dread fortification, they had survived the inferno. Now, they were dying.

Arms of sorcerous stone shot out from the Varanspire wall,

grabbing warriors and dragging them to their deaths in the solidifying wall. Boiling spawnflesh spurted from the mouths of daemonic gargoyles decorating the ramparts, splattering down on the warriors below. Coated in liquid horror, the spawn-flesh assumed the shape of lesser daemons that assimilated the warriors' dissolving forms. Braziers situated either side of the gate smouldered with a debilitating fog that, when breathed in, afflicted the victim with blistering burns to the skin, an agonizing blindness and a lung-curdling cough. Arrow slits sang with the thud and whoosh of crossbows and monstrous spear-shooting ballistas. Each bolt was crafted from hell-forged iron and carried a bound daemon within. Even if a striking bolt or spear failed to kill an approaching warrior, the blood-mad daemon that bled from the iron to possess the injured victim shredded both their flesh and soul.

Zuvius ran towards the fortress with his warband following, while the knights, butchers and swordsmen who had taken shelter behind the shield wall stomped across the bridge after him. Zuvius didn't care whether this was out of a desire to kill him or to attack the Varanspire. Once they were in range of its dread defences, intentions would matter little. The Chaos fortress was a challenge that could not be ignored. The Chaos warriors accelerated across the bridge. The energy of their charge was almost infectious: blood knights in full plate, wasted warriors in leper's robes, barbaric pleasure-seekers whose flesh was stuck with pins and shards of bone, and sorcerous champi-ons like himself, wielding daemon-forged blades. The growing horde charged along the walkway. The fortress wall grew higher above them and the monstrous gate hove into view, shimmer-ing in the heat of the broad moat.

A great arch lined with iron teeth, it was sealed by a series of warped portcullises, each lowered one behind the other.

Through the grille of the bars Zuvius could see the warriors of Archaon, armoured silhouettes in thick plate mounted on fearsome steeds. They waited, weapons sheathed, seemingly unconcerned. They were confident in the Varanspire's defences. Zuvius snarled. He would make them pay for their arrogance and serve Archaon all the better for taking their place. No warrior would breach the Varanspire while the Prince of Embers stood in their path.

Suddenly he was amongst bodies – the unfortunates who had failed to breach the Varanspire's defences before him. Zuvius would not fail. Their remains were trapped amongst a forest of iron shafts and ballista bolts embedded in the stone. Zuvius could feel the raging daemons bound to the iron reach out for him in their fury. Savages and warriors who had shed their plate sprinted ahead of Zuvius, desperate to get out of the killing ground. They could not, however, for the fortress was designed with such desperation in mind.

Within seconds, the vanguard of the horde was dead. Such was the power behind the crossbows and the infernal ballistas that within a blink, daemon-bound bolts and spears were thudding into the stone about them. Marauders were thrown off their feet by shafts that hammered into their chests. Black projectiles hit the ground about Zuvius' feet while shards of stone showered him where the missiles from ballistas shattered the walkway. A daemonic roar could be heard with their passing. Half-stifled screams and grunts of sudden death filled the air as Chaos warriors were impaled by the missiles and staked to the bridge.

There was no avoiding such an onslaught. Mallofax, who soared above the stabbing storm, had called it carnage; the bird had not been wrong. Aspiring champions, pledged to all manner of Dark Gods, died with brutal indifference. They had braved the lethality of the realms to reach the Varanspire and now it was their undoing. Alongside them, Zuvius heard members of his own warband dying. He ran on through the forest of iron and the impaled warriors. The heart-stopping whoosh of a ballista bolt nicked Zuvius' ear and thudded straight through the battered breastplate of a Hexenguard knight. Zuvius heard the daemon in the missile rip the armoured warrior apart in seconds.

Step after feverish step took the Prince of Embers on towards the gate. It grew before him, its iron teeth threatening to swallow him whole. Madmen and driven warriors of darkness ran beside him. Behind them pounded a swollen blightking of Nurgle, who seemed to soak up bolts and the Varanspire's daemonic heralds with his diseased flesh. As they neared the gate, the hail of bolts from above began to ease. Confidence welled up once again in Zuvius and those about him.

Suddenly, Sir Abriel's shield flashed before him. The Tzeentchian knight put his willowy fingers on Zuvius' chest to slow him. The prince heard the thud of several opportunistic bolts slam into the shield – daemon iron that had been meant for him. He didn't usually waste sentimentality on the Hexenguard but immersed in the death and destruction, he found himself grinning hysterically at his father's former captain of the guard.

When the ballista bolt came, it sheared the shield in two and did much the same to Sir Abriel. Skewered through his ruined chest and down into the stone, the groaning knight was pinned. Zuvius wasted a few precious moments trying to pull Abriel free before coming to his senses. The knight was all but dead already; Zuvius would not end the same way.

'Sorry, old friend, but this is the price of entrance,' the prince told the warped knight as the bound daemon ravaged what was left of him. With screams echoing about him, Zuvius ran for the gate.

A huge Khornate knight in baroque plate smashed into the portcullis with his colossal axe, causing the metal gate to shake. Feverish berserkers thrashed at the grille with their axes, while pus-swollen warriors of the Lord of Decay put their backs and bellies into lifting the colossal portcullis. It would not move, however. Even if it had, two more lay behind it, as secure as the first. With a metallic squeal, the hell-knights beyond the gates thrust the length of their fellspears through the gate grilles and skewered the Chaos champions hammering to get in. With infernal discipline, the knights withdrew their weapons and allowed their victims to fall before thrusting forth and impaling those that took their place.

Dark champions, filled with a warrior's ecstasy at surviving the sorcerous flames and the storm of bolts, threw themselves at the fortress gate. Sparks flew where their hammers bounced off daemon-forged metal. Light-armoured deviants covered in tattoos, chains and studs reached through with their cruel blades, attempting to slash at the machinery that raised the gates, but nothing worked. Archaon's hellish garrison were ready for them. The interlopers would die at the gate. With a whoosh of steam, a foul liquid cascaded down the walls and turned the besiegers to screaming statues of melting flesh. All the while, the skin of champions blistered as they stumbled blindly through the diseased smoke of braziers.

Zuvius felt the fight leaving the attacking horde. Even dread warriors such as these needed some expectation of success, but the Varanspire gave them none. For a moment the prospect of braving the ballistas back across the walkway began to assume a grim appeal. Zuvius knew he had to rally the besiegers. He had to find an advantage.

'My sorcerers,' Zuvius called. 'My Unseeing, move on. Show me what you can see through this wretched gate.'

The Prince of Embers knew the cost of the sacrifice and accepted it. Before the Varanspire and under the gaze of the Three-Eyed King, he had to relinquish the trappings of a Tzeentchian warrior. Those that fought for Archaon cared not for the Dark Gods they formerly served or the warbands that in turn served them. Their only concern was the wish and whim of the Everchosen of Chaos – for to be one of his knights was to forsake all other things.

The Unseeing moaned as they stumbled through the bodies before the gate. They flinched as they bumped into the grille and laid their gnarled hands on the bars. Several died immediately, the cruel points of fellspears bursting from their backs. Reaching through the warped grille, the wretch-sorcerers struck out their palms.

Tattooed symbols burned in their flesh as the horror of their visions was unleashed on the armoured warriors beyond. The screams of the Varanspire's hell-knights fortified the resolve of the faltering champions of Chaos trapped outside the fortress walls. Through the grille, Zuvius could see the twisted silhouettes that the Unseeing had created. As a fresh cascade of boiling oil came down the towering walls, the sorcerers' screams joined those of their victims – robes were set alight and flesh was burned from bones.

'Get back!' Zuvius called, gesturing to the knights of the Hexenguard and the rest of the champions clustered at the gate. He raised his glaive. The gates would resist a sorcerous blast from the daemon-forged weapon, but the stone of the wall might offer a different opportunity. He adjusted his aim, pointing the glaive to one side of the portcullis.

The metal eye of the pommel opened and Zuvius blazed a continuous stream of lightning at the wall. It crackled and glowed with the blinding power of the arcing blast. As the sorcerous stream ceased, Zuvius walked up to the point of impact. All about the side of the portcullis the stone of the gate had turned to a dark glass. Jabbing at the smouldering crystal with the pommel, the prince shattered the wall around the edge of the portcullis grate.

The Hexenguard filed through first. The Tzeentchian knights found only warped sculptures of mangled flesh, bone and plate on the other side. The horde swarmed the opening, a lord of Khorne pushing past in his blood-dripping cloak and great horned helm to lead the way. Newly filled with resolve and a desire both to impress the Everchosen and destroy the unworthy among his servants, champions of all powers and patrons followed him. Zuvius watched pleasure-bound killers enter, armed with blades that glistened with poison. Hulking sacks of indomitable pestilence followed, with the cerulean-skinned warriors of Tzeentch. Barbarian berserkers jangling with skulls clawed at each other to be the first to the fighting within. They were a horde of unwitting puppets, all serving as a distraction for the Prince of Embers.

As Zuvius entered and moved through the gallery of twisted death the Unseeing had sculpted in the barbican, he found Mallofax. The bird had risked the sky-bound furies to fly over the wall and gather intelligence for his master of the trials to come.

'Speak,' Zuvius commanded.

'Daemons, my prince,' Mallofax told him, hopping from statue to statue. 'The legions of hell, fighting for the Everchosen.'

As the barbican opened up onto another stone walkway, Zuvius found that his horde had run straight into the determined resistance of the hell-knights who had escaped the gaze of the Unseeing, and a throng of daemon shock troops – things unleashed to immediately check the advance of any besieger entering the fortress.

Beyond the barbican troops, the lord of Khorne had dived straight into combat, his cloak and monstrous axe wheeling about him in a spatter of blood. Inspired by his fearless example, the champions of other dark gods fell in behind him – the Chaos lord was the point of a wedge that the horde was driving through the ranks of savage Varanspire daemons. Horned plaguebearers tore warriors of Chaos limb from limb with their diseased claws. Pallid nightmares of claw and dread feminine form snapped off heads with cruel elegance. Fury-red fiends of horn and claw danced death through the horde, wielding hellblades in devastating arcs of destruction. The lord of Khorne found himself fighting for his life against a trio of bloodletters, turning a storm of swords aside with brutal swings of his axe.

No less devastating were Archaon's Knights of Ruin. Decked in plate of black and gold, they were broad and powerful, and thrust their fellspears through champions of Chaos, sometimes two or three at a time, impaling them like stuck boars.

The Hexenguard moved about their master, giving Zuvius the protection of their shields while sweeping through lesser daemons with longswords. As change-blessed flesh and bone stretched, the arcs of the tapering blades surprised the infernal creatures and opened up throats and bellies. As a plaguebearer clawed through the Hexenguard shields, the daemon batted one of the knight's heads from his armoured shoulders with a diseased hand. It beat another into the ground with a fist before pulling out a jagged, rusted cleaver and swinging it with droning abandon at Zuvius.

Like his former patron, the Prince of Embers had a special hatred for the Lord of Decay's foetid daemon foot soldiers. Bringing the blade of his glaive down, he knocked the creature's weapon to the floor before slicing its hand from its gangly arm. With the foul thing at a disadvantage, Zuvius brought the pommel of the glaive around to smash the daemon in the face, before turning the shaft in his hands and ramming the blade straight into its swollen belly. Pushing through the shields of his Hexenguard protectors, Zuvius forced the plaguebearer back. Rot-infested entrails tumbled from the thing's cleaved form. Slamming it into the back of one of the Everchosen's ruinous knights, Zuvius turned the glaive blade like a key, bursting the rest of its putrid organs.

Feeling the blow, the blood knight turned around. Despite the weight of his thick plate, the warrior moved like a striking serpent, his ensorcelled blade a blur of runes and dark steel as it smashed A'cuitas aside. The knight seemed drawn to the Prince of Embers' confidence and lethality, recognising the competition. Perhaps, Zuvius thought, he had seen him issuing orders to the horde outside the gate and gain entrance with his crackling power. The knight stared at the prince through the eye slits of his helm, the ornate headdress of metal horns thrumming with dark power.

Zuvius felt the intensity of the knight's attentions. He was hungry for the kill. The prince's life was his to take and every second Zuvius was allowed to breathe was a grievous insult to the Everchosen of Chaos. His sword was a stabbing, sweeping, cleaving instrument of cold steel. Relentless in the economic savagery of his attacks, the warrior backed Zuvius towards the barbican wall, away from others of his warband and the horde that might help him. Away from the other dark knights of the fortress who might take the honour of the kill.

Working his glaive around, Zuvius turned the cuts and swings of the ensorcelled blade aside. The knight moved with incredible speed and assurance, pressing the prince to his limit. He felt the warrior's attacks burn with the desire to end him. Zuvius backed into the barbican wall and sparks flew as the knight carved his blade into the stone. The prince ducked and weaved around into an alcove doorway.

'Expect to get no further,' the knight hissed through his helm. A haft-ringing deflection knocked Zuvius' weapon aside. A brief stream of lightning scorched and crackled away to nothingness on the smooth stone. The knight had the measure of him now. He wouldn't allow Zuvius to press his sorcerous advantage.

As the murderous thrusts and stabbing attacks forced Zuvius through the spike-inlaid doorway and up a crooked spiral of stairs, the prince felt the dread knight gearing up for the kill. Even with the advantage of higher ground, Zuvius could not get past the warrior's defensive sweeps. It was as though his weapon were part of him, moving with speed and force to knock the glaive aside.

As the walls opened out onto a stone landing, Zuvius readied himself for the end. Archaon did indeed only select the very best warriors for his ranks. As their blades clashed and the knight backed Zuvius across the landing, barbican archers in dark helms and with bare, scarred chests moved their bows, arrows and ballistas across the stone floor. With the sound of battle within the walls alerting them to a breach, the archers were intent on moving their deadly weaponry over to the arrow slits on the other side of the landing so that they could once more target the horde below.

'Think never to wear the dark plate of the Everchosen,' the unhallowed knight spat as he attacked. Sparks lit up the landing as Zuvius turned the ensorcelled blade away, each deflection a little slower, each lethal lunge of the blade a moment closer to ending the prince.

As they reached the end of the landing, Zuvius saw the knight's eyes widen with surprise and hostility. Instead of skewering Zuvius, the rune-encrusted blade pointed towards an archer standing behind the prince. Turning, the prince saw that the archer was standing next to an unloaded ballista and was holding the heavy, iron bolt above his head like a cudgel.

'This dubious honour is mine,' the knight shouted at the archer, warning him off.

Zuvius knew that this was his last chance. This knight of ruin, this warrior acolyte of the Destroyer of Worlds, would slay him. Touching the pommel of the glaive to the metal of the knight's weapon, Zuvius allowed the briefest stream of lightning to course through the blade. The sword leapt from the knight's gauntlet with a sudden shock and rattled across the floor, away from them both.

As the knight and Zuvius stared at one another, the sorcerer thrust the crowning blade of A'cuitas back, stabbing the archer through the chest. Without looking, Zuvius listened for the cacophonous clatter of the heavy bolt on the floor. Zuvius knew what to expect next. The knight was so skilled with the sword, the prince wagered, that he wouldn't continue the combat without it.

Grunting his hatred, the knight made a run for the ensorcelled blade. Zuvius was right behind him. With the haft of the glaive in both gauntlets, Zuvius thrust the weapon over the knight's head. As the warrior's ornate helm was knocked to the floor, Zuvius hauled him back. The knight reached for his blade, but it was just out of reach. Zuvius pushed the glaive's blade to the knight's throat, and the warrior was forced to grasp the weapon at his neck instead.

Without his helm, Zuvius could see the knight was some kind of albino, with unnaturally pallid flesh. His mouth opened, gulping for air, and the sorcerer caught a brief glimpse of his black tongue and needle teeth as he bucked around. Like a tormented animal, the dark knight – who had been so deliberate in his murderous bladework – reared with Zuvius on his back and flung them both at the wall. Zuvius held on for his life as the knight backed and battered them both against the stone. Heaving the shaft of A'cuitas ever closer, his arms burning with the effort, the prince felt something give, and the knight suddenly go limp. Riding the cascade of hell-forged plate and muscle to the ground, Zuvius held the knight there for a few moments longer, just to make sure. Getting to his feet, Zuvius turned his blade about in his gauntlets and struck the dread knight's head from his shoulders.

'You fought well,' Zuvius told the corpse. 'Just not well enough. The honour might have been yours but the pleasure was mine.'

Archers came around the corner armed with their bows and improvised weapons. Turning A'cuitas on them, Zuvius arced lightning from one killer to another, turning each into a wall-splattering eruption of blood.

Leaning against the glaive, Zuvius took a moment to catch his breath. At the arrow slit he heard the flap of wings. Mallofax settled in the opening, watching his master with beady, black eyes.

'Where have you been?' the prince asked.

'Our siege does not go well, my lord,' Mallofax squawked. Zuvius went across to the arrow slit and peered down at the walkway leading from the barbican. The Varanspire's daemonic shock troops were taking the Chaos horde apart. The Hexenguard were all dead. Champions of different fell gods fought side by side against the Everchosen's monstrosities, killing the dread things when they could. Only the Khornate lord in his blood-baroque armour and gore-drizzling cloak seemed to be making headway. With his axe dripping with infernal ichor, the bodies of bloodletters, plaguebearers and daemonettes twitched at his feet. Zuvius thought on the mess he had made of the archers who had been about to open fire on the walkway.

'The siege goes better than it might,' Zuvius corrected the bird.

Zuvius looked down on the horde below, the champions of Chaos doomed to become little more than a daemon-slain distraction. His gaze followed the walkway spanning the exterior wall and the next. While the Everchosen's knights, sorcerers and daemons haunted the fortress corridors and clung to the architecture like warped gargoyles, the colossal courtyard in between blazed with torches: an assembly ground for monstrous hordes, led by countless champions and Chaos lords who fought under Archaon's banner. They waited to be summoned to battle at the Everchosen's order, somewhere in the Mortal Realms, while other armies of darkness arrived with the spoils of war to take their place.

There was no way that the invading horde could fight through such numbers and horror. Zuvius would have to find another way. The horde could still serve his interests as a timely distraction. He would not tolerate a challenger for the Everchosen's attentions, however. Scooping up the iron bolt the archer had dropped on the floor, Zuvius loaded and cranked the ballista. He could feel the hate of the bound daemon radiating off the cursed iron. Aiming the weapon down through the arrow slit, he lined it up with the back of the Khornate lord that was still leading the fighting.

Allowing the Blood God's champion to finish one of Archaon's black-armoured knights with a bludgeoning swing of his axe, Zuvius fired the ballista. Mallofax flapped his wings at the sound and hopped onto the prince's shoulder.

The iron bolt speared through the warrior's back and out

from his chest, and the lord of Chaos staggered. The released daemon savaged at the warrior's soul while a daemonette leapt on him, scything with her claws, but the Khornate champion somehow fought on. Tearing the creature from his pauldron, the Chaos lord smashed her into the ground. Falling to his knees, he took the legs out from beneath another daemonette as she ran at him. Dropping his axe and falling onto all fours, the Khornate lord was surrounded by stalking bloodletters. The daemons waited for a moment and then pounced, tearing into the Blood God's champion with horn and claw, pulling free his skewered heart and snarling skull.

'What now, my prince?' Mallofax asked.

'Now we find the Everchosen of Chaos,' the Prince of Embers told him.

The Varanspire.

Orphaeo Zuvius negotiated the leagues of fang-lined battlements. He stood in the monstrous claws of tower turrets, watching greater daemons on the wing, hunting furies in the storm-wracked skies.

In search of Archaon, Zuvius explored the citadel, its towering heights and corrupting depths. There, all the Chaos Gods and Archaon, as their undisputed champion, were celebrated. Shrines and temples dedicated to the Ruinous Powers turned Zuvius' heart black. Labyrinthine libraries of sorcerous tomes threatened to claim years of his life, while crowded fighting pits were places of perpetual death. Zuvius walked through miles of corridors sizzling with dark intent. He found lavish chambers that were nests of writhing daemonflesh, and stagnant ruins in which time almost stood still. Indeed, the heart of the Varanspire barely seemed to observe the natural laws at all – an architectural nightmare crafted in darkness, stone and fire.

On the courtyard expanses he passed beneath banners depicting the symbols of the Everchosen and the unruly hordes of ruin: spawn, savages, Chaos knights, enslaved monstrosities, charismatic champions and dark warlords, all serving dread Archaon. Mallofax warned his prince of lesser daemons and infernal beasts haunting the fortress corridors ahead.

While the diversionary sacrifice of his warband and the besieging horde had allowed Zuvius within the Varanspire's walls, it had been his patience and cunning that had allowed him to traverse the walkways and courtyards, the ramparts and corridors. When he needed to, the prince murdered with silent impunity, strangling the lesser guards of the fortress garrison with the A'cuitas' haft and stabbing the blade up under chins, through backs and into helms.

With every treacherous blow Zuvius got nearer to his goal, until he walked straight through the monstrous gates of the citadel spire itself. Mallofax hopped and flapped down empty corridors ahead of his master.

Lost in this hellscape, each twist, turn, deathly drop and corrupting flourish was dedicated to the Everchosen of Chaos. Only the strangest of daemonic creatures stalked the dream-like depths, feverish abominations writhing with tentacle. Daemon monstrosities that struggled to keep their form, erupting with mouths and limbs that spewed forth sorcerous flame, drove Zuvius on through the insanity. Magical hellfire not only thundered up corridors and through chambers but scorched the very nature of reality itself. Zuvius stumbled away from the heat, light and sound, driven down into one corridor and then the next, until he could no longer escape the corruptive bloom of daemon flame coming at him from all directions.

As the booming inferno enveloped him, Zuvius simultaneously lost and found himself. Blinking the nightmare from his eyes, the Prince of Embers stumbled across a gargantuan chamber of black marble that he couldn't remember having entered before. It was dark magnificence given form. Mallofax hopped and staggered behind him across the polished floor. A forest of colossal pillars rose to the ceiling and Zuvius stumbled between them. Into each was crafted the horror of screaming faces.

Pushing himself between two pillars, Zuvius suddenly caught sight of the back of a monstrous throne, a thing sculpted of darkness and ossified ambition, a thing that radiated unholy power and struck a chord of dread in the Prince of Embers' heart.

'This is it,' Zuvius said to Mallofax. 'This is a throne room fit for the Everchosen of Chaos. A place of doom and dark majesty. We have made it, Mallofax.'

Zuvius staggered about the corruptive splendour of the throne, keeping his distance as he moved around in front of it. The throne itself was blinding in its dark brilliance and the prince found himself crashing to his knees in exhaustion and dread.

'Mighty Archaon,' Zuvius managed, his helmet off and forehead to the floor. 'You have summoned and I have answered. I have travelled far and fought hard in your name, all to take a place at your unholy side. Archaon, Everchosen of Chaos, Destroyer of Worlds and men: I supplicate myself before you. I pledge myself to you in bringing an end to this world and all others.'

'You seek Archaon?' a voice came, burning with age and sorcerous power.

Zuvius brought up his head and stared into the radiating darkness. He got the impression of a gaunt figure rising from the throne, at one with the unholy dread of the object. It walked down the steps towards the kneeling Zuvius. The prince rubbed the darkness from his eyes. He could make out a skeletal figure and sorcerer's robes. The thing's features were warped, and blinked with a thousand eyes. Zuvius burned under its fell gaze.

'I seek Archaon,' Zuvius confirmed, holding his hand out in front of him to ward against the darkness, and getting to his feet.

'In a fortress he has barely set foot in?' the sorcerer said. 'Before a throne upon which he has never sat?'

'Archaon is not here?'

'And never shall be.'

'I don't understand,' Zuvius told the sorcerer honestly. 'I am–'

'You are blind and foolish,' the sorcerer said. 'That is all that matters. How came you to be in this place?'

'I followed the crows,' the Prince of Embers said.

'For where the Everchosen treads, the crows indeed follow,' the sorcerer said.

Zuvius heard it. Faint at first. The distant flapping of wings. The caws of hungry carrion birds. The sound grew, booming about the cavernous chamber. Suddenly they were everywhere. Birds, black of feather and sharp of beak. A storm of crows swarmed through the pillars in all directions – flying at Orphaeo Zuvius, the Prince of Embers. A squawking Mallofax was lost in the thunder of the flock. Zuvius was lifted from the ground but remained in place, being shredded from all angles. They ripped his armour from his form and tore at his skin with their beaks and talons. Zuvius screamed as they pulled the remaining hair from his scalp and his eyes from their sockets. Like a torrent of darkness, they baptised him in death.

Zuvius crashed back down to the marble floor. Black feathers floated down beside him, an agony on his raw flesh. He felt blood spill down his face from the empty sockets and drip to the floor. He heard Mallofax squawk his misery from nearby.

'My prince...' the bird said, but got no further.

The sorcerer moved painfully close to the Prince of Embers and leaned in, causing Zuvius, blind, to angle his head awkwardly this way and that, trying to fix on the presence.

'Your trials are over,' the sorcerer told him. Orphaeo Zuvius didn't know whether to laugh or cry. Instead he settled on a dumbfounded silence. 'What did you expect? Some kind of dark coronation? The Everchosen of Chaos here to recognise you personally for your dread service? Service to Almighty Archaon is recognition enough.' Zuvius nodded slowly in his private agony.

'Don't worry,' the sorcerer said as he left him, the horror of his voice growing distant. His words were laced with a dark amusement. 'There are none so blind as those that will not see.'

The Prince of Embers knelt there, the sorcerer's parting words echoing horribly about the colossal chamber. They were everywhere, melting into his mind behind the empty sockets of his eyes. There, on his knees before the empty throne, Orphaeo Zuvius came to know the true nature of damnation. He had forsaken all in his search for the Everchosen of Chaos and Archaon, in turn, had forsaken him. Letting the torturous darkness where his eyes used to be sink down into his soul, the Prince of Embers became one with the potent doom of the place. The wicked laughter of insanity. A haunting whisper in the fortress depths. A cautionary tale never told.

BLOOD AND PLAGUE

David Annandale

In a dead land, the cold arena waited. Echoes of battles past and civilizations forgotten lined its cliff walls. The land did not remember the glories that had been. It remembered their loss. It remembered their fall. And it muttered to itself with the whisper of tombs. The whispers spread across the floor of the arena: broken archways, depressions of absent foundations, doors to emptiness. Eroded walls faded to nothing, sentences trailing off into silence.

Above the cold arena, on a projecting spur of rock, a sorcerer watched the whispers. He watched the land beyond. He watched as the waiting came to an end.

The Many-Eyed Servant faced south, seeing much further than the arena. The carriers of his vision flew over the land. A multitude of fragments became a composite panorama of the battle to come. From the east and west, warbands approached through the canyons of vanished waterways and time-gnawed sepulchres of civilisations. 'They are almost here,' he said.

Heavy footsteps crunched the stone behind him. A presence loomed at the daemon's back. The Many-Eyed Servant's master had come. He said nothing, but the daemon sensed his satisfaction. The Everchosen had arrived to witness the final display.

'Where have you brought us?'

Copsys Bule thought before answering. Fistula's words were less a question than an accusation. They had marched for a day and a night since passing through the gate. Until now, Fistula had said nothing to challenge the lord of plague's command. Since their escape from the seraphon, Fistula had been less and less inclined to hide his anger and impatience. The blightlord had, for a time, been willing to accept that abandoning a second battle to the Stormcast Eternals was the right price to pay for the greater glory of joining the forces of Archaon. But that promise still showed no sign of being fulfilled. Instead, they travelled through nothing. The land was cracked, bare stone. The gate had brought the Rotbringers to the floor of a wide, twisting canyon. The riverbed had dried out centuries before. The journey between the cliffs took them through the traces of fallen cities and immense, fading graveyards. There was no life at all. Bule had abandoned a realm bursting with the gifts of Nurgle's garden for a wasteland. No disease could flourish here. There was nothing here to decay. There was only the slow erosion of wind, and the fading into a greater silence. The groans of this realm's flesh had been spent long ago.

But this was the way. The call of Archaon was as clear to Bule now as it had been mysterious before. The land held no promise, yet Bule followed the certainty of destiny.

'We are where we must be,' he said. 'I have not brought us here. Archaon has. The blessing of Grandfather Nurgle has. There is no reason for anger, Fistula. Rejoice instead, and learn patience.' Fistula fought well, but he had too little experience of the larger ebb and flow of war. Plague waxed and waned, but in the end, it consumed all. To deny this was to fail to understand the nature of disease. Rage was useful, but had its limitations.

Bule's exhortation had little effect. The blisters on Fistula's bald head crowded each other with suppurating anger. Bule watched Fistula's grip tighten on his blades. He gauged the other Rotbringer's stance. Are you going to attack? Bule wondered. He followed his own counsel and remained patient. His armour was heavier than Fistula's. He had the advantage of bulk. He could absorb a first blow. But there was no need to precipitate a struggle; ahead lay glory for all. He would lead by example.

'You don't hear the call?' Bule asked.

'No.' More anger in that single word.

'Then put your faith in the path we have followed.'

'From one retreat to another?'

'The call I heed led us to that gate. Now it takes us to a culmination.'

Fistula grunted, but he plodded on. Bule looked back over the rest of the band. It was a much smaller horde now, consisting of only those who had followed him into the polluted river to find the gate beneath the foundations of the humans' temple. The newly constructed symbol that rejected Nurgle's gifts had concealed in its heart a cancer: the key to a greater victory. The loss of the rest of the warband, abandoned to the Stormcasts, had been a small price. Patience would see the coming of a greater bloom; of this, Bule was sure. Did the rest of his warriors share this certainty? Did they have faith, or did they doubt like Fistula?

He pushed the question aside. Though the canyon stretched onward, twisting in its grey death, the summons was clear to him. The flies that birthed from his head and swarmed about him buzzed with greater intensity. Faith would soon no longer be necessary. It would give way to proof.

If not around the next bend, then the one after that. The march through desolation would end soon.

Bule lengthened his stride. His gut bounced and roiled with his steps. Putrid gases rose from the rotting sores in his flesh. The garden was alive in him, and he would see it flourish in service to Archaon.

There were too many silences. Some were offensive to Ushkar Mir. Others were dangerous.

The snarl of his breath tried to fill the silence of the land. The absence of blood and fire was a frustration so intense it was agony. He saw bones. He saw skulls. But they were old, meaningless. They crumbled to nothing beneath his steps, giving off puffs of grey dust. There was no war here. If there had been violence once, even its memory was buried in stone. The emptiness of the canyon and the emptiness of the days: these were the silences that offended the exalted deathbringer.

It was the silence of Danavan Vuul that was a potential threat. The bloodstoker had said nothing for many hours now. With each day that had passed since Mir's last trial, each day absent of any foe, each long day in the empty land, Vuul had said less. They were still in the Realm of Death. The longer the march had gone on through this cursed canyon, the more Vuul's silence had expressed his doubts about the direction the Bloodslaves were taking. His face was hidden by his helmet. In his heavy crimson armour, he marched with a steady gait, leaning forward as if ready to break into a charge. Ushkar Mir monitored his every step out of the corner of his eye. He was braced for an attack. He contemplated killing Vuul, terminating the threat before it declared itself. He would have already done so were it not for the call. Archaon's summons pulled him forward. He would find the Everchosen here, and soon. There *was* battle in this realm, and Archaon was at its forefront. The scent of war and bloodshed had brought him this far. It was immaterial whether the rest of the warband felt the summons too. Destiny was close, and the moment was coming when there would be an enemy to shatter.

Mir stayed his hand. In so doing, he surprised himself. Regardless of Vuul's anger, his ambition was obvious and dangerous. He resented Mir's status as one of the Exalted. He made no secret of that, and obeyed orders with grudging reluctance. Two days ago, Mir would have treated the prospect of a prolonged period without a foe as intolerable. He would have assumed Vuul would move against him. He would have killed Vuul at the first opportunity.

Now he didn't. For perhaps the first time in his life, another goal superseded self-preservation. The greatest need to was to find Archaon, and to become his champion. To achieve that goal would make him stronger yet, ensuring his survival and perhaps the immortality of his name. But now he wondered if perhaps he was reaching for something even greater than that. To fight alongside a being who refused to be the vassal of any single god would be a personal victory beyond any other. The brass band over his eyes burned his flesh. The endless pain of the metal and the miracle of his continued sight were perpetual reminders of his unwilling allegiance. Khorne owned him. His existence was devoted to the reaping of skulls for the Blood God, and so it would ever be.

Until he could achieve his vengeance.

But to be a champion of Archaon, to be among the number who fought for Chaos under the banner of the warrior who was a force unto himself – there would be pride in that achievement. There was no such thing as redemption. The concept was meaningless. He had witnessed the immolation of all such hope. He would grasp instead the chance to shed blood no longer for the sole benefit of Khorne.

The prospect of soon standing before Archaon subsumed all other thought and so he kept his eye on Vuul, but he did not instigate the duel. He had no patience for such a pointless delay. Even his axes were eager to reach their destination: Bloodspite, black as old blood, and Skullthief, red as a fresh arterial fountain, each containing a bloodletter daemon. The perpetual rivals for greater slaughter vibrated with their hunger, and they pulled him forwards. They too wished to fight for Archaon. Let Vuul stew in impotent rage. Let him witness the truth.

The canyon took another turn and beyond it, revelation unfolded. It opened up into a vast bowl, with a second entrance to the west. A great host lined the top of the north wall, but from the floor of the arena, he could not judge its full size. It extended along the entire wall of the arena, and he could hear the clamour of ranks upon ranks. Black smoke rose in the distance, and from somewhere in that direction came the screams and moans of prisoners.

Mir had never beheld such an army before. He saw exalted deathbringers and skullgrinders. He saw a warrior in huge and terrible crimson armour, a warrior who could only be a Lord of Khorne. And these powerful servants of the Blood God stood beside those sworn to the Plaguefather, and the Changer of Ways, and the lost God of Excess. Vuul even saw the tall, angular shape of one of the Great Horned Rat's corruptors. The most powerful knights of Chaos in all its forms were gathered in a unity Mir could barely comprehend. They looked down upon him and they waited, for they did not command.

They followed a being greater than all of them.

'I never imagined...' said the slaughterpriest Orto. He who had been so confident in his preaching of Khorne's will was at a loss.

You serve Khorne utterly, Mir thought. This army serves Archaon. You knew this was our goal. But you never imagined? Is your faith inflexible, slaughterpriest? Can it not survive paradox?

Below the host, a stone staircase descended to the floor of the arena. The staircase was huge. Its width took up half the cliff. It was badly eroded. It had become a majestic ghost.

A narrow spur projected far into the air from the centre of the north wall. On it stood a towering figure in black armour.

Archaon.

And at the sight of that being, that supreme warrior of Chaos, Mir too thought, I never imagined.

The Everchosen spoke.

Bule guessed what he would say. The lord of plagues saw the other warband enter the arena at the same time as his. Even though Bule knew the test that lay ahead, Archaon's words rooted him to the spot. The voice, terrible in power, echoed across the arena. It was more than the voice of destiny. It was the voice of a being who had made destiny his slave.

'Champions,' Archaon said, 'I welcome you to the Ossuar Arena. You have fought well. Now you are at the end of a journey. One will be found worthy to join my Varanguard. One.' Archaon paused. His great horned helm tilted downward. He was gazing at the two warbands.

'You will exact your own judgement,' he said.

Across the line of the Everchosen's warriors, war horns lifted. The arena resounded with the deafening blast of the call to war.

The air trembled and cracked. The moment had come for the act of killing to return to this corner of the dead lands.

At the signal, Bule turned his gaze from Archaon and signalled to his warband. They began a rolling charge across the arena. The enemy was clad in armour the colour of blood and fire. Warriors of Khorne. He focused on their leader. Hundreds of yards separated the two forces, and Bule could make out few details of his rival. He was easy to identify, though, as he led his attack, fronting the warband's collective howl of rage. In contrast to his followers, he wore no armour. A brass band covered his eyes. It gleamed, though no sun pierced the heavy clouds. His flesh was marked with burning runes. He was already outpacing the rest of his band. He was fast. Faster than Fistula.

The Bloodbound were a real threat. No matter. Here, at last, was the destiny that had guided Bule through three realms. No one would stand between him and his apotheosis. He would strike this pretender down, and, at Archaon's side, he would see the Grandfather's garden flourish as never before.

Bule answered the snarl of the Bloodbound with his own roar. He revelled in its wet ratcheting. It was the sound of disease at war. He would drown the rage-possessed in the joyous flood of pestilence.

Behind him, his Rotbringers joined in his call.

Plague rushed forward to clash with Blood.

Then, from the skies, came a storm of wings.

There was his challenge. The putrid worshippers of Nurgle. Their charge made Mir snarl with disgusted rage. Their gait was a shambling rush. Their stench washed through the air in waves. Their blood would be a polluted stew. Khorne cares not from whence the blood flows, he thought. Nor does he care for its purity, as long as it flows.

The Rotbringers were one more threat to his survival. He would tear them apart, and he would join Archaon.

He ran across the uneven floor of the arena, leaping over empty tombs and crumbled walls. As he did, he saw movement on the spur of rock. He looked up. Archaon had stepped back. A daemon moved to take his place at the end of the spur. It was a thing of skeletal majesty. Mir could feel its manifold gaze burning down on him from a hundred angles at once. The daemon spread its arms wide. A flapping cloud came into being around the daemon. It spread and swooped down into the arena, bringing winged night with it.

It was a gigantic murder of crows. Thousands upon thousands of the birds. They cawed and whirled. They were everywhere. They covered the space of the arena. And as they beat their wings and gave voice to their raucous song, the land began to change.

The ground rippled. It dipped and rose, transforming into hills and gullies. Stone became malleable. It turned into a liquid, then smoke. It lost its form. Barrenness gave way to convulsive life. Naked stone became muck. Mir's boots sank past his ankle. Clouds of insects descended on him. Trees speared out of the mud. They unfolded branches heavy with rotting leaves. Growths twisted the limbs, and from them, things squirmed to be free, worms with pale, grasping hands. The trees reached out to each other, and the worm-things clasped and clawed across the growths, and a tangle of wood, soft, rotten, yet resilient, surrounded the warband. Blackened vegetation flowed around their legs. It was a rising tide of dying mulch. It fell apart, blossomed, sickened and died, then rose from its own decay in the space of a breath.

Mir could no longer see the enemy. The Rotbringers had vanished behind the wall of embodied putrescence. The crows

dived through the canopy. They perched on branches and circled above the warband. Some of the birds were rotting as they
flew. Others were on fire. They all had too many eyes. They
cawed their mockery. Mir slashed at them and at the vegetation blocking his way forward. His advance slowed to a crawl.

'You have turned Khorne against us!' Orto shouted. 'Archaon
favours the followers of Nurgle.'

'Are you already defeated?' Skull answered. In the blood
warrior's words, Mir heard his own thoughts given voice.
Khorne had rendered him mute, but Skull always spoke for
him. Skull, whose loyalty was so unshakeable, it had to be a
form of enslavement. 'Do you abandon your duty to the Blood
God?' Skull demanded.

Vuul answered before Orto. 'The transgression is Mir's, not
ours,' he snarled. To Mir he said, 'We followed you and this
is our reward.'

Mir swung his axes. Branches fell, burning at their touch.
I will have your silence and your effort, or I will have your
head, he thought.

Skull said, 'The enemy is close, and Ushkar Mir will not let
a few trees stand between us and their skulls.'

Mir paused and faced Vuul. He parted his jaws, his teeth
ready to tear flesh. He felt Vuul's gaze on his face. There were
no eyes for the bloodstoker to see, but Mir knew his band of
brass blazed in the foetid shadows of the forest. Vuul hesitated,
then, with a snarl, he turned back to hacking at the growths.

Vines tangled around Mir's arms. He tore the lanyards
apart. Spores burst from the ragged ends. The air thickened
and sought to choke him. He spat it out and forced his way
through the wall of rot. With each slowed step, his anger grew,
and the forest began to shrivel at his touch.

He moved faster, a vector of wrath burning through the

woods. He still could not see the Rotbringers. Nor could he hear them. He could barely hear his own troops over the shrieking of the birds. The stench of putrescence drowned out the scent of his prey's blood.

No matter. He drove forward. If he did not reach the foes himself, the foes would come to him. And his rage would reap the harvest of their skulls.

The land erupted with violent death. Rivers of flaming blood ran between hills of skulls. Through the darkness of the crows' wings, everything was the red of fire and the crimson of gore. Bule had been running across a barren plain, and then it had heaved skyward, stone transforming into bones soaked in blood, steaming and burning. Bule struggled up the slope. Skulls and femurs rolled and shifted. The ground tried to swallow his legs in avalanches of remains.

The Rotbringers reached the top of the rise. The walls of the arena had vanished. Bones, blood and flame stretched out to burning horizons in every direction. Overhead, the crows wheeled. Their many eyes glittered and judged.

'We are abandoned,' Fistula said.

There could be no garden here. There was no life. Only the perpetuity of pyres and the scarlet flow of rage.

'We are challenged.' Bule said. He would not despair, though the omen of the transformation was an ill one. Let it be a further trial, then, another means by which he would prove himself worthy of serving Archaon, and of the blessings of Grandfather Nurgle.

'Look,' he said, pointing, 'we have an opportunity.'

The Bloodbound were further away than they had been before the land had transformed. The wall of the arena had vanished, and the battlefield was infinite. Still, the Khornate warriors were on the same heading. There was something odd about their advance. They moved more slowly than Bule had expected. Their gestures were strange. They were slashing at the air as if battling invisible enemies.

'What are they doing?' Fistula wondered.

'I don't care, as long as it does them no good.' Bule thought for a moment. The Bloodbound warband looked strong. Whatever the confusion of the warriors' gestures, they were striking forward with the coherence and force of a battering ram. Bule had little doubt that a head-on collision would go against him. That would be playing to the strengths of the wrathful. Neither band was very large. The possibilities for manoeuvring were few. But they still existed.

'Embrace the enemy with the generosity of Grandfather,' Bule ordered. He would take advantage of the Bloodbound's apparent distraction. 'Advance to meet them, encourage their charge, then split up and hit their flanks.'

Fistula nodded. Of course he's pleased, Bule thought. He will lead half our band.

It was a risk, but one he saw no way to avoid.

Bule resumed the charge. He bellowed and stormed down the hill of bones. The footing was treacherous. He stomped hard on the shifting bones, shattering them, splashing through rivulets of blood, imposing his bulk on the burning land. The distance between the two bands narrowed. Though both struggled, it seemed as if the field were contracting once more. The crows called their excitement as the champions hurled towards each other.

We're closing too fast, Bule thought.

There was nothing but the forest, nothing but the black, viscous, rotting density of the vegetation. Mir heard the Rotbringers, but could not see them. The sound of their tramping was muffled by the vegetation. There was no way to gauge their distance.

And then the forest fell away, shrivelling and burning at his touch, and the Rotbringers were before him. He roared. His hatred fuelled by frustration, he shot forward, axes raised. They screamed their hunger. The warrior at the Rotbringers' head was huge, a festering mass of muscle and bulk. The spikes of his armour squirmed with rotting meat. His helmet was featureless except for a down-curving horn and a cluster of three eye-shaped holes. Mir saw in the design the idiot implacability of an insect, and his jaws parted in anticipation of the foe's blood.

The Rotbringer was faster than he looked. He took a step back and pivoted to the right. Mir's momentum carried him forward, too powerful to alter course. Skullthief slashed into the Rotbringer's torso. Dark, stinking blood erupted into the air, boiling from the strike. The axe blade scraped against ribs. The Rotbringer shouted in pain, but kept moving, pulling free of Skullthief. Behind him, a second warrior, lighter in build and armour, broke left. He was very fast. He escaped harm. The knight coming up behind him was not as lucky. Mir brought his two blades together. The daemons within, as frustrated and raging as he, bit deep into the rotting, rusted armour. The double sweep slashed through flesh and bone. The knight's head flew off. Blood fountained over Mir. It was thick with parasites. He snarled and batted the slumping corpse aside and the head rolled into the muck and vegetation. The plants rotted to nothing, as if the touch of the dead plague-bringer broke their hold on reality and they withdrew before the greater force of wrath.

Behind the fallen knight, a trio of marauders hurled themselves at Mir. They hacked at him with blades dripping with filth. The edges of his wounds turned black. The pain squirmed.

He roared. Rage turned his vision red. It burned his veins clear of the infections. He brought Bloodspite down on one marauder's skull, splitting it in two. Skullthief took another's sword arm off at the shoulder. The wounded Rotbringer howled but pushed in closer, his rotten blood washing over Mir. Insects and worms tried to burrow through the brass. They succeeded in smearing his vision. Behind him, the rest of his band pushed forward.

But as he swiped the slime from his face, he saw that most of the Rotbringers had moved out to the left and right, flanking his warriors.

The wound burned. Not with the generous malignancy of Grandfather Nurgle's munificence. It burned with a destroying fire, one that put the torch to the beauty of decay and left nothing but bone and ash. Bule hissed. His breath was pained and angry. The Bloodbound had hit so hard, so fast. Bule had seen them coming. He should have been able to judge when to move out of the way. But the distances in the battlefield were fluid, treacherous. He could not trust them. Fistula was right – there would be no blessings to look for from Nurgle. Everything was up to Bule. He would not find the garden in this landscape of skulls. It would be up to him to bring it here by fertilizing the ground with the blood of the wrathful.

Reeling from the blow of the Bloodbound champion, he moved in an arc away from the enemy horde. He glanced back. Just over a third of his knights followed him. The marauders took the brunt of the Bloodbound charge. They would be dead in moments. That was all the time he needed. On the other side of the enemy, Fistula kept pace with another third of the warband, mirroring his manoeuvre. The Khornate fighters smashed through the Rotbringers that stood in their way.

That's right, Bule thought. You have broken us in two. Hold that belief.

He angled back in, ploughing through the bones, splashing through blood, bringing the weight and disease of his troops against the rear flank of the Bloodbound. The enemy turned, eager in rage to meet the challenge. But the ragged line was narrow. A concentrated wedge of Rotbringers hit it from both sides. Plague-ridden Chaos knights clashed with Khornate ones. Rotting armour and slimy, rusting blades met iron glowing red with the forge of anger. Barbarians in joyous states of decay fought counterparts whose faces were frozen in a rictus of perpetual wrath. Bule raised his battle axe. A green miasma spread out from it. The air itself sickened. Some of the foe began to stumble even before he made contact. One doubled over, choking with violent, rib-shattering coughs. His lungs, already half dissolved, pushed out through his straining jaw.

Bule brought his axe down. The pain in his chest faded into the background as the blade smashed down through a skull-reaper's shoulder and halfway down the torso. The warrior's face screamed with hatred and pain. He struck at Bule with his other arm, wielding a sword the length of a man. It bled its own ichor. The blow struck just above Bule's pauldron. The skullreaper had been aiming for his neck, but was weakening from more than loss of blood. The axe's venom was running rampant through his body. Anger was impotent against the surge of transformative decay. Bule absorbed the blow and hit the skullreaper again in the other arm. The Bloodbound fell. Bule stepped over the still-breathing body. Where the blood of the Khornate warriors flowed, the land cooled. The low flames that flowed like oil over the mounds of skulls dampened. The bones crumbled into mulch. Shoots burst from the ground, pendulous with growths.

'Break the hold of wrath!' Bule shouted. 'Let the garden flourish in victory!'

To his right, he heard a snarl so fanatical in its rage it withered the sprouting vegetation.

Mir decapitated another marauder and turned back in time to see the rear half of the warband caught in a vice. Where the Rotbringers attacked, the diseased vegetation exploded with a new exuberance of rotting life. Vines and branches rose in tangled exultation towards the sky of crows.

He snarled at Vuul. The bloodstoker was fighting at his shoulder, flaying a Rotbringer knight with his great whip.

'Why are you here?' Skull said to Vuul. 'Lord Mir commands you go back up the line. Hold the centre.'

'And you?' said Vuul, challenging.

'*Do it.*'

There was a single moment's hesitation. Had there been a second, Mir would have attacked. But Vuul turned and saw the imminent collapse. The triumph of the enemy was too hateful to be borne. He raced down into the thick of the fray.

Mir killed the last of the Rotbringers at his position. The blood warriors around him paused, uncertain. They were poised to lend support to Vuul and push back the enemy attack. Mir shook his head. He gestured with Bloodspite. *With me.* Skull, the skullgrinder Kordos and the rest of the leading warriors followed as he turned right, off the clearing forged by the battle, plunging back into the festering green. He knew exactly where the Rotbringers were now. He would use the obscurity of the foliage against them. He would even turn their own manoeuvre against them. He would smash their illusions of strength. They flanked us, he thought. Now we flank them.

He wanted the skull of the Rotbringer champion. Killing him

meant more than achieving the task set by Archaon. It meant more than destroying the principle threat. Skullthief had tasted the champion's blood, and it was hungry for more. Bloodspite, envious, sought to steal its twin's kill. Mir shared their hunger and their frustration. The Rotbringer should already be dead at his feet. The absence of the corpse was an insult.

The forest was thick with disease and insects. Almost immediately, Mir's sight was reduced to a few steps in front of him. All directions were the same. The sounds of the struggle were too close to muffle now, though. He knew where he was going. Nurgle's profusion would do nothing now to impede the path of rage.

He slashed through vegetation. It barely slowed him. He moved in a fated arc. There was no doubt, no confusion. He came in behind the lord of plague's contingent. Around the struggle, the land was in flux. Vegetation burned and fell away, revealing a terrain of skulls. Blood flowed between the bones, turned black, and fertilized the ground. Growths and flame blossomed, the marks of the gods battling each other for supremacy with the same fury as the warriors. The Rotbringers had their backs to Mir. He could catch them in their own trap, crushing this part of the horde with greater numbers, then annihilating the other.

On the point of beginning the attack, Mir stopped. He raised his right arm, calling a halt.

'Why do we stop?' Kordos asked. It took much to move the skullgrinder to speak. His confusion must have been great. Since when did the Bloodslaves stop mid-charge?

'Why do you question Lord Mir?' asked Skull.

Kordos didn't answer. Mir turned his head in Kordos' direction for a moment, letting the skullgrinder know he had Mir's attention. Then he faced forward again.

Vuul was fighting with ferocious skill. The Rotbringers attacked on two fronts, but the bloodstoker held them off. His whip and torture blade were blurs. His voice rose in a howl of thirst. He took the skulls of the enemy in a frenzy of blows. He cut through the Rotbringers as though they were no more of an obstacle than the forest. He was a towering storm of wrath.

Archaon had said there could be only one champion.

Mir had understood what that meant, but he had pushed the consequences aside until now. The priority was the defeat of the Rotbringers. Afterwards, he would deal with any of his warband still standing. But now, as he saw Vuul fight, his priorities changed. Vuul was fighting too well. His rage was fuelled by desperation and ambition. He understood the import of Archaon's words too. Vuul sought to become the Varanguard.

Skull and the others with Mir obeyed when he signalled them to stop. Did they realize what he was doing and why? Did they understand what awaited them? Or were they too blinded by their dedication to Khorne? Perhaps they thought no further than the next kill, the next skull. Perhaps they dared not think any further. Certainly they dared not challenge him. To do so would be to invite the end of their lives even sooner.

So they obeyed. Even Kordos. They stopped. And with Mir, they waited.

Vuul fought through the violent roil of battle to reach the lord of plagues. Fire clashed with thick green fog. There were too many warriors in the way. Mir watched another Rotbringer, a blightlord, close in on Vuul. He was lightly armoured. He was fast. His lips were pulled back in a snarling rictus. His body was riddled with sores, but his rage was so great that it rivalled that of the Bloodbound he cut down.

Vuul sensed the approach of the blightlord and turned to meet him. The bloodstoker blocked a dual-bladed attack with the hilt of his blade. The Rotbringer stepped back, pulling his swords away. He feinted forward as Vuul lashed out with the whip, aiming at his neck. It was a trap, and Vuul fell into it. The blightlord took another step back. The whip went wide. The blightlord tangled it with one of his swords and yanked. Vuul stumbled forward. The blightlord came in and brought his other blade down on the bloodstoker's right upper arm. The sword cut deep, slicing through armour, flesh and bone. The arm hung limp, swinging on the end of a flap of skin. His whip fell to the ground.

Vuul's wrath gave him speed. He still had his torture blade. He stabbed forward. 'Behold your champion, Everchosen!' he cried. The Rotbringer sidestepped. The blade glanced off his torso, hacking away a chunk of flesh. It was not enough to slow the blightlord down.

Archaon sees nothing in you, Danavan Vuul, Mir thought.

The blightlord brought his right blade up, into Vuul's forward momentum, and used the bloodstoker's mass to ram the tip through the left eye-slit of his helm. Vuul stiffened. His war cry turned into a stuttering, wordless howl. Then it stopped. His knees buckled. The blightlord yanked his blade free, and blood gushed forth. On contact with the air, it turned into a black froth. Tumorous fronds unfurled to embrace his corpse.

The blightlord moved forward, leading his forces through the few Bloodbound that separated him from joining up with his chieftain. One of them was Orto.

'Blood for the Blood God!' the slaughterpriest shouted. 'Skulls for the Skull Throne!'

His zeal was unbroken. Mir knew that the Orto had found his path – he too understood how the contest must end, and he welcomed that meaning. He kept to the simplicity of fidelity to Khorne. He fought for the Blood God, and only the Blood

God, to the end. He swung his bloodbathed axe with a speed that defied its size. The heads of rotted knights and barbarians flew in its wake. But there were too many, and the blightlord drove his blades into Orto's back.

Mir roared. *Now!* His game was over. His rivals were falling. Time to finish off the others. He ran forward, blood boiling with the taste of victory.

Bule saw Fistula kill the bloodstoker. A few moments later, as the two groups of Rotbringers made contact, crushing the remaining Bloodbound between them, he heard the roar of the Bloodbound champion. The flames shot higher with the Khornate charge. Blood geysers erupted on either side of the warriors' path.

Bule had seconds before the impact. There would be no evasion this time. The Bloodbound had been slow to arrive, though. The Rotbringers now had the numerical advantage.

But Bule turned away from the enemy. He had seen Fistula kill the slaughterpriest.

He had seen the skill, the speed and the rage. The skill and the speed were threats. The rage was an opportunity he must seize.

'Fistula betrays us!' he shouted. 'He is apostate! Look how he abandons Nurgle for Khorne!'

Fistula blinked in astonishment, his blades deep in the corpse of a blood warrior. His battle rage gave way to blank surprise, and then returned, greater than ever, as he realized what Bule was doing. He snarled, freeing the swords, and played right into Bule's hands. The violet blotching of his face and the contorted tendons of his neck were clear for all to see. He had always been the impatient warrior. His faith in Nurgle had been a crusading one, but only in the sense of the destruction of the Plaguefather's enemies. He had shown little interest in the cultivation of the garden.

Now his anger doomed him.

Bule hurled the accusation. The Rotbringers heard and saw Fistula's reaction. And Bule acted. He did so without pleasure. He swung his axe because he must, because only he could be Archaon's champion, and Fistula's visible wrath meant this was the moment his apostasy was plausible, and there was no chance Fistula could turn the warband against Bule.

He also swung the axe with conviction. Fistula's rage *was* suspect. Bule *believed* the blightlord was a threat to the garden.

Even taken by surprise, Fistula's reactions were fast. He swiped a blade across Bule's torso. He tore the wound left by the Bloodbound champion wider and left a new furrow, dragging down deep into Bule's gut. The filth on the blade reacted with the filth in Bule's blood. Strains of plague did battle. Bule welcomed the conflict. It could only bear fruit, wonderful and dark.

Bule accepted his injury, gave thanks to Nurgle for the violent spread of infection, and smashed the massive axe blade down on Fistula.

The blightlord managed to jerk his head out of the path of the blow at the last second. It did him little good. The axe shattered his chestplate. It shattered his sternum. It split him open. He flailed. His arms batted at the weapon buried in his body. Their movements were so loose, so independent of one another, it was as if Fistula's mind had been divided too, each half pulling at one set limbs.

Fistula staggered backwards, choking and gargling. Bule yanked the axe free and brought it down again. This time he smashed Fistula's skull. The blightlord collapsed, his body erupting with maggots and rot. Its shape softened. The flesh rippled, then crumbled. Blood spread over the land. Where vegetation had grown from the death of Bloodbound warriors, it burned at the touch of Fistula's blood.

'Behold his treachery!' Bule yelled, though his belief in his lie collapsed. Fistula's blood had the same effect as that of his brothers in disease. Bule shouted to keep the lie alive in the minds of his warband just a bit longer.

Then the Bloodbound champion was upon them, and Bule abandoned all thoughts of strategy. There was no deception, no forethought.

There was battle, and there was his faith in Grandfather Nurgle.

And that was all.

Mir led the charge into the Rotbringers, and Chaos embraced the conflict. The land heaved and bucked. It burned and flourished. It was bone, it was muck, it was brackish stream and it was flaming blood. The order of the warbands broke down at once. There were no longer enough warriors on either side to maintain coherence after the initial shock, and as the numbers fell, the significance of Archaon's words was felt by all. Mir embraced the disorder. From the moment he struck, from the moment Bloodspite and Skullthief began to feed, he saw only red. Every presence on the battlefield was a threat. The existence of any other being filled him with desperate rage. He waded in, killing any warrior within reach.

To Mir's right, Kordos laid waste to the plague warriors with the burning fist of his anvil. He fought in silence, he killed in silence, until the anvil buried itself in the corpulent body of one of his foes. The Rotbringer slumped, his corpse smouldering, and the collapsing mass held the brazen weapon for a moment. Kordos grunted in anger, and that was the last sound Mir heard from him. The rhythm of his blows was disrupted just long enough for the huge lord of plagues to attack his flank. Mir saw Kordos' death coming just as he cut down another barbarian. Two steps to the right and he could have joined Kordos, blocking the lord of plague's attack.

He stepped forward instead. He heard the axe blow. The shattering of armour and the rending of flesh. When he heard the axe hit again, he knew Kordos was dead.

Mir fought on, killing his way toward glory, each corpse another step toward vengeance.

The land mirrored the storm of the war. It rose and fell with greater violence, as if Bloodbound and Rotbringers fought on the heaving chest of a great beast. It burned and flourished. It was turbulence itself.

Mir kept his feet. He lost himself in murder and wrath. He howled in an ecstasy of rage. He filled the air with his hatred for his enemy, hatred for his rivals, hatred for the other Bloodbound, hatred for himself. And the air answered. A fresh storm broke. Thunder roared, and blood lashed down in torrents and vortices. It blinded. It filled lungs. It surrounded Mir in a perfection of violent death. It turned blades away. He was coated in the bloody manifestation of his hate.

Every warrior fought for his own survival. Mir no longer knew whom he was killing. Nothing mattered except that those who stood before him fell to his blades. His axes, maddened and drunk on gore, screamed for more. And the storm of blood battled with another tempest, one of pestilence. A diseased wind battered Mir. It shrieked in his ears. It forced itself into his lungs. It was hot with decay. Each breath took in a legion of parasites. He burned the sickness out with the fever of his hate, and then in it came again.

The threat made him more furious yet. He slashed as if

he would kill the air itself. He became part of the vortex of blood. Every blow was lethal. The death fountains of his enemies anointed him with victory and survival.

He saw no faces, only prey. Only shapes to be torn apart. Only skulls to be severed from their necks.

But then one spoke to him. One word, in the moment before the slavering Skullthief made the killing stroke. One word, in a voice so familiar, so in tune with his thoughts, that he had come to think of it almost as his own.

'Lord–' said Skull. Then Mir killed him.

He paused, suspended in his blood haze. He stared at the severed head of the blood warrior. Pale blue eyes in pale blue skin looked back at him with the final glimmers of life, and in them Mir saw not rage, but betrayal and grief.

What happened could not be helped. Only Mir could survive this war. Only Mir could be Archaon's champion.

But this was Skull, who in all the warband had displayed a loyalty that went beyond an alliance of convenience. A loyalty that Mir now recognized, too late, as the last thing of value, the last thing unconsumed by wrath, that he would ever know.

He was vaguely aware of replacing Skullthief on his belt and picking up the head. Then he fell into the crimson fire once more, and there was nothing else. He killed and he killed and he killed. He was incoherent with rage and self-loathing. The world fell into ruin. All was storm. All was chaos. All was blood.

No longer for the Blood God. Blood for himself.

Killing and killing and killing.

Blood and blood and blood.

And…

And then Bule was alone. Alone against the being of wrath.

The storm raged on. Flame and pestilence whirled around

him. The earth on which he stood shifted from loam to bone to blood to rock to all and none. There were bodies everywhere, rotting, burning and being devoured by the shifting land. The horizons had vanished. He and the Bloodbound champion faced each other in the midst of the collapse of all form.

The exalted deathbringer stood with an axe in one hand and a skull in the other. The head had been used as a weapon, and was a battered, smashed relic, but Bule could see it had been one of the Bloodbound, not a Rotbringer. The death-bringer looked at the skull with his head cocked, almost with regret.

How many of his own Rotbringers had Bule killed? He did not know. The answer did not matter. What mattered was the fulfilment of destiny. What mattered was to ascend to Archaon's side as a warrior of the Varanguard.

His mind cleared of battle frenzy. He braced himself for the charge of the deathbringer. Bule was no match for his speed. This warrior was faster and more powerful than Fistula. Bule could not evade. He would not get the first blow in, but he would, with the Plaguefather's blessing, get the last.

Against the quick, he had always used his great bulk. He won by being the hardest to kill.

The deathbringer dropped the skull and seized his other axe. He turned his maddened eyes to Bule and rushed in. He was a thing of crimson hate. His blades howled with him.

Bule braced for the impact. He stood with all the strength of a warrior for Grandfather Nurgle. He knew the fevers and the bodily erosion of a legion of diseases. They made him strong, for Nurgle valued the great resilience of life, and its ability to decay into ever more bounty, ever more life. Bule gathered the great endurance gifted to him by the Plaguefather. He would let fury spend itself against the bulwark of illness.

The deathbringer hit. He stabbed the axes low. He plunged both blades deep into Bule's exposed belly.

It was exposed because it was a trap. Bule's organs had long ago ceased to function in any mortal fashion. They were reservoirs of disease. His body was the carrier of pestilence. He was beyond the reach of ordinary weapons, no matter where they stabbed him. Time and again, foes had plunged their blades into his festering mass only to find their weapons stuck, and themselves left open to his counterblow.

This time was different. Wrath itself was upon him, with speed and fury and the frenzy of boiling blood. The deathbringer's axes had their own will. They were a higher order of death-dealer. They went too deep. They burned too profoundly. They severed something too important.

Bule felt himself come undone. The strength went out of his legs. He lost feeling in the lower half of his body. His knees must have buckled because he was sinking toward the ground, drawing the wounds even wider. The exalted deathbringer's face twisted into an expression of hate-filled triumph. The weakness spread up Bule's arms. He dropped his axe.

He had lost without landing a single blow.

No, he thought. Not like this. I will not fail you, Grandfather. I am still your gardener.

He held on to the most fundamental fact of his being. Death was coming to Bule, but *Bule* was just a name. He was a lord of plagues. To the end, this was his truth, and so he took all that he was, all the vast strengths bestowed upon him by Nurgle, the power that was more important than his axe, more important even than endurance, the essence that shaped his physical form into a poor mirror of its full reality. He became infection. As he fell, he reached out for the wounds on the Bloodbound champion's body. His arms were weak. His blow was glancing.

But infection needed only the slightest touch to take root. All it needed was a point of ingress. All it needed was blood.

Bule found the other champion's blood. And with the totality of his being, with the pure transmission of disease, he stole this blood from the Blood God.

The land became quiet. Fire, rot and bones became simple stone again. The empty wastes of the arena returned. The crows flew off, vanishing against the dark of the sky. The Rotbringer fell at Mir's feet. He spasmed and twitched, still alive but fading quickly. There was no need to strike again. Even so, Mir prepared to mark his triumph with the decapitation of his foe.

He tried to raise his arms.

He could not.

He staggered back from the body. Something crawled over his flesh and through his veins. He shook so hard that he lost control of his limbs. His lungs could not draw air. He was suffocating. His gasp was the sound of iron dragged across stone.

Mir wheeled away from the Rotbringer. The stairs of the arena seemed leagues away. But Archaon stood on the end of the rock spur once more. The Everchosen waited for his champion to climb up and claim his prize. Mir would climb.

Except he was on all fours. The tremors had him in their jaws. Cold and fever hit him in waves. Thick, bloody mucus poured from his nose and mouth. He crawled toward the stairs. They were too far, too far. Behind him, he heard the Rotbringer drag his carcass forward with slow, pitiful scrapes.

Mir gasped. Everchosen, he thought. The victory is mine. Free me of this pestilence. Induct me into the Varanguard. Heal me, he thought. Let me live.

'The final blow was mine,' said the Rotbringer, his words barely audible. 'Let me serve.'

Mir collapsed onto his stomach, racked by coughs. There was nothing either of them could do. Archaon knew who the victor was. He would raise that warrior up and save him.

Archaon's laughter rumbled across the arena. 'And thus do both exact judgement. Well done. On this day I witnessed more than a struggle between wrath and pestilence. You presented me with the contest between survival and fealty. It was instructive. And, for both of you, futile. I chose my champion before your arrival.'

No, Mir thought. His anger flared, but it could do nothing for him now. He watched Archaon walk away and out of his sight. Darkness fell over his eyes. In his last moments, he regarded the monstrosity of his years, and he recognized the fitting pointlessness of his end.

He thought he heard the laughter of crows.

The Many-Eyed Servant watched Mir and Bule die. And then it was done. He had witnessed every moment of the contest across the realms. He had looked through the eyes of insects and crows, and he had seen all there was to see. The compound tableau of vision was complete.

Except it wasn't. There were gaps. He had not seen through the eyes of the combatants themselves. Their thoughts were closed to him. So were Archaon's.

The Everchosen stopped up beside the sorcerer. 'More eyes, Gaunt Summoner,' Archaon said, in answer to an unasked question. 'I always need more eyes.' He gestured to the corpses below. 'They were blind. My champion is not. And it is time he assumed his duties. Return us to my fortress.'

'My lord,' said the Many-Eyed Servant. He moved his arms in eldritch signs. Mystic energies gathered around him and Archaon. They grew into a great pillar of fire. It rose to the heavens. And with a clap of implosive thunder, the cold arena vanished.

'Rise.'

Orphaeo Zuvius stood. He knew he was in the throne room. He was conscious of his body. It was healed, it was strong, and yet it retained a wound. His sight was odd. It was off-centre. He raised his fingers. He moved them toward his eyes, and when he did, his vision turned and he saw his own face from the perspective of his shoulder.

He was looking through Mallofax's eyes.

The blue daemon bird watched what Orphaeo needed him to see. A blue jewel sat in Orphaeo's right eye socket. A pink one occupied the left.

Orphaeo tilted his head back, and Mallofax looked up at Archaon. 'Why have you spared me?' Orphaeo asked.

'Spared you? I have made you my champion. And why? Because you have vision. Because you think to look and see where others race to pointless combat and die. You sought me here, not on the battlefield. For your trespass, I have punished you. For your vision, I have blessed you.'

'But you have stolen my sight.'

'Have I? Look further.'

Through Mallofax's eyes, Orphaeo examined his face again. He considered the jewels. Their facets. So many planes and angles. So many perspectives.

Of course.

With understanding came more sight. He saw as Mallofax, and he saw as the warriors under his command. He was in the fortress. He was outside its walls.

He was everywhere he would send his forces.

All the facets of the battlefield would be his.

'Do you see?' Archaon asked.

'I do, Everchosen. Oh, I do.'

'Then it is time to go to work, champion. I have wars for you to witness and to shape.'

SEE NO EVIL

Rob Sanders

The searing gaze of the Many-Eyed Servant travelled far. Nothing was beyond his regard. He could see an entire people put to the blade and moments later the cavernous emptiness in the heart of the man who had ordered such an atrocity. He saw what the Everchosen could not see, and went where the Everchosen could not be.

Archaon exercised his omnipotence through the black-hearted loyalty of those who were pledged to the Chaos gods. The realms were nothing without the mortal souls infesting them, and souls could be corrupted, bought and bartered. Those wretches already lost to the myriad corruptions of existence found deeper damnation in Archaon's fell ranks.

The Many-Eyed Servant peered through the storm of a land long sundered. A place the Everchosen's armies had conquered an age before. A haunted corner of the realms, empty of the people who had existed there – for either they had been assimilated into Archaon's conquering hordes, or their skulls now made up the bonemeal beaches of the shoreline.

The Many-Eyed Servant's gaze had passed across this dead place before. There he had seen something that he knew would anger his master and shake the realms with his fury. What the Gaunt Summoner saw was a land retaken by an enemy force. For now the darkness of these craggy fortifications had been scalded away by columns of lightning reaching down from the heavens. From these blazing conduits came the Stormcast Eternals. The God-King's weapons of war. Sigmar had been busy and so had the forges of the Celestial Realm, crafting immaculate plate, weaponry and souls to wield them.

The Stormcast Eternals appeared on a dead peninsula called Cape Desolation. They took the fortresses lining the hellish coast without raising a weapon, and had clear plans to expand their invasion. They would bring freedom to the people of the darkness beyond the peninsula – the Shatterlands – which the Everchosen had held in his crushing grip for a thousand years.

The Many-Eyed Servant whispered what he seen to his master.

'There is a light in the darkness, Exalted One.'

'Light is but a brightness of the moment,' the Everchosen said, his words burning on the air. 'The spark of flint. The strike of lightning. It passes. Darkness is forever.'

'This spark,' the Many-Eyed Servant said, 'has started a fire, my lord. A fire from the sky that threatens to rage through the Shatterlands and bring hope to peoples beyond. The God-King's warriors rain from the heavens and have made landfall. Our bastions along Cape Desolation are theirs.'

'Sigmar's warriors,' Archaon said, 'in the Shatterlands?' The Many-Eyed Servant heard both searing outrage and relish in his master's voice. 'Its people will come to know the exquisite torment of hope dashed and the terror of lights extinguished.

'Send word to my warlords, my champions and the fell kings of the surrounding regions. Summon my unholy Varanguard. I shall lead the Knights of Ruin myself in a counter invasion. Those bastions shall be mine again. The God-King's light shall be banished and his warriors shall flee for the skies. I want Sigmar to know that he will find no purchase in lands forever dedicated to the Chaos gods.'

Peering down through the tumultuous skies of the God-King's storm, the Many-Eyed Servant could see his master. Riding atop the monster Dorghar – an abominable creature of twin-tail, colossal wings and three terrible heads – Archaon led the way through the holy tempest. With his cloak streaming in the maelstrom and the Slayer of Kings held out in front of him, the Destroyer of Worlds rode out the storm at the head of his fleet.

A thousand dreadships coursing through the crash and squall of a spectral sea, all flying the flag of the Everchosen. The sea was a ghostly swarm of lost souls, the crash of waves and the hiss of the surf the sound of spiritual suffering.

Thrashing with their galley oars and with flayed-flesh sails full of sacrifice-bought winds, the armada surged on towards the black peninsula. Each ship carried hordes of Chaos warriors and Archaon's own Knights of Ruin – thousands of dark templars, clad in plate of black and gold, utterly committed to the Everchosen's service and the absolute destruction of his enemies. Among them was a worthy warrior the Many-Eyed Servant recognised from a past trial – the sorcerous warrior they called Orphaeo Zuvius, the Prince of Embers, now a knight in the Everchosen's service.

The Prince of Embers burned for battle.

Standing on the deck of the dreadship *Aftermath* – so named

for the death and destruction left in its blood-churned wake –
Orphaeo Zuvius felt the surge and drift of the vessel through
the spectral sea. Crafted from the torched wood of treelord
ancients that groaned their suffering still, the landing galley's
black prow cut through the ghostly seas. Riding the swell, he
looked to the flesh-sails, filled with the doom-laden winds that
took the Everchosen's armada on towards the skull beaches of
Cape Desolation. Bloodreavers scrambled up and down the
rigging of raw tendons while masts of braced bone creaked
with the weight of wind and sail.

Zuvius made his way across the deck. His plate was black
and gold and hell-forged to fit his slender frame. While one
pauldron bore the crafted symbol of Archaon, the other had a
metal spike. On the spike perched the familiar Mallofax, a reptilian bird of blue feather and black heart. It had been Mallofax
that had guided the Prince of Embers down his destined path
and into Archaon's dark service. The wind ruffled the intense
blue of the bird's plumage.

About the main mast the deck was crowded with warriors of
Chaos – Varanguard like Zuvius who had proved their worth
to the Everchosen. The bloodreaver crew gave such warriors
and their monstrous, armoured steeds a wide berth. The planks
smouldered where the hooves of the mounted Varanguard held
firm to the deck. The ruinous knights bled malevolence and,
despite the subtle differences in their appearance and the myriad blessings of their dark gods, all wore the black and gold of
their master. He was the Exalted Grand Marshal of the Apocalypse and they were his instruments of doom.

Zuvius mounted his own steed, Hellion. A muscular abomination that seemed mostly horse, Hellion blinked multiple dead
eyes that ran the length of its fang-filled snout. Horns erupted
from its malformed skull and its transparent hide revealed the

ghastly inner workings of the beast's grotesque body. Hellion's spiked hooves clopped across the deck. Zuvius' daemon-forged glaive A'cuitas sat in a saddle sheathe like a spear ready to be drawn in the charge.

Around the prince, warriors of the Varanguard were making preparations. Some were readying weapons and armour. Others were bringing their steeds to heel with vicious tugs on the reins. Some were even mumbling dark prayers to the Ruinous Pantheon, bidding the gods to grant them worthy foes and a merciless victory for their Everchosen.

Nearby, Zuvius saw fellow former acolyte of the Great Changer, Aspa Erezavant. Like him, the prince had forsaken his dread god in favour of service to Archaon. Through the Everchosen, Zuvius had pledged his soul, blade and talents to the unified forces of Chaos. Aspa Erezavant never spoke of such a pledge, however. The Varanguard warrior said nothing. He never did. There was only flesh where his mouth used to be.

Zorn the Brazenfleshed, however, always had something to say. A knight of dread threats and bombast, the Varanguard had once belonged to the Blood God. Now he commanded the *Aftermath* for the Everchosen, ensuring the vessel – in coordination with others cutting through the souls of the spectral sea – landed their Varanguard and meatshield hordes on the beach.

'By the fell gods,' Zorn roared through the storm at the ship's bloodreaver crew, 'if you don't get more flesh to the wind I'll flay your hides for extra sail!' He turned to a pair of bloodreavers attending to the rebellious tiller. 'Hold your course, damn you. And you,' the Varanguard warrior bellowed at a bloodstoker called Killian, 'get below decks. More power on the stroke. Take your lash to the oar crews. I want them sitting in a pool of their own blood. The Exalted Grand Marshal demands from them everything they have to give. Gods help the wretch who holds back his best from the Everchosen of Chaos!'

Zuvius watched the Varanguard warrior knock a passing bloodreaver brutally to the deck and then deliver a vicious kick with his armoured boot.

'Fetch my weapons and my steed!' Zorn roared at the unfortunate.

'The Everchosen watches,' Sarsael Hedra said. 'The Brazenfleshed bids to be first on the beach for our master'. The Varanguard slipped his helm down over the oily flesh of his handsome face. The warrior's words were slick with suggestion – insolence even. No one would actually level such an accusation at Hedra, however. He had killed too many in Archaon's name.

'I think he just might be,' Kadence Salivarr said, looking from the saddle out across the ghostly waves at the rest of the fleet. His eyes were bright within his twisted helm. Like Salivarr, Zuvius could see that the *Aftermath* was pulling ahead.

'Not if I get there first,' Sarsael Hedra said, pulling on the reins to line up his fell steed with the ship's prow. An armoured mountain of filth, Vomitus Grue, shook the deck with the boom of his laughter.

'The Everchosen watches,' said another Varanguard warrior through the ranks of mounted knights. Known as the Unslaked, his words were barbed much like his blood-stained blade. 'He sees all. He hears all. He hears the prattling of his warriors. Witless boasts to calm the nerve and steady the cowardly soul.'

The deck fell silent but for the clop of hooves and scolding tongue of Zorn the Brazenfleshed. The Prince of Embers moved Hellion around, edging the steed ahead of Sarsael Hedra's own. He licked his lips with a silver tongue.

'The Varanguard will see the dark will of the Everchosen

done,' Zuvius said, his voice assured and even. 'Each according to his gifts. We can all trust in that – as the Exalted Grand Marshal puts his trust in his Varanguard.'

Kadence Salivarr nodded his helm slowly at Zuvius. As the storm raged about them and the ship, that seemed to be the end of the matter. The dark templars waited. Waited to disembark, to take the beach and then the bastion beyond for their dark master. If every warrior of the Varanguard did their duty well, each fortress along Cape Desolation would be taken back in the Everchosen's name. The warriors of the God-King would be naught but the blot of an afterglow on the eye. The Shatterlands beyond the dark peninsula would belong stone and soul to the Chaos powers once more. The Varanguard about the Prince of Embers weren't wrong though. Archaon and his sorcerous servants would be watching. They always were. Orphaeo Zuvius aimed to give them a sight to see. The Prince of Embers would make it his honour to lead the warriors of the *Aftermath* in their charge up the beach, behind the Everchosen himself, who would ride on ahead and strike the first terrible blow.

As well as the unhallowed ranks of the Varanguard, the *Aftermath* carried a small horde of Chaos killers to help take their section of the beach and soak up enemy fire: hulking khorgoraths of the Red Death, Tzeentchian sorcerers of the Glass Spire, and spindle-limbed bloodletters of twisted horn and daemon wrath. The largest contingents were the indomitable plague-bloated warriors of the Rank and Vile, led by a sack of corruption called Bloatus Belch, and the Chaos knights of the Mazarine in their glowing blue plate, directed by a two-faced champion called Vitas and Volitae. Even the Fleshblessed, the Slaaneshi spawn shackled below decks, had their role to play in the battle to come. But they were all nothing to Archaon's chosen.

A bloodreaver walked past Zuvius with his eyes on the deck. He carried a crude spyglass in his hand for scanning their landing at the beach and the approach to their target fortress, called the Ebon Claw. Unlike Zorn the Brazenfleshed, Zuvius needed no glass. Isolated straggles of blue hair danced in the wind, while the remaining threads of his skin squirmed over the red raw flesh of his face. His silver tongue licked at scorch-smeared lips. The prince's crow-pecked sockets now contained jewels instead of eyes – sorcerous gemstones, one blue and one pink to honour his former patron. These eyes saw for Archaon now, the labyrinthine facets of the precious stones giving him unparalleled vision.

He could see the spectral sea lapping up along a beachhead of weathered skulls. He took in the Ebon Claw beyond, a craggy edifice of petrified, black stone. Its battlements were razored like flint, while its towers were jagged like the crooked fingers of a grasping talon. Across the phantasmic waves, Zuvius saw other dreadships of the Everchosen's armada, carrying knights like himself to take the Ebon Claw and all the other enemy-occupied forts along the coast of Cape Desolation.

Zorn had instructed the bloodstoker and his bloodreavers to keep the tiller trained on the lightning stream coursing down through the stormy skies into the Ebon Claw. It was just one of many pillars of searing power that carried the God-King's warriors and their reinforcements into the bastions that punctuated the peninsula coast.

The dreadships converged on the shoreline. Zuvius could feel the rancid excitement on the air. Below decks, the spawn of the Fleshblessed were whipped to an ecstasy while bloodreaver oarsmen surged the galley towards the beach. The oars of the *Aftermath* tangled with those of another closing dreadship. Every knight of Chaos in the fleet wanted to be the first to reach the beach and earn the approval of Archaon.

Peering down the coast, however, Zuvius saw that his unhallowed master was busy. He had already reached the peninsula on the back of his monstrous daemon steed. The beast flapped his giant wings and soared across the battlements. While most would flee before the sight of the Everchosen astride his monster as they might a city-razing dragon, Sigmar's Stormcast Eternals stood like golden statues: cold, implacable and unimpressed. As Dorghar banked, Archaon swept helms and heads from shoulders with the Slayer of Kings. Dorghar stove in towers with his lashing twin-tail and tore away sections of battlement with his great claws, sending Stormcasts raining to the ground.

'Pass the word,' Zorn the Brazenfleshed called down the length of the ship. 'Prepare to disembark and fight for your lives.'

Zuvius heard Bloatus Belch and the Tzeentchian Vitus and Volitae readying their warriors below decks. He knew that the Red Death would barely be able to contain their fury and that the predacious bloodletters would be hissing their anticipation of the kill. The Varanguard would go first, however, for there were no servants of Chaos worthier than Archaon's dark templars. And among the Varanguard ranks, there would be none as worthy as the Prince of Embers. Zuvius promised both himself and his Exalted Grand Marshal that.

'The honour is mine,' Zuvius hissed to himself. He worked Hellion around, lining the beast up for disembarkation. He could hear raised voices beyond.

'My lord...' Bloodstoker Killian said.

'Hold your damned course,' the Brazenfleshed spat. Zuvius looked down the coastline. Dreadships were taking in sail and stowing oars, coursing through the shallows the rest of the way to the shore. The *Aftermath* would not take such precautions on the approach. Zorn meant to hit the coastline at ramming speed and ride the galley as far up the skull beach as he could get.

As the vessel coursed through the shallows ahead of the armada, Zuvius saw bloodreavers wind their arms and legs about the rigging. The Chaos warriors below the decks began to chant their bloody expectation, while the ruinous knights settled into their saddles and stirrups, ready to follow the Prince of Embers.

'For the Everchosen,' Zuvius roared, kicking his heels into Hellion's flanks. It was as much a challenge as an announcement. 'May he and all who follow in his shadow know absolute victory this dark day.'

Standing up in the stirrups, Zuvius urged his steed down the length of the ship. With the steed's spiked shoes tearing up the deck, the unnaturally swift and strong beast hit a gallop by the time it passed the mast. Dread knights of Chaos watched the prince thunder by, readying their own steeds for impact. Even on Hellion, Zuvius felt the *Aftermath* shudder as the vessel's keel bit into bonemeal and then the shattered skulls of the beach. He readied himself for the inevitable. In the contest between the galley and the land, the land would eventually win.

The prince's timing was perfect. The *Aftermath* had rammed its way out of the shallows and cut into the skull beach. As the vessel ground to an abrupt stop, the mast let out an excruciating creak and the flesh-sails billowed the other way. Steeds stumbled and bloodreavers were thrown from the rigging. Hellion made his jump just as the full force of the impact struck. Clearing the bulwark, the monstrous steed soared across the skulls. Hitting the beach of shattered bone at a gallop, Zuvius slipped the glaive A'cuitas from its sheath and spun it in his gauntlet. His exalted master had been the first to achieve an enemy kill on the cape. Zuvius would be the second. At his side, keeping pace with the monstrous steed, flew Mallofax.

'Find me a way in,' Zuvius said. The bird squawked an acknowledgement before taking to higher altitudes. Looking back, Zuvius saw that only now the other dreadships were slowing in the shallows and lowering their ladders for disembarkation. The *Aftermath*, however, with her keel torn out and hull well and truly beached, was disgorging her fell cargo. Inspired by the prince's example, the knights of Archaon's chosen had followed Zuvius and were riding up behind like a tidal wave of blade, plate and doom.

The khorgoraths of the Red Death hadn't waited for bloodreavers to open the vessel's fang-lined boarding-maws. The monstrous creatures of red flesh and fury had smashed their way through the hull and were lumbering up the beach towards the enemy. While the Fleshblessed spawn were unleashed upon the beach and made their mindless approach at unnatural speed, Bloatus Belch and the two-faced Tzeentchian exited the vessel through the holes the khorgoraths had left behind. They led their warriors past the sorcerers of the Glass Spire and out onto the bonemeal. Bloodstoker Killian cracked his whip and blew a horn, prompting the *Aftermath*'s bloodreaver crew to grab their blades and leave the ship.

Racing towards the Ebon Claw, Zuvius could see the golden shapes of the Stormcast Eternals. The God-King's warriors had been busy. The black talon of petrified stone was now but a derelict shell. Like the petals of a dead flower, the sharp walls and cragged towers of the fort had given way to new fortifications built within the ruins. About the column of lightning streaming down, new and glorious fortifications had sprung up – domed citadels of silver and gold. Immaculate structures of globed indomitability, at odds with the petrified jaggedness of the surrounding fortifications. It was as though the Ebon Claw suffered some kind of taintless cancer, with towers of metal, light and storm blooming amongst the twisted architecture of the malefic bastion.

Zuvius read the enemy's defence of the fortress. Archers in glorious plate and their watching lords took position on razor-sharp battlements and looked down on the beach approach through crooked arrow slits. Meanwhile, destroyers in burnished plate collapsed the fortress gateway, turning the entrance into a barricade of smashed rubble with earth-shaking blows from their crackling hammers. Atop towers and derelict ramparts, Stormcasts waited for the Chaos invaders with glaives and great shields, their impassive stillness an invitation to death.

Suddenly everything was gold and bone. Zuvius resisted the urge to haul upon the reins as the beach exploded before him. Hitting the ground and throwing skulls and bone shards into the air with the force of their landing were the warrior-heralds of the God-King. Launching from the walls of the Ebon Claw, armoured warriors had flown down to the shoreline, dropping with the force of a meteorite shower crashing to the ground. Their wings were a spread of lightning blades whilst they clutched a pair of ornate hammers in their gauntleted hands.

Zuvius would not be stopped. Urging Hellion on into the warrior heralds, the prince extended A'cuitas out in front of him like a spear. Zuvius crashed into his foes.

The knight's glaive punctured its way through a faceplate, impaling the skull of a landing herald. The Prince of Embers allowed himself a flesh-smeared smile. As the weapon skewered the head clean off the armoured warrior, Hellion rammed his horn straight through the breastplate of another and tossed the enemy aside. With the death of each Stormcast, soul-lightning leapt for the sky with a satisfying crack and flash. Battering another Stormcast aside, Hellion turned the warrior into a staggering mess of celestial plate. Allowing the glaive shaft to slide forward in his grasp, Zuvius smashed the heavy metal pommel of the weapon down through the herald's helm. Braining the warrior with the bulbous counterweight, Zuvius saw another flash of lightning rocket up to the heavens.

Thundering through the heralds' freshly landed ranks, Zuvius heaved on the reins and turned Hellion about. He would ride them down from behind, pounding their plate into the skull beach with his mount's hooves.

The warrior-heralds had recovered quickly, however. Having turned to receive the knight's attack, they threw their celestial hammers head over haft at Zuvius. It was all he could do to lean out of their pulverising path. As one smashed his gauntlet, while another grazed his pauldron. Zuvius didn't see a hammer flung at the last moment towards his head.

Smashed in the face, Zuvius almost tumbled from the saddle. His skull felt as though it had been split in two and though he fought to stay alert, consciousness started to slip away from him. The prince shook his head. He could not allow himself to fall. He would be butchered by the God-King's warrior heralds.

Zuvius was suddenly at the eye of a storm of hammer blows. Hellion reared and the prince tried to turn the beast while fending off as many of the strikes as he could. He heard something crack in his side as both plate and bone gave in to the force of a righteous smash. Zuvius grunted. There was nothing his serpentine words or silver tongue could do to get him out of this. Hellion was drowning in a sea of plate, while heralds smashed at Zuvius, attempting to pierce his hell-forged armour and drag him down.

Zuvius briefly entertained the blasphemous notion that he was finished. That his service to the Everchosen would end here on Cape Desolation. Zuvius turned A'cuitas about in his gauntlet and clutched the shaft under one arm. Aiming the pommel at the advancing heralds, the prince unleashed a crackling arc of lightning. The Stormcasts trembled for a second as the sorcerous energies of the daemon-forged glaive coursed through them before exploding in a shower of blood and crackling soulfire, their spiritual essence rocketing for the sky.

Untouched by the arcing bolt, a surviving herald lifted his hammers to pound Zuvius into the bone beach. The prince put his glaive between him and his enemy, deflecting the hammer heads with the shaft. Pulling the glaive back with sudden violence, the prince cut the crowning blade through his enemy's throat before heaving it back to take the herald's head off his armoured body.

As the bloody mist cleared, Zuvius saw other newly landed warrior-heralds racing for him, hammers held in both hands. Zuvius felt thunder rolling up the beach. His brothers in corruption had arrived. Riding their monstrous mounts like a black wave crashing up the beach, the knights of the Everchosen's calling crashed through the God-King's ranks. While some warrior-heralds managed to land blows on the armoured steeds or knock the warriors of Chaos from their saddles, most succumbed to the earth-trembling charge. Fellspears sheared straight through plate and the blessed flesh within. Daemon-forged swords and great ensorcelled axes chopped down the Stormcasts as the line of steeds passed through, sending columns of lightning arcing for the heavens.

The horde from the *Aftermath* stormed the beach after their Varanguard, making their way towards Zuvius. The spawn of the Fleshblessed, gibbering with expectation, and the bloodreavers ran ahead of the mob. The Mazarine and the lumbering fury that were the khorgoraths of the Red Death weren't far behind, with the Glass Spire sorcerers and Bloatus Belch's Rank and Vile making more sedate progress up the beach. They would all play their part in the horror to come. As a meatshield before the mighty Varanguard or as scavengers devouring the scraps Archaon's chosen left behind, the horde would find service to the Dark Gods.

As injured warriors tried to get to their feet, more heralds glided across the charging columns of knights to fortify their number. Zuvius turned Hellion about and raced off to join the mounted ranks of the Varanguard, leaving the warrior-heralds to be swamped by butchers, monstrosities and dread swordsmen.

Cape Desolation was a vast shoreline of bone and darkness, swarmed by the Chaos hordes of Archaon's monstrous army. It was swallowed by the charging ranks of Varanguard, their mounted number shattering the skulls of the beachhead and closing about the twisted forts lining the peninsula. The Everchosen was everywhere, soaring through the storm, setting the monstrous Dorghar on fortification after fortification. As Archaon cut Stormcasts from the ramparts with blazing sweeps of the Slayer of Kings, the daemon mount tore down sigmarite towers erected amongst the razored ruins of Chaos bastions.

To any other mortal in the nine realms, the sight would have shredded their minds and turned their hearts white with terror. Like the fires of doom, the Everchosen and his World Enders had arrived. Suffering and death awaited all in Archaon's path. The God-King's Stormcasts were not just any other mortals, however, if they were mortal at all. Crafted of immaculate plate and righteous flesh, the Stormcasts were Sigmar's cold wrath incarnate. They knew no fear and lived for the sole purpose of driving the scourge of Chaos from the realms.

All along the coast, the beach was lit up by streaming shots of celestial energies. Flights of skybolt arrows blazed up out of the fortresses before dropping back down onto the beach in searing volleys. Lightning blasts created craters in the shattered skulls and blasts were shot through rough arrow slits from boltstorm crossbows. Zuvius rode up through the lines of mounted knights and the blinding storm of celestial energy being visited upon the approach to the Ebon Claw.

'Damn these armoured curs,' Sarsael Hedra roared from the saddle as Zuvius pulled level with the dread knight.

'Hiding behind our walls with their craven weapons,' Vomitus Grue rumbled from along the line. Aspa Erezavant, who was riding up behind, said nothing. Drawing ahead of the Prince of Embers, Sarsael brought up his warpsteel shield. Riders along the line did the same. Skybolt arrows rained from the sky, stabbing into the beach about the hooves of the knights' steeds and fizzling to nothing against the surface of their shields.

'Behind their breastplates they fear us,' Zuvius roared. 'Let us be the realisation of that fear in flesh and blood. Let us besmirch these lands once more and send the Stormcasts shrieking back to their God-King.'

'For the Everch–' Zorn the Brazenfleshed called, riding up behind them. The red-skinned knight never got to finish his proclamation as both he and his blood-sweating steed disappeared in the blast from a thunderbolt crossbow.

As lightning struck the beach, reaching out from the impact site with spidery arcs of energy, armoured warriors went down. Steeds crashed into the skulls, throwing their Varanguard riders, who died in crackling cages of arcing power.

Zuvius and Sarsael's steeds jumped the fallen. As Hellion crushed skulls to bone dust on the other side, Zuvius hauled the reins from one side to another, avoiding more sizzling arrows dropping from the sky. The Prince of Embers spat his disgust. The Stormcast Eternals aimed to thin out the Ever-chosen's warhordes before they even reached the bastion and mounted their siege. Varanguard were dying. The approach to the fortress was a lightning-scalded killing ground of havoc and confusion. With Zorn the Brazenfleshed and a number of veteran Varanguard dead, the Prince of Embers felt the eyes of the Everchosen on him. Archaon swooped overhead astride his daemon mount, momentarily drawing the lightning storm of fire from the Ebon Claw. Zuvius would not fail his dread master.

'With me...' Zuvius started to say to Sarsael Hedra, but the dread knight was dead – a skybolt arrow finding its way around his shield to skewer his horned head.

'Come on!' the Prince of Embers called down the line. Sav-agely digging his boot heels into Hellion's ghastly flesh, Zuvius drew ahead of the charge. Galloping headlong through the celestial streams, explosions and lightning traps, the ruin-ous knight led by example. Other warriors in gold and black plate similarly urged their steeds onwards through the tem-pest of light. In cutting down the amount of time spent on the approach, Zuvius hoped to limit their casualties. It was imperative that the Chaos forces arrived to besiege the forts in unstoppable numbers. With the lightning column blazing down into the Ebon Claw supplying fresh Stormcast Eternals, the Varanguard would have to overwhelm the Stormcasts there and cut off the God-King's reinforcements.

As the charge entered the deep shadow of the Ebon Claw, the bolts and shafts of celestial energy began to dwindle. With Archaon's chosen all but to the walls, the angles became too tight for the Stormcast archers. Instead Zuvius felt the arrow storm pass overhead, destined for the advance of Archaon's hordes making their way up the beach. It was a gauntlet that Bloatus Belch and the Tzeentchian Vitus and Volitae would have to run.

Zuvius slowed Hellion before the petrified black rock of the Ebon Claw's walls. Above, the magnificent sigmarite towers reached up out of the jagged talon of the fortress' damned architecture. Zuvius hauled on the reins and had his steed come to a stop on the shattered bone of the beach. As Archaon's chosen arrived at the fort walls they did the same, drawing their daemon-forged battle-axes and ensorcelled sword blades.

Zuvius heard the flap of wings. Landing on the prince's pauldron spike in a cascade of cerulean feathers was Mallofax, returned from his reconnaissance. From his singed wing, Zuvius could see that the bird had also suffered the attentions of Stormcast archers.

'Speak, bird,' Zuvius said as the creature got its breath back. 'How many?'

'Hundreds, at least,' Mallofax squawked, 'with reinforcements coming down from the sky.' Zuvius looked up at the column of lightning blazing out of the heavens into the fortress. It was going to be a problem. The Varanguard would have to find a way to cut it off.

'Does the host have a commander?'

Mallofax squawked his incredulity. 'They all look the same to me.'

'A Stormcast,' Zuvius pressed the bird, 'surrounded by banner men, coordinating defences, issuing orders...'

'Yes,' the bird said. 'There's one sat astride a great reptile.'

'Where?'

'The courtyard,' Mallofax squawked. 'With the main body of the host.'

Zuvius snarled at the thought of the enemy commander so close beyond the wall.

'Entry?' he demanded of the bird.

'All the entrances have been collapsed,' Mallofax said, hopping about on the pauldron spike as grit rained from above. 'There's no way in.'

'There's always a way in,' the Prince of Embers insisted. He had besieged all manner of fortresses. Not even the Everchosen's own Varanspire had stopped him.

'The Stormcast fortifications favour the north and west structures, reinforcing the demolished towers there. The walls are thinner,' Mallofax said, 'more dilapidated on the southern side.'

Zuvius nodded his approval, grit pitter-pattering off his plate.

'Fly,' he told the bird. 'Bring the sorcerers and breachers for the walls. We shall need a shield of tainted meat before us as we enter.'

The Ebon Claw blazed with energies launched from the jagged ramparts and Stormcast towers. Mounted Varanguard charged up to the walls, leaving smouldering mounds of corrupt flesh and hell-forged plate in their wake – Knights of Ruin and their mounts who had failed to run the blinding gauntlet of the Stormcast archers. With many veteran Varanguard dead on the beach or struggling their way up it, Archaon's chosen had stalled. They needed an objective. All that faced them, however, was the petrified black stone of the fortress wall.

Zuvius watched the warhorde advance up the beach. While the spawn of the Fleshblessed made a maniacal dash across the open, crossbow-blasted ground and the horrific khorgoraths of the Red Death cared little for the searing streams and explosions, the rest of the horde followed the Glass Spire sorcerers. The Tzeentchians used their unnatural talents to create changes in the landscape about them. Moving their willowy arms and fingers in strange patterns, they caused the skulls of the beach to tremble and part to admit glowing blue shafts of crystal.

Creating natural shields for the advancing hordes, the sorcerers strode up the beach with Bloatus Belch's Rank and Vile, the Mazarine knights and the bloodreaver crew of the *Aftermath*.

Moving from outcrop to crystalline outcrop, the warhorde made good progress. The bolts and streams of lightning blazing from the Ebon Claw scorched the crushed-bone beach about them. There were casualties across the killing ground, however. Mindless spawn were reduced to charred meat by the eruption of lightning storms. Slow moving members of the Rank and Vile exploded in plague-swollen splendour as streams of celestial energy struck their outliers.

As crystal shuddered up through the skulls to absorb the worst of the lightning storm and the warhorde took advantage of the cover, the surviving warrior-heralds on the beach smashed into the mobs of Chaos warriors. The warhorde was a monster, ravenous for its first taste of slaughter. While the heralds fearlessly ran at the ruinous horde, they were enveloped by corrupt killers and torn apart. Khorgoraths snatched up the Stormcasts, wings and all, and hurled them furiously into the bone-shattering surface of the conjured crystal. The knights of the Mazarine went toe to toe with the warrior-heralds, while bloodreavers slit their throats. Those Stormcasts unfortunate enough to smash their way into the Rank and Vile found a host of implacable foes. Their diseased flesh soaked up all the punishment the God-King's servants could mete out, all with the rancid smiles of their jovial patron plastered across their pox-marked faces. With the blaze of fallen Stormcasts shooting for the sky, the warhorde made their approach on the fortress.

The Varanguard known as the Unslaked sidled his steed aggressively up against Zuvius' own. He had seen Zuvius despatch his bird for the hordes following the Varanguard up the skull beach.

'Zorn would have smashed through that barbican,' the Unslaked stated.

'Zorn's dead,' Kadence Salivarr called across the storm.

'The Stormcasts will expect it,' Zuvius told the Unslaked. 'While we're excavating the rubble from that gateway, they'll rain down destruction upon us. Look,' Zuvius said, indicating the way in which the Stormcast fortifications had grown up out of the shattered stone of the Ebon Claw. He then pointed at the approaching sorcerers of the Glass Spire and the shafts of crystal they were drawing up through the beachhead. 'There will be losses beneath the barbican. There will be no siege. We shall create our own entrance. Large enough to admit a meatshield and our mounted ranks. We shall rush the Stormcasts from within.' Zuvius saw Vomitus Grue and Aspa Erezavant nod their approval. Salivarr stared at the Unslaked, who seemed to rage within his helmet.

As a storm of celestial energy blazed from the ramparts, something else dropped down from the battlements. Before the Unslaked could respond, towering Stormcasts in ornate armour landed about the knights and their steeds. Dropping down from the castle walls, the Stormcasts carried massive battle hammers that seethed with celestial power. A huge warrior landing with assuredness next to Zuvius brought his colossal hammer down on Hellion's back with a blaze of power. The steed almost buckled, staggering away from the Stormcast warrior. As Zuvius recovered his balance and hauled Hellion back, the Stormcast turned swiftly on Zuvius.

The prince thrust his glaive at the God-King's warrior with enough force to skewer a gargant. The Stormcast was swift as well as huge, however, and twisted his ornate helm to one side to avoid the glaive blade. Knocking A'cuitas aside with the shaft of his hammer, the Stormcast spun around and landed a hammer blow on the prince's leg. Knocked back with Hellion into the unforgiving stone of the fortress wall, Zuvius felt both the wind and all sense knocked out of him. His armour plate was buckled and a pain in his thigh blazed to agonising intensity.

Struggling to see through the pain, Zuvius just got his head out of the way of a hammer blow that stove a hole in the stone of the exterior wall. As Zuvius hauled Hellion away from the wall and the plunging arc of the great hammer, he could see hulking Stormcasts and Archaon's chosen fighting a ferocious battle along the fort wall. Another huge Stormcast landed nearby, falling into a crouch to absorb the distance of the drop. Zuvius rode up behind him, thrusting the glaive down, stabbing him in the back. Punching the heavy blade through the golden plate, Zuvius feverishly stabbed him twice more before kicking him forward. Crashing faceplate first onto the skull beach, the dead Stormcast turned into a vaulting arc of lightning.

With blood on his teeth and scorch-smeared lips, Zuvius pulled Hellion around. He shot the first Stormcast a contemptuous grin. The towering warrior swung the hammer about him, stepping forward to smash the knight to oblivion. The prince allowed the Stormcast to advance. He kept Hellion moving and jabbed at the warrior with his glaive to keep his attention.

'Erezavant,' the prince said finally, 'just kill him.'

The Stormcast turned to see another of Archaon's chosen behind him. The dark knight's eyes said everything. They narrowed, serpent-like, right before the strike. Erezavant already had the broad and smoking blade of his ensorcelled sword up and ready. At Zuvius' words, Aspa Erezavant swung the cursed weapon and cut the top of the Stormcast's head off. As the sorcerous smoke cleared, the warrior's open helm and skull were revealed to the sky.

The Stormcast crashed down onto his knees and fell face forward. By the time the spirit of the God-King's servant had blazed away, Erezavant was gone – on the bloody trail of another foe.

Turning, Zuvius saw the Varanguard fighting hard against Stormcasts who were dropping down the rough wall from the ramparts. The fighting was bloody. Stormcasts hammered monstrous steeds to death before pulverising their trapped riders with polished, crackling hammers. The dread knights of Archaon fought back, spearing lone Stormcasts or hacking them apart with daemon-forged blades. Vomitus Grue, whose fell blessing was to know no pain, took several blows to the head with a lightning-wreathed hammer. Almost knocked from the saddle, the indomitable warrior leant down to grab the armoured Stormcast by the helm and smashed him repeatedly against the fortress wall.

The battle was turning. The Stormcasts were fearless and powerful but while they were undoubtedly the living weapons of a god, their god was not with them. Archaon, the Exalted Grand Marshal of the Apocalypse and demigod of Chaos, fought side by side with his dread armies. Every damned wretch on that beach simultaneously adored and loathed the Everchosen. He led by example, inspiring his slaves to darkness with monstrous acts of destruction, and through the heart-stopping incentive of fear. Battle-hardened champions, lords of Chaos and abominable daemons dared not fail him and, if asked to, would walk into certain death for Archaon.

'Come on!' Zuvius roared back down the beach, riding around to the south wall through throngs of knights and Stormcasts in desperate combat. Kadence Salivarr gave chase,

Vomitus Grue and Aspa Erezavant on his heels, and the Unslaked in their wake.

Mallofax had returned. With him he had brought the war-horde: spawn, monstrosities, daemons and men of dark purpose.

As Zuvius and two other ruinous knights carrying fellspears impaled a trapped Stormcast in an excruciating three-way skewer, he saw the Glass Spire sorcerers approach. Ripping A'cuitas out of the unfortunate warrior, the prince left him to the other two warriors.

'Sorcerers,' Zuvius called. 'The Everchosen has need of your wretched talents.' Salivarr and the Varanguard drew up behind the Prince of Embers.

'My lord,' the first of the robed creatures said, his eyes on the ground.

'The Stormcast have denied us entrance to our own fortress,' Zuvius said. 'I want you to create another. I'm assured the wall is thinner and weaker here. Bring forth your creations and split the stone apart.'

'At once, my lord,' the Glass Spire sorcerer said, signalling to nearby enchanters with his third arm. Zuvius turned to see the knights of the Everchosen's calling and the monstrous horde gathering at the south wall of the Ebon Claw.

'Well,' Kadence Salivarr said. 'Tell them.'

Zuvius spat at the beach of skulls.

'This miserable scrap of land is ours,' the prince said. He slapped the petrified stone of the wall beside him. 'This is ours. The realm is ours and all others beyond. Ours by dark right. By right of conquest. Ours for the taking. The warriors of the God-King trespass on unholy ground.'

Zuvius directed the sorcerers of the Glass Spire to work their dread magic. 'For corruption's sake, for the coming end, for Almighty Archaon. Bring it down.'

Shafts of blue crystal burst from the wall of the Ebon Claw. The columns of crystal sheared away sections of the wall. Working their way through the rock like a wedge, they pulverised the crumbling material in between, creating not only a large, ragged entrance but also crystalline columns to support it.

'Now!' Zuvius roared.

Bloatus Belch ordered his Rank and Vile in through the breach. Putrid warriors, green and distended with disease, they wore rusted scraps of plate and mail. Smiling like mad men, the blightkings pushed on.

Archaon's chosen held back, despite their eagerness to let loose. Such dread warriors could not be wasted on a wall breach. The cankered and inexorable troops of the Great Lord of Decay were perfect for such a duty. Unrelenting, uncaring sacks of rancid filth that would soak up the worst the Stormcasts had to throw at them, a rancid meatshield advancing before the mounted doom of the Varanguard.

Over the wall, Zuvius could hear movement – the trembling of stone beneath boots and the rattle of plate. The breaching of the south wall had been unexpected but the Stormcasts had hundreds of warriors within the fortress ready to respond and repel enemy invaders. As Bloatus Belch allowed the rusty chains of his flail to fall ready from his meaty, green fist, he filed in with his warriors. There was unremitting death and destruction to be had within and the blightlord wanted to be part of it.

As Zuvius heard the clash of Stormcast weaponry on the corrosion-pitted blightblades of Belch's soldiers, he knew that the Stormcasts intended on destroying the interlopers without mercy and plugging the breach. With countless warriors inside the courtyard surging towards the south wall, the Prince of Embers knew exactly what to do. The khorgoraths of the Red Death had thus far only been unleashed on the last of the hammer-wielding Stormcasts outside of the walls. Now it was time to set them against the packed ranks of hallowed warriors within.

The hulking creatures of the Red Death enlarged the ragged entrance with their muscular bulk. With them Zuvius sent the daemon bloodletters, the fast and rangy killers being the perfect complement to the destructive khorgoraths.

A Mazarine knight and one of the bloodreavers suddenly disappeared in a flash of celestial energy. Arcs of lightning crackled through the tight ranks of Fleshblessed spawn and blightkings. Looking up, Zuvius saw Stormcast archers on the battlements above, aiming bows and crossbows.

'More,' Zuvius growled at the Glass Spire sorcerers. 'And take care of those.'

As the Tzeentchian sorcerers drew on their powers, spikes and shafts of crystal erupted up through the black stone of the fortress. Crystal-braced holes opened up in the wall, while the ramparts above cracked and sheared away, plunging the Stormcast Eternals earthward.

Above, Zuvius felt the mighty beat of Dorghar's wings as the daemon steed took Archaon swooping overhead. The Varanguard roared their jubilation. The prince took this as a good sign. The Everchosen was departing to visit his monstrous wrath and that of his daemon upon the other bastions. He was leaving the Ebon Claw in the hands of his Varanguard, having seen them breach its walls.

It was time. The Varanguard needed to overwhelm the defenders with a single, decisive action. They had not landed their hordes and taken the beach to be target practice for the Stormcasts. The enemy held fortified positions and could afford to wait them out. Besides, within the fortress the enemy would think twice about loosing into their own lines.

Archaon was watching. Expecting. Zuvius felt the dark energy about him. It was the seething desire of the Varanguard to see their warlord's will be done.

'For the Everchosen!' the Prince of Embers roared across the ranks.

Archaon's chosen stormed the breach, clutching monstrous spears, warpsteel shields and hell-forged blades that smoked with murderous expectation.

The air was thick with lung-shredding dust. With A'cuitas held ready for the thrust, Zuvius charged through the breach. Within the fortress, Zuvius saw that crystalline shafts had ripped up through the foundations, burying nearby Stormcasts in rubble.

The Ebon Claw was a pit of unrelenting slaughter. Death waited but moments away for all fighting within its walls. There were Stormcast Eternals everywhere – their plate almost blinding as it reflected the light storm funnelling down from the sky and into the scorched ground of the courtyard. Crackling silhouettes ventured forth from the lightning column, becoming searing realisations as their boots touched stone. It became clear to Zuvius that the God-King's hallowed warriors had no intention of giving up the fortress. It was carnage – with Stormcasts and warriors of Chaos barely having room to raise their weapons.

As Zuvius rode through the wreckage, hammers came crackling up at the prince's head. Leaning out of their path, Zuvius evaded them, allowing them to pulverise the petrified stone. The prince cut two of the Stormcasts down. A third leapt into his path, swinging a blazing mace. Zuvius pulled back on the reins. He drew Hellion out of the way of the bludgeoning, angular edges of the weapon before kicking the Stormcast back at the wall. The precarious stone above his foe came loose and buried the celestial warrior while the Prince of Embers dug his heels into his steed's side, prompting the beast to surge on.

From rock dust Zuvius entered a haze of blood, cooked in the air by the passage of skybolts shot down into the courtyard from the battlements. The prince had been wrong about the Stormcast archers. Confident in their aim, they were unafraid to fire into the seething melee below with the furious energy of their lightning bows.

Zuvius scanned the brutality and bloodshed. Stormcast warriors with mighty warblades were hacking at the Knights Mazarine, battering them back with their sigmarite shields, while the khorgoraths of the Red Death snatched up the golden warriors and tore off their heads. Bloatus Belch was dead, a Stormcast hammer still buried in his plague-swollen corpulence. His Rank and Vile advanced still, soaking up the God-King's wrath. As hammers knocked sprays of flies from their mouths, stove in ribcages and splattered pus-ridden limbs, the blightkings fought on. They relentlessly hacked and stabbed with their diseased blades, the smiles of Grandfather Nurgle on their maggot-eaten faces.

The Glass Spire sorcerers were held high above the rabble, impaled on the long blades of Stormcast glaives, the last of their number bringing down ramparts and stone stairwells with their crystal blooms to reveal the polished metal of Stormcast towers and fortifications.

Bloodstoker Killian and his bloodreavers, however, hopelessly outclassed by divine warriors in full celestial plate, were fighting rabidly. Driven on by the lash, they rolled fearlessly under the lumbering weaponry of the Stormcasts, despite suffering continuous losses. They came at their foes in gorethirsty throngs: gouging throats, plunging reaverblades into backs and feverishly stabbing Stormcasts in the sides of their helms.

Zuvius caught sight of the Fleshblessed. The monstrous spawn swarmed over the golden paladins like a plague of deranged spiders. Putting their extra limbs to good work, they prized plate from the warriors and tore out throats, hearts and entrails. For their part, the paladins wielded mighty axes that lopped limbs and heads from the wretched spawn. Above the din of clashing blades and battle, the Fleshblessed took their grotesque talents to the ramparts. Leaping from paladin to wall, the abominations clawed, hauled and swung their way up the ramshackle architecture of the fortress. Latching onto Stormcast archers, the plague of spawn tore warriors from their footings. As the Stormcasts crashed down onto the battlements and then fell the distance to the crowded courtyard, the Fleshblessed suffered shafts of celestial energy and crossbow blasts. Those who survived leapt for the armoured archers and began tearing at heads and limbs.

A rogue shaft of celestial energy from a skybolt bow caught Zuvius in the back, causing the prince to snarl his pain. As a hammer landed a glancing blow on his pauldron, knocking him to one side, Zuvius clasped his glaive in one gauntlet and against his arm. Flinging the glaive around in a furious arc from the saddle, the Prince of Embers cut the Stormcast in half.

There was polished plate everywhere. Weapons clashing. Blades thrusting for the kill. Hammers decapitating Chaos invaders. Tzeentchian knights fought side by side with bloated blightkings. Bloodreaver savages died in their droves amongst Slaaneshi spawn thrashing their lives away to defend them. Love and fear of the Everchosen in equal measure pushed the warhorde on to feats of suicidal valour. No-one wanted to be left alive, should the invasion of Cape Desolation be a failure. Not at the mercy of the Everchosen's boundless wrath.

Through the hordes emerged Archaon's chosen. Pale

reflections of the Everchosen himself in their dark plate, they were almost the opposite of the Stormcast Eternals.

The Varanguard fought like tempests of black-hearted vengeance. Charging through the Chaos ranks and into the enemy with the cold confidence of warriors undefeated, they thrust their fellspears through throats. They battered Stormcasts to smashed armour and bloody pulp with their warpsteel shields. They hacked limbs and immaculate helms from shoulders with tight and ruthless strikes of their daemon-forged blades.

Turning Hellion amongst the mayhem and desperation of battle, Zuvius raised A'cuitas to stab and blast the God-King's warriors out of his path. Shrugging off glancing blows of polished blades and the sparks of lightning hammers, the prince heaved his steed around to find his weapon raised at other Varanguard. Aspa Erezavant said nothing. Kadence Salivarr spoke for both of them.

'Hold, brother,' the knight called, knocking aside the disciplined thrust of a Stormcast glaive. Zuvius could hear the rancid boom of Vomitus Grue's laughter through the clash of blades as he watched the plague-ridden warrior almost spear one of his own kind.

'This isn't working,' the Unslaked said, riding up between them. 'As fast as we send these craven filth back to their weakling god, more of them arrive.'

Cutting a Stormcast's head from his shoulders with an elegant sweep of his blade, Salivarr nodded his agreement.

'We need to kill all that we can,' Zuvius answered. He gestured to the column of lightning blazing down into the fort, before bringing A'cuitas brutally down through an attacking herald. 'But more will follow, while that conduit remains open. Find and destroy their lords. No doubt they hold the key to such sky-rending sorcery. Spread the word. Let us justify the Everchosen's faith.'

As Zuvius and the Knights of Ruin took the fight deeper into the courtyard, the sky lit up with souls rocketing for the heavens. As the Stormcasts disappeared in blazes of lightning, Zuvius found their comrades to be undaunted.

Seizing a glaive blade that had sliced into his side, Zuvius held the Stormcast who wielded it steady. The prince's grimace of pain turned into a triumphant snarl as an enraged khorgorath of the Red Death bit the golden warrior's head off, only to have his prey disappear in a flash of lightning. This seemed to infuriate the khorgorath even more – the thing already stuck with the quivering shafts of spears and glaives. The monster swept the advancing line of Stormcasts aside before settling upon one to beat into the courtyard floor.

'Feast!' Zuvius commanded a nearby horde of bloodletters. At the Varanguard's command they jumped onto the remaining Stormcasts, who were swinging their glaives at the Prince of Embers. The rangy daemons tore at heads and plunged their brazen blades into metal then flesh. 'Blood for the Blood God...' Zuvius said in mock gratitude.

The prince's jubilation was short lived. Although the horde seemed to be soaking up the worst of the Stormcasts' punishment and Archaon's Varanguard were intent on cutting a path of bloody death through the enemy, the celestial warriors still came. Reinforced by the lightning column, it was only a matter of time before the battle turned in the God-King's favour. The forces of the Everchosen had thrown hordes in their entirety at the fortifications along Cape Desolation. With the ability to replenish their warriors within the walls, however, the Stormcasts had the advantage. The day would be theirs unless the dark warriors could even the odds.

Looking up through the bloody mist of the crowded courtyard, Zuvius saw Stormcast reinforcements take their positions.

The derelict ramparts of black stone, speared by the silver and gold of sigmarite towers erected through the fort, were crowded with the God-King's warriors. Silhouetted against the blazing column of lightning, the prince saw a Stormcast lord riding a reptilian beast giving orders to a skull-helmed warrior. Zuvius calculated that his only chance to destroy the conduit was to kill the lord.

'Varanguard,' Zuvius called to Archaon's chosen. 'There upon the battlements. Let's take our fight to a foe deserving of our hell-forged steel.'

Zuvius saw Vomitus Grue headbutt a paladin in the faceplate and toss him to the Rank and Vile before urging his powerful steed up the rubble of the south wall. Like Grue, other knights in their plate of black and blood-splattered gold finished their present foes before making for the battlements.

Zuvius saw the Unslaked mount the shattered steps of a half-demolished stairwell. He fought through the axe-wielding Stormcasts holding it from the Knights Mazarine. Meanwhile, Kadence Salivarr's elegant monstrosity leapt up through the ruin of the south wall, bounding and balancing from purchase to precarious purchase. All the while, the Varanguard warrior stabbed and slashed his blade through surrounding Stormcasts.

The Prince of Embers grunted his derision. Zuvius would be damned anew before offering up such a prize to his brothers in darkness. As he saw an opportunity to reach the battlements ahead of them he raced away, only to be suddenly torn backwards.

A Stormcast hammer had struck him in the shoulder, puncturing the pauldron and hooking him back. Tensing his thighs about the saddle and clinging to the reins, Zuvius held on. As the pull of the hammer hauled him and the steed around, the immaculate gauntlet of a Stormcast smashed him across the face. Zuvius reeled. His face was already a mess but now his nose was broken and blood-splattered.

'Unholy wretch,' the Stormcast said through the mirrored finish of a glistening helm. His words crackled like the divine metal of the Stormcast weaponry. Swiping again at Zuvius, the celestial warrior cracked his cheekbone and ripped the thin flesh of his face where the ornate gauntlet caught him. 'The spawn of corruption. You are a thing of evil.'

'Indeed I am,' Zuvius snarled before being savagely hammered in the jaw by the Stormcast's righteous fist. Blood and teeth went flying, tapping and spattering against the glorious pauldron of a nearby paladin.

'The God-King comes to claim what is his,' the Stormcast snarled. 'Soul, stone and sky. All belong to Sigmar. Do you hear me, creature?'

As the skull-helmed warrior rushed to attack once more, the Prince of Embers was ready. Clutching his glaive close to its crowning blade, the knight used the momentum of the next savage tug to thrust A'cuitas down into the Stormcast's chest. Zuvius pulled him close and watched as blood streamed from the mouth slit of the skull helm. Zuvius thrust again with the glaive, down through the diaphragm and into the gut. The prince felt his foe tense with every plunge.

'Yes,' Zuvius told him. 'I hear you.'

Zuvius ripped the glaive out of the warrior. The Stormcast staggered back, a bloody hole in his chest that cascaded gore down his beautiful suit of armour. The prince pulled the hammer from his ruined pauldron and dropped it on the ground with disgust. He didn't like the feel of the celestial weapon.

'Hear this,' Zuvius spat. 'Now I go to ensure that your God-King forfeits his claim.'

Leaving the Stormcast to waver and stagger in his last

moments of life, Zuvius rode across the courtyard. Barging Stormcast and warhorde warriors aside with Hellion's armoured flanks, the prince used the shaft of his glaive to smash a lunging Stormcast aside. As another took a swing at him with his grandblade, Zuvius leant down out of its devastating path. Jabbing the blade of A'cuitas through his faceplate, Zuvius rammed the glaive home in the warrior's skull. Leaving a trail of vaulting lightning storms in his wake, Zuvius reached the other side of the courtyard.

Jabbing his armoured heels into Hellion's sides, Zuvius prompted the beast to leap up onto a collapsed section of wall, then from the back of a mortally wounded khorgorath, who roared its blood-gurgling defiance. As lightning shafts scorched the stone about him, the Prince of Embers thrust his glaive up into an armoured archer who fell forwards into the courtyard. Urging Hellion on, Zuvius risked the scrabble up the twisted architecture of the wall. A monstrous leap demolished the structure below. As Zuvius held out his glaive to balance, Hellion's hooves reached the battlements and carried the knight to stable ground.

At last, the Prince of Embers saw the Stormcast lord. He was backed up onto the steps of a gold, sigmarite citadel. The crowning tower was the tallest of the God-King's fortifications.

His reptilian mount wore extravagant gold plate like its master. Zuvius was sure that he was the leader of the warriors fighting for the Ebon Claw. He was not alone in that assumption. While the armoured bodies of Archaon's chosen lay about the battlements where the Stormcast lord and his beast had slain them, the Unslaked, Vomitus Grue and Kadence Salivarr still lived, and they had surrounded him.

Zuvius promised himself that victory would not be theirs. Pushing Hellion on, Zuvius raced for the tower. Leaping the razor-edged crenulations between battlements, he dodged several shield-bearing warriors of the God-King. Hellion cleared a section of wall demolished by a mace-swinging Stormcast just moments before and leapt the opportunistic gladius sweeps of others desperate to put themselves between the Varanguard and their lord. As Hellion leapt back down onto the battlements, Zuvius thrust his glaive through two of the Stormcasts. As their swords clattered to the floor, Zuvius ripped A'cuitas free. With lightning souls erupting about him, the Prince of Embers drove his armoured steed on towards the tower.

Everything hurt. Every twist and turn was agony. Every muscle screamed for respite. But Zuvius would not relent.

As Zuvius reached the ruined tower at last, Vomitus Grue died. The pestilent knight had felt no pain when the great hammer of the Stormcast lord smashed him aside. He had felt nothing as the reptilian beast breathed storm-lightning into his pox-scarred face. Zuvius didn't know if Grue had felt the beast's jaws tear his head off and spit it into the courtyard below, but it didn't matter. The body followed moments after.

Kadence Salivarr and the Unslaked tried to take the Stormcast lord together. With their daemon-forged blades a deathtrap of cleaving and thrusting lethality, the Stormcast reared his beast and smashed the blades aside with the crackling power of his colossal hammer. The lord kicked the Unslaked's bloody mount back while breaking the back of Salivarr's beast with a downswing of his mighty weapon.

The reptilian mount backed up the tower steps and leapt clear over the two knights, bounding about them to get into a better position.

As a warrior-herald landed nearby to come to his lord's aid, Zuvius skewered the Stormcast and kicked in his faceplate, sending him toppling over the sharp battlements. The Unslaked attacked next, and tried to unseat the Stormcast lord. Instead, his horned helm was smashed to brain-dribbling scrap by the Stormcast's hammer. Kadence Salivarr tried to bring his infamous bladework to bear, but was felled by the thunderbolt blast of a crossbow bolt in the back.

As the smoking shell of the dark knight crumpled before the Stormcast lord, Zuvius drove at him. The Stormcast hauled on his mount's reins and pointed the head of his hammer at the Varanguard before him.

'No,' the Prince of Embers told him. 'It shall be you to taste oblivion.'

Such words seemed to provoke something in the Stormcast lord. Digging his heels into the scaly flanks of his steed, he urged the beast on.

Zuvius roared his defiance at the Stormcast who stood up in the saddle, his hammer aloft. Hellion wanted to charge but Zuvius kept the reins tight in his armoured grasp as he turned the shaft of A'cuitas about in his other hand.

As the Stormcast lord charged, Zuvius pointed the pommel of A'cuitas at the ground. The metal eye opened and a blaze of dark lightning scorched the stone battlements, turning them from black to a glowing red, melting the stone in the Stormcast's path. As the reptile's claws met the molten stone they sank, before becoming trapped as the stone cooled to glass. The beast's momentum suddenly arrested, it threw its rider from the saddle and over its head.

As the Stormcast lord hit the battlement floor face first and skidded to a halt before Zuvius, Hellion bridled. The golden warrior's hammer skimmed across the stone and fell into the courtyard. The Stormcast rolled over. Zuvius held the point of his glaive over his scuffed helm.

'Unworthy,' Zuvius told him, before stabbing down. A lightning storm raged about him as the Stormcast lord died.

The reptilian beast roared its grief and anger at Zuvius, straining to tear its legs free. It opened its jaws wide to unleash its lightning at Archaon's chosen.

'Enough,' Zuvius told it before spearing it through the mouth.

Zuvius urged Hellion to the edge of the battlement. He looked down into the courtyard. He waited. The warhorde fought on against the Stormcast defenders, while other knights arrived behind them, too late to take their part in the glory and destruction of the celestial lord. Among them was Aspa Erezavant, the silent killer whose blade dripped with gore. The battle had turned. While the wretched warriors of Chaos had to step through a carpet of their own dead, the Stormcasts were being backed up to the column of lightning.

The prince's smeared lips curled. The celestial lord was dead but the column went on burning and with it came endless reinforcements.

He had been wrong.

Zuvius furiously looked across the battle, across the golden paladins fighting for their God-King and the living corruption attempting to destroy them. He saw the Stormcast Eternal who had been speaking to the Stormcast lord earlier. The indomitable warrior was still alive and deep in prayer.

'You...' Zuvius said. He realised this warrior must be controlling the column of light. He lifted A'cuitas up like a spear, took aim and threw it. The Stormcast looked up just as his comrades tried to warn him. The glaive squealed down through the skull-helmed warrior's armour, impaling him to the ground and silencing his prayer.

As the skull-helmed warrior became a coruscation of surging, spiritual energy blazing for the skies, the column of lightning stuttered and disappeared, leaving only burnt air and a sharp afterglow. Zuvius had severed the conduit. The Stormcasts remaining were as indomitable as ever but the tide had turned. The forces of Chaos fell upon them in droves as the followers of Archaon butchered their way to a crude victory.

The Prince of Embers heard the flap of wings. It was Mallofax, returned after the worst of the fighting. The bird rested on Zuvius' ruined shoulder guard.

'You saw?'

'I saw, my lord,' the bird squawked.

'The Stormcast in the skull helm?'

'Aye, master.'

'Then fly to the other fortresses, to the other hordes,' said Zuvius. 'Tell our Varanguard brothers how to sever the storm. Tell them how the God-King's warriors can be defeated and driven from this miserable land.'

With the beating of wings, Mallofax peeled off into the sky. Orphaeo Zuvius leant back in the saddle. With his injuries, he almost fell. Aspa Erezavant nodded at him before urging his steed back down the ruined steps leading from the battlements.

Zuvius looked down into the courtyard and to a victory declared in blood and lightning. The Ebon Claw was theirs.

Weary, Zuvius had one more thing he needed to see. He steered Hellion up the glorious steps of the sigmarite tower, to the highest part of the Ebon Claw, and stared out across the dark peninsula. Cape Desolation belonged to the Everchosen. The columns of lightning connecting each of the fortresses were being snuffed out like the flames of distant candles. He could hear cheering, sorcerous chanting and the screams of the dying. They all came together in an unholy cacophony.

Zuvius felt a ravenous pride eat away at him as he looked out across the Varanguard swarming the conquered peninsula. He felt part of something abominable and powerful. He had been a warrior, pledged to Chaos. An acolyte of dread Tzeentch.

A blind man leading the blind, without true purpose. Alone among wretches, he had become complacent. Content in personal damnation.

He understood that he would never know the meaninglessness of spawndom or the monstrous powers gifted by the Great Changer. He was not the one but the one among many. Only in service to the Everchosen of Chaos had the Prince of Embers come to know the true power of damnation. Damnation of all for all. The harnessed strength of corruption, the glorious darkness of a fell blade wielded by the greatest of their kind. Archaon was a dire warlord who united not only the Varanguard behind him, but all servants of the Dark Gods as he stormed through the victim realms.

A dark silhouette in the rising dust, the Prince of Embers could see his master. Archaon. A horned shadow in his monstrous plate, his daemonsword and runeshield held in tight as he prepared to take once more to the air. The daemon steed launched into the sky, extending the great expanse of his wings. While Sigmar's tempest continued to rage across distant skies, over Cape Desolation all was still.

Orphaeo Zuvius watched the Everchosen and his daemon steed fly high over the Ebon Claw. Gliding on Dorghar's powerful wings, Archaon steered the monster towards the dark lands beyond. Zuvius nodded to himself. There would be more fighting. More killing to come. The arrival of the God-King's Stormcast Eternals would have given people living beyond the peninsula hope – hope for a realm without the tyranny of a ruinous overlord like Archaon. As the Prince of Embers took up his glaive and turned Hellion back down the steps, he came to realise that hope was a truly terrible thing.

ABOUT THE AUTHORS

David Annandale is the author of the Horus Heresy novel *The Damnation of Pythos* and the Primarchs novel *Roboute Guilliman: Lord of Ultramar*. He has also written the Yarrick series, several stories involving the Grey Knights, including *Warden of the Blade*, and *The Last Wall*, *The Hunt for Vulkan* and *Watchers in Death* for The Beast Arises. For Space Marine Battles he has written *The Death of Antagonis* and *Overfiend*. He is a prolific writer of short fiction, including the novella *Mephiston: Lord of Death* and numerous short stories set in The Horus Heresy, Warhammer 40,000 and Age of Sigmar universes. David lectures at a Canadian university, on subjects ranging from English literature to horror films and video games.

David Guymer is the author of the Gotrek & Felix novels *Slayer*, *Kinslayer* and *City of the Damned*, along with the novella *Thorgrim*. He has also written The Beast Arises novel *Echoes of the Long War* and *The Last Son of Dorn*, and a plethora of short stories set in the worlds of Warhammer and Warhammer 40,000. He is a freelance writer and occasional scientist based in the East Riding, and was a finalist in the 2014 David Gemmell Legend Awards for his novel *Headtaker*.

Guy Haley is the author of the Horus Heresy novel *Pharos* and the Warhammer 40,000 novels *Baneblade, Shadowsword, Valedor* and *Death of Integrity*. He has also written *Throneworld* and *The Beheading* for The Beast Arises series. His enthusiasm for all things greenskin has also led him to pen the eponymous Warhammer novel *Skarsnik*, as well as the End Times novel *The Rise of the Horned Rat*. He has also written stories set in the Age of Sigmar, included in *Warstorm, Ghal Maraz* and *Call of Archaon*. He lives in Yorkshire with his wife and son.

Rob Sanders is the author of *The Serpent Beneath*, a novella that appeared in the *New York Times* bestselling Horus Heresy anthology *The Primarchs*. His other Black Library credits include the The Beast Arises novels *Predator, Prey* and *Shadow of Ullanor*, the Warhammer 40,000 titles *Adeptus Mechanicus: Skitarius* and *Tech-Priest, Legion of the Damned, Atlas Infernal* and *Redemption Corps* and the audio drama *The Path Forsaken*. He has also written the Warhammer Archaon duology, *Everchosen* and *Lord of Chaos* along with many Quick Reads for the Horus Heresy and Warhammer 40,000. He lives in the city of Lincoln, UK.

WARHAMMER
AGE OF SIGMAR

THE REALMGATE WARS
WARDENS OF THE EVERQUEEN
C L WERNER

WARHAMMER
AGE OF SIGMAR

THE REALMGATE WARS
WARBEAST
GAV THORPE